Praise for Vonna Harper's
Shifters' Storm

"SHIFTER'S STORM is not for the faint at heart, the powerful emotions emanating from each of these characters is shared in vivid detail. The sex scenes are both haunting and so erotically charged you will hope you have someone or something close by to put out the fire... I was immediately drawn into this book and enjoyed every minute I spent with the characters."

~ *Fresh Fiction*

"This was a wonderful story, with all the elements in place to develop further into a series. I've no idea of the author's intentions, but in my most humble opinion, this [setting] and idea were far too sublime not to expand and explore possible relationships from the resulting 'clan'. Highly recommended."

~ *Whipped Cream Reviews*

Look for these titles by *Vonna Harper*

Now Available:

Bloodhunter
Predator
Night Hunter
Shifters' Storm
Studs

Shifters' Storm

Vonna Harper

Samhain Publishing, Ltd.
11821 Mason Montgomery Road, 4B
Cincinnati, OH 45249
www.samhainpublishing.com

Shifters' Storm
Copyright © 2011 by Vonna Harper
Print ISBN: 978-1-60928-621-7
Digital ISBN: 978-1-60928-513-5

Editing by Linda Ingmanson
Cover by Scott Carpenter

This book is a work of fiction. The names, characters, places, and incidents are products of the writer's imagination or have been used fictitiously and are not to be construed as real. Any resemblance to persons, living or dead, actual events, locale or organizations is entirely coincidental.

All Rights Are Reserved. No part of this book may be used or reproduced in any manner whatsoever without written permission, except in the case of brief quotations embodied in critical articles and reviews.

First Samhain Publishing, Ltd. electronic publication: August 2011
First Samhain Publishing, Ltd. print publication: July 2012

Dedication

Shifters' Storm is all my Samhain editor's fault. I was minding my business, doing something terribly important, when Linda Ingmanson threw me a challenge. Okay, two challenges. "How about trying a ménage?" she emailed one day. When I responded with, "Huh?" she threw up another gauntlet. "Shape-shifters are sexy and popular. How about trying one of those?"

A few more less than intelligent "Huhs?" from me and total lack of sympathy on Linda's part and things started germinating inside my uncontrolled and uncontrollable brain. I'm not sure how ménage and shape shifting started meshing together, but I knew enough to come along for the ride.

And if readers have as much fun reading *Shifters' Storm* as I did creating it, I'll cancel that hit I've ordered on Linda.

Chapter One

Dew touched with ice oozed out of the ground to caress Rane Haller's hiking boots and send cool fingers up her jeans-clad legs. The message was simple and inescapable. Winter had snuck up on fall and was overtaking it. Once winter won the inevitable battle, snow would start to blanket the woods she loved, despite what had happened here.

Winter was coming too soon, she acknowledged as she continued along the deer trail that slipped deep into the Chinook Mountains where she'd grown up. She needed more alone-time in the wilderness. Needed answers.

And justice.

Her kind of justice.

Sucking in air that smelled of cold, soil and pine needles, she stopped and listened. To the left and above her, a Clark's nutcracker pulled bark from the top of a Ponderosa. The gray-black bird probably assumed the solitary human was unaware of its existence, but Rane heard things people unaccustomed to a forest didn't.

She also caught a hint of the dried fox dung to her right, and because she knew where to look, she spotted the ground squirrel all but buried in decaying pine needles. Unless nature's order had been turned on end, the squirrel would soon be hibernating. In the meantime, it was trying to pack on weight.

Dismissing the rodent, bird and what a red fox had left behind, she continued climbing. Her destination this October morning was a high meadow that owed its rich grasses to an underground spring and was a favorite grazing spot for deer and elk.

Elk.

Gripping the shoulder straps on her backpack, Rane concentrated on toeing outward. Her butt was sticking out, but it wasn't as if there was anyone around to see. If she spotted someone, her first move would be to take her rifle from her pack, release the safety and aim. Only then would she concern herself with trying to determine who was sharing this space with her.

Acknowledging her actions saddened her. As a child, personal safety had never once concerned her. Yes, her mom had cautioned her to keep an eye out for cougars, and she couldn't remember when she hadn't known not to get between a female bear and her cubs. Except for those remote possibilities, the only thing she'd had to concern herself with was not breaking a leg.

How things had changed.

She'd included a waterproof sleeping bag and enough food for four meals in her pack, but as she continued to put the yards behind her, she again acknowledged her hope that she wouldn't have to spend the night out here. It wasn't as if she was afraid of a solitary night in the wilderness, but if she rolled out her sleeping bag, it meant she'd failed in her attempt to find the elk, or more to the point, Songan.

Songan. Native American for strong.

Her mother used to caution her not to let her mind wander while hiking and always keep her attention on where her feet were landing, but two hours into her journey, it was hard to stay focused. It was also nearly impossible not to think about what standing close to Songan would do to her system.

Body-blowing.

Shaking her head, she concentrated on the feel of cool, clean air caressing her lungs. It would definitely help if she could channel the air between her legs and bring the temperature there down a few degrees. That way, when she finally caught sight of Songan, she'd be able to concentrate on what she had to do and not the wanting.

Why hadn't he gotten in touch with her lately, damn it! Granted, this time of year his thoughts were on fucking, nonstop if possible, but he had to know what she was going through.

Didn't he?

Another shake of her head didn't come close to unjumbling her thoughts. Pausing, she looked ahead. She was still on the decades-old deer trail that showed no sign of petering out. Even if it did, she could still reach the meadow. Granted, she'd been to it only a couple of times, and not since she was a teenager, but that was another benefit of having had the Chinook Forest as her playground. She didn't get lost.

Another half hour of planting one foot ahead of the other brought her to the top of the long slope. The lush grassy area dotted with silver-barked aspens was just beyond this last bunch of trees, but like the deer who'd provided her with a clear path to her destination, she knew better than to expose herself. The fresh scent of elk and deer dung blended with fern, moss and foxtail barley. The uninitiated might believe they'd reached a peaceful place, a safe haven, but she didn't dare think that. Yes, predators such as cougars, foxes, coyotes and bears were around, but the true threat came from humans.

Shivering, she reached for her mother's rifle. No! She didn't dare let the word *threat* swamp her, not now.

Head cocked, she listened. Within seconds she'd identified and dismissed the normal meadow sounds. At the same time, she'd honed in on a distant and nearly imperceptible snuffling. Turning her head one way and then the other, she determined it was coming from the meadow's east side. Nostrils flaring, she sought to capture the scent she knew went with the faint sounds, but the wind was blowing in the wrong direction. Determined to assess the situation, she held her weapon steady as she slipped around the tree she'd been using as a shelter.

Fall had erased the rich green that painted the grasses during spring and summer. Shades of gray touched everything in the approximately five acre space, making it difficult for her to discern details. Now that trees no longer stood between her and the sound, she concluded she'd heard a bear. The creature was walking slowly and cautiously, which concerned her. Most times, especially if they were unaware of human presence, they blundered around ruled by their bellies and propelled by their noses. Adult bears took it for granted that they had no natural enemies in the forest. If they wanted to lay claim to a grub-filled log or dine on an animal carcass, they did, and woe to anything that got in their way.

Carcass?

Bile rose in Rane's throat, and tears burned her eyes. Much as she hated the wave of emotion, she knew better than to try to deny it. Grief demanded its own time and weight. When, after too long, sorrow backed off enough to allow her to think, she set about trying to separate the bear from its surroundings. The creature was still sniffing the earth, but now it paused between steps, making her wonder if it was stalking something.

The breeze shifted, then shifted again, and she smelled the bear. There was something off about the odor. A lack of unity. If it wasn't for the other smell she'd just detected, she would have set about trying to determine what didn't fit about the bruin. However, the second scent was suddenly so strong it overpowered everything else and tightened her fingers around her weapon. Again she had to fight the urge to cry out, only this time her reaction had nothing to do with grief and everything to do with alarm. Bits and pieces of instinct and intelligence wove together in her mind and provided her with the unwanted explanation.

Blood and gore. Violently expelled body fluids.

She didn't fault the bear for being drawn to death any more than she'd ever been upset by the sight of buzzards. Carnivores did what nature had designed them to do. But before she let the bear do his job, she needed to see what had been killed and how.

Firing into the air might chase off the bear, but she didn't want to telegraph her presence. She had no choice. She'd observed enough of the area's blacks to be relatively certain this one would choose retreat over confrontation. That was one of the plusses to being deep in the wilderness. The wildlife here hadn't become conditioned to human presence.

The *off* bear smell as well as the death stench guided her search. Studying the meadow's east edge, she spotted a dark shape. At this distance, she knew better than to go by first impressions, but the bear seemed unusually large. It was just her luck that she'd have to run off a male in his prime. At least bear breeding season was behind him. Hopefully his testosterone level had dropped so his balls no longer ruled him. After determining the direction the bear was walking, she studied the ground until she made out a motionless mound some hundred feet ahead of the bear.

Sticking to the trees ringing the meadow would increase the

amount of time she needed to reach what she now knew was a carcass, but she knew better than to conclude she and the black had the area to themselves. Other critters were fine. In fact, she'd love to see some deer right now, but something on two legs was a different story.

She'd recently been given stark proof of the evil man was capable of.

Stopping, the bear turned and rose onto its hind legs, obviously studying her. Huge! Even with so much distance between them, she had no doubt the beast would make the local record books. Hands shaking a little, she sighted through the rifle's scope.

"Oh shit. Shit."

Still cursing under her breath, she acknowledged the chill down her spine. What had she been thinking? This was no shy and unassuming black. The rich auburn fur alone told her that. More to the point, this creature had to go twice what a black weighed and sported a massive shoulder hump.

A grizzly.

Couldn't be! The breed hadn't been seen in Oregon for decades.

But it was.

Even as she noted the thick legs, small ears, long, tapering muzzle and take-no-prisoners body, something else occurred to her. The beast's full attention was on her, which meant he wasn't aware of any other humans in the area. Much as she relied on her own senses, she had even more faith in his, and he was telling her she had nothing to fear from one of her kind.

Her safety where he was concerned was a different matter. She could die today, a victim of claws and fangs. The rifle she'd hauled up here was probably worthless. If she hit it, all she'd do was make it mad.

Could she turn tail and get the hell out of here?

The strongest gust of wind so far brought her a metallic stench that sent shock through her already overloaded system. Blood. A lot of it. Undeniable proof of a savage death. More information sorted itself out in her mind. Whatever had died was pretty big. There was something *stale* about the smell, which told her the death hadn't happened within the past few hours.

Her nerves tightened, and her awareness tunneled until only she and the bear existed. Lowering itself back onto four legs, it woofed.

Didn't expect to see you here, it seemed to be saying.

"I didn't expect to see you either," she whispered.

"Don't be afraid."

Her heart lost rhythm, then reset itself. If she'd been anyone else and didn't know about the rare creatures that called the Chinook Forest home, she would have been convinced she was hallucinating.

"I don't want to be," she admitted.

"Come closer." The grizzly briefly turned his attention to the carcass. *"You need to see."*

Driven by a force she didn't comprehend, Rane started toward what in essence was a killing machine. Even if it charged, she doubted she'd shoot, because the grizzly was at home in a forest where it no longer belonged.

Her legs felt strong, and despite the uneven ground, her hips moved effortlessly. The combination of smells became more complex and deeply layered. Everything in her said she was supposed to be doing this insane thing. Erasing the distance between her and the great, rich-coated creature was all-important. As a Forest Service employee specializing in wildlife biology, she'd seen a grizzly up close, but that one had been drugged. Helpless.

When maybe fifty feet separated her from the massive beast, she dug her boots into the soft ground. She felt disconnected from herself and reality as she untied the backpack fastenings around her waist. If she was wrong about the *connection* between her and the bruin, she'd never be any older than today. Holding the rifle with first one numb hand and then the other, she slipped free of the pack's weight. Momentarily unbalanced, she concentrated on standing upright. Once her equilibrium was restored, she again assessed the scent coming from the creature. She knew what a bear smelled like. This one was that, all right, and more.

The grizzly's beautiful coat was thick and long, preventing her from getting a clear picture of the amount of fat, bone and muscle underneath. This time of year, healthy bears were putting on weight to insure they'd survive all but the harshest winter. Contrary to what many people believed, they didn't spend the winter in deep hibernation, especially at this elevation, but their activity level decreased dramatically.

Looking into the small but shining eyes, she realized they were black instead of brown as they should have been. The bear was fully alert, but it was more than that—an intelligence.

"What are you?" she managed.

"I don't know if you can understand."

Shocked, she glanced over at the inert form. The instant she did, she could no longer breathe. Sick and scared, she stared. She barely recognized her strained, "No, no, no."

"What is it?"

"An elk. Dead." The inadequate words were all she was capable of.

"Yes."

"Did you—"

"No."

Whether she believed the grizzly or not didn't matter. He might stop her from getting closer to the body, might swipe her out of existence. Despite the danger, she studied the carcass.

The elk lay on its side with its head at an awkward angle. Its eyes were closed, its slender legs useless. Its belly was well rounded. From where she stood, she couldn't see its sex organs, but its unimpressive antlers told her it was—had been—a young male.

"Not you, Songan," she managed. "Thank God, not you."

Despite her relief, cold sweat coated her spine, and for several seconds she couldn't hear anything for the roaring in her ears. Then, because she needed to know what had killed the youngster, she took three forward steps. The grizzly again rose onto his hind legs, revealing large, dark, nearly hairless sex organs.

Standing the way he was, the beast was close to twice her height, with claws capable of digging trenches in the earth—or her flesh—and startlingly white, potent teeth. His nose twitched, and his ears swiveled toward her, then back. She remained most aware of his eyes. Not only weren't they the right color, they were larger than they should be and full of depth.

"Get down. I can't handle this," she said, her voice dropping at the end. Surprised by her admission, she was slow to comprehend that he was indeed again lowering himself. He wasn't obeying her, never that. In fact, if she could believe the way his ears were working and his head's sudden sharp jerk to the left, she'd suddenly become unimportant to him.

Repositioning the rifle so it was at the ready, she strained to locate what had captured the bear's attention. A sharp crash nearly tore a scream from her. The bear whirled in that direction.

Even before the bull elk with the split-the-forest-size rack burst from the evergreens at the edge of the meadow, Rane knew what she'd see. Just the same, time snagged and nearly stopped. She smelled the rut on the elk, the prime in his thick neck. Clear of the underbrush now, he hammered himself to a stop, every inch shimmering and muscles threatening to burst through flesh and hair. No matter how many times she'd seen an elk up close, their potency awed her. In contrast to his dark brown legs, face and neck, the rest of his body was blond, the hair shaggy. The monster-size bull stood a three-second charge away.

A rutting bull elk's bugle was a beautiful thing, eerie and erotic all in one, but the sound grinding out of the massive lungs and throat had nothing to do with seduction. Instead, it was all challenge. Letting the grizzly know he was ready for battle.

This didn't happen in the natural world. An elk, which at his core was a prey animal even though a bull could be five feet high at the shoulder, attacked only to save his life or that of another of his kind. He'd charge another male elk to claim a cow in estrus but not a grizzly.

Again she nearly screamed. Then, chiding herself for almost playing the feminine card, she scurried backward. This was between two wilderness lords. Her only role was as audience.

Instead of charging the again upright bear, however, the elk plodded toward the carcass. His laborious movements were familiar.

"Songan," she whispered.

Chapter Two

Rage and confusion ran through the nine-hundred-pound elk. He might not know the name of the large, rich brown animal he'd nearly attacked, but something imbedded deep inside him told him the creature was unlike any he'd ever seen. Too big. Too intelligent. Dangerous and a threat.

A threat to what, the bull pondered. He lost the question when the slight, two-legged creature made a noise. He didn't understand the sound coming from the pale throat. At the same time, it was familiar. Keeping his head high and antlers angled toward the great beast, he tried to make sense of the two-legged one's smell, but other scents overran it. The fanged and clawed bear stank of challenge and might. In contrast, the wind-borne aroma that had brought him here spoke of surrender. Death. Gore.

Trying to comprehend took so much effort. The death stench warned that the same thing might happen to him, but how could he decide whether to flee or fight when he didn't know what had stopped the fallen elk's heart?

His blood ran hot with the sexual need that had driven him for days and distracted him from the question he dimly perceived to be vital. As the sun was rising this morning, he'd stepped into the middle of his harem, not to lead them to the nearby creek but because two cows were licking their sides and sex. They'd briefly tried to evade him, then stopped and set their wide-spread rear legs.

Bugling, he'd approached from behind, reared, planted his front legs along the first one's sides and curled his buttocks inward. His long, heavy cock first stabbed between the cow's rear legs and then rammed into the dripping, soft opening. Once, twice, three times he'd thrust deep. As the cow started to collapse, he'd backed away from her and headed toward the second one.

Mating twice had only fed his need to keep spilling himself until he was too spent to stand. Nostrils quivering, he'd been looking for another receptive cow when something beyond the drive to impregnate gripped him. Reluctantly turning his back on his harem, he'd let a sharp distant blast lead him to this meadow.

The retort hadn't been repeated, but deep inside resided the understanding that he was more than four legs, a heavy rack and hungry cock. That other thing needed answers.

His compulsion to learn the truth had was still so powerful he dismissed both the great newcomer and the two-legged creature.

Not wanting to do what he had to, he approached the dead elk. This one's antlers were half the size of his. That and the narrow chest and slender neck told him this male hadn't yet seen its second winter. Dark blood had pooled around a ragged hole behind his shoulder, but although he couldn't quite make sense of that, Songan had no trouble determining what else had been done to the young male. The sex organs had been removed.

Rage as powerful as any rut urge engulfed him. Whirling, he again faced the oversize creature he now recognized as a bear but with a coloring he'd never seen. He couldn't save the young elk, but he could avenge—

Pawing the ground so dirt and grass flew about, he lowered his head. The strange bear hoisted himself onto his hindquarters and swung his front legs up and out. Deadly claws raked the air. A sound like thunder burst from the gaping mouth.

The two-legged creature gasped. Out of the corner of his eyes, the elk saw that she—he knew that much—was aiming what looked like a branch at the sky. The branch bellowed, the sound nearly identical to what he'd heard this morning, only much louder. Startled, he turned his attention from the bear to the she-creature. Lowering the thunder-branch, she pointed it first at the bear and then him.

She started chattering, her mouth and throat moving, eyes saying she was afraid but not terrified. Even with everything he was trying to make sense of, he admired her courage.

Her eyes carried more than warning and determination, and as her chattering slowed and then quieted, he studied the huge brown bear. The creature was back down on all fours and staring at the *she*. It tipped its head to the side as if trying to make sense of the now soft sounds. No longer having to concentrate on how much of a threat the grizzly presented helped cool the elk's blood, but it was more than that. With every breath he took, he dismissed more of the death and bear smells and became more aware of the *she*.

Her. Female. Touching him in ways he needed. Triggering memories.

"Songan," she said. "Songan."

Feeling as if she might splinter into a thousand pieces, Rane repeated the shape-shifter's name in the singsong tone she'd relied on over the years. It could be her imagination, her need to make order out of today's craziness, but she swore she was getting through to him. One thing she was certain of, the beautiful bull elk who was her friend and sometimes sex partner was focused on her instead of the grizzly or the inert body. Knowing she didn't dare do the same added to her fear that she might not be able to hold everything together. Dismissing the grizzly could get her killed today.

Determined to put an end to the standoff, she leveled the rifle at the bear while continuing to mutter Songan's name. Something about the grizzly still felt off. Its—his—eyes hinted at impossible intelligence for an animal. Her stomach tightened as a possibility occurred to her, but that would have to wait.

Taking a deep breath, she yelled, "Go!" at the grizzly. Teeth clenched, she fired, aiming several feet over his body. Her arms jerked upward, and for an instant, she couldn't see anything. The bear, sounding startled or angry or both, roared.

"You heard me! Go! You're not wanted here."

The beast reared and dropped to the ground with a thud. His lips curled back, exposing his teeth.

Willing her arms to hold steady, she fired again. This bullet streaked less than a foot above the bear's back. The echo went on and on. Instead of attacking her or running away, which was what she was hoping for, she swore the beast's eyes told her not to panic.

"Go, please. I don't want to kill you, so just get the hell out of here!" Like her puny deer rifle could bring down a thousand-pound monster.

What she was tempted to interpret as a frown pulled the grizzly's eyes together. His attention flicked to Songan, then back on her. She swore he sighed before slowly and regally backing away. After a final look at Songan, the mass of muscle and bone turned and loped away. Moments later, he'd disappeared into the close-growing evergreens marking the end of the meadow. Despite that, his essence remained. He was still in the area.

Now that the immediate threat had been dealt with, Rane waited for relief to weaken her muscles. Instead, regret closed around her. Irrational as the thought was, she wanted the beast to return. If he did, she imagined herself slowly approaching, reaching out and touching the great body.

As far as she knew, the elk shifter hadn't moved while she was dealing with the bear. Accustomed as she was to Songan's behavior when he was in elk form, she knew not to expect much of him intellectually. Right now all that truly mattered was whether he knew she was part of his world.

After a final look in the direction the grizzly had gone, he approached the carcass. His graceful head topped by a massive rack hung as if he was reluctant to acknowledge what couldn't be denied. It took effort for her not to touch Songan in sympathy, but experience had taught her to have patience when he was like this. Shifting her gaze, she noted that the dead elk had been shot in the side behind its front legs. Seeing lacerated flesh where its sex organs had been again made her sick to her stomach.

"Who did this?" she muttered around clenched teeth. "What kind of bastard..."

The bull elk she'd come here in hopes of finding stepped between her and the carcass. She wondered whether he was more concerned with protecting one of his kind or shielding her. His eyes darkened, and he again lowered his head as if the weight of his antlers was more than he could bear.

"I'm sorry. This was the work of poachers, damnable killers. I can't call them human."

Until now she hadn't had time to consider that whoever

had shot the young elk might still be around, but with the grizzly no longer constituting a threat, if it was, she was able to concentrate on other things. If the hunter or hunters hadn't put considerable distance between themselves and what they obviously had no more use for, they'd heard her shoot. They might have even heard her cry out. Songan and she were vulnerable. Maybe as much as her mother had been.

"It's too late to wish I'd been quiet," she told Songan as he continued to regard her. "The damage is done. Oh, I'm so sorry I said that." She jerked her head at the carcass. "That's real damage."

The magnificent elk, who was much more than that to her, looked down at what could have been one of his offspring.

"Do you know what I'm thinking?" she continued. "Do my words make sense?"

With her attention fully on him, she searched her memory for what Songan had looked like the last time she'd seen him like this. Her mother still lived—had lived—in Forestville, and Rane had tried to see her every few months. Each time she did, Songan and she *hooked up*, but if her memory was right, she hadn't seen him as an elk for a couple of years.

"You've matured," she told him. "All bulked up. You're also full of fire because it's *that* time of the year." She reluctantly nodded at the inert form. "I'd hoped I'd find you here. The meadow's a favorite place for the herd this time of year. But I wasn't sure—I know what bulls are like during rut. Nothing takes them from the females. Not even death."

The elk continued to study her. His eyes made her think of wet and impenetrable obsidian. Suddenly weary, she lowered her rifle to the ground. Then she pressed the base of her hand to her forehead. Memories of the days and nights with Songan washed over her, and pressure of another kind ground into her.

Maybe her sexual awareness was nothing more than needing to distance herself from the nightmare she'd been living and responding to Songan's high testosterone level. Maybe.

"I've been looking for you. I need your help." Feeling exposed by her admission, she ran her hand into her hair, disrupting the thick, shoulder-blade-length mass as she did. "Maybe human concerns mean nothing to you this time of year. Maybe you don't know what happened."

Only a few minutes ago, she'd considered herself part of the world she'd grown up in. Now she felt as if she'd lost touch with everything except pure male animal. She'd stare at him as long as he stared at her, and when that was over and he'd gone back to being nothing except a bull elk, what? Return to her mother's empty house? Continue to be alone while the desire for justice overwhelmed her.

"Songan," she whispered. "I need you."

The elk shuddered. She'd seen the transformation and knew what to expect. Still, it had been awhile, and she'd forgotten how much power was involved.

Even though she knew it wasn't true, as he jerked and shivered, she half believed he'd been struck by lightning. Wave after wave of movement rolled down the rut-swollen neck and through the solid body. The waves came faster and faster until she could no longer distinguish where one ended and another began.

Similar to a balloon robbed of air, the form before her shrank and morphed from rich golden brown to flesh color. Front legs transformed themselves into arms. The massive rack disappeared. One heartbeat, she was watching an elk. The next, the man she'd given her virginity to stood naked before her.

Recalling that he'd need several minutes to adjust to the change, she clenched her fingers and studied six feet three inches of muscled male. The last time she'd seen Songan, which had been some six months ago, she'd talked him into stepping on the scales. He'd weighed just over two hundred pounds, but it looked as if he'd put on at least twenty more, every ounce of it muscle.

When in human form, which was about half of the time, Songan and his fellow shifters gravitated toward physical labor. Political and economic factors had led to a decreased need for timber in recent years, but several tracks of mostly lodgepole pine had opened up for harvesting this year. Her mother's e-mails had kept her up-to-date about work on the new logging roads into the area and the massive, expensive equipment that now did what hundreds of loggers had once accomplished. Despite those changes, the two women had agreed there'd always be a need for men who understood trees and the dangers inherent in working among them.

Even as he stood naked with his hair-dusted belly and muscled ass, Rane acknowledged that Songan was one of those strong, brave, and resourceful men. He belonged in the wilderness even more than she did.

He needed a haircut and hadn't shaved for days. His thick, long, red-black hair had been combed by the wind. The way he stood with his legs spread and his arms out from his sides made her wonder if he felt as if the world was tipping under him. She could only guess what changing felt like. He gave no indication he was aware of her as he took in the meadow with its slender, white-barked aspens and the large pines surrounding them. Obviously he was reluctant to leave his animal half.

Songan had an erection. She'd never seen a more potent cock, all dark prominent veins and thick foreskin ringing the base of his cockhead. Thinking about how she loved to slide the sleek foreskin about made her hands sweat.

"Songan, it's me, Rane."

"I know."

His eyes no longer had that faraway and unfocused look, but his unemotional tone told her he hadn't completed the transformation. He'd once explained that he felt as if he belonged nowhere while morphing from human to animal or back again, and although he'd said nothing about being alarmed by the experience, she didn't see how it could be otherwise. He didn't want to be touched until he was fully in one body or the other.

She'd waited long enough. She had to remind him of what they'd once had.

Otherwise, he might never understand her need for him.

Her legs had grown weak. Either that or knowing what she was asking of them had stripped strength from them. Whichever it was, she had to concentrate on walking. As a result, when she looked up at him, she was closer than she thought she'd be.

Warmth flowed from his naked form to reach and caress her skin through her clothing. If the cool mountain air had made an impact on him, he gave no indication as he placed his broad, strong hands on her shoulders. She'd left her backpack and rifle behind. Except for the clothes she suddenly wanted nothing to do with, she and Songan were equals. Hopefully alone.

Will you help me? was what she'd believed would be the first thing to come out of her mouth once they stood face to face. But sex had always defined their relationship. It still did.

"You're back," he said.

"My mother—you can't be surprised to see me."

"I'm sorry, Rane. Sorry about what happened to her and what's happening to me right now." Letting go of one shoulder, he cupped his cock. "This time of year, I can't fight the elk in me. I wanted to be there for you, but—"

"I know." Strangely, staring at what she could see of his cock was easier on her nerves than looking into his eyes. All except needing to have it buried inside her. "Remember, I was here when you matured. The first fall when the rut hit you—"

"I wanted to fuck your brains out."

"Not just want. You did."

Maybe he was no longer interested in going down memory lane. More likely sex held the upper hand as he pulled her against him. Her face mashed into his chest. Even as she turned her head so she could breathe, his cock grinding at her belly loosened and moistened her pussy.

Clouds were starting to gather, a brisk wind pushing them and bringing a faint, distant scent of snow. Except for acknowledging the cool air, she paid little attention to the change. It would take a lot more than a breeze to kill the desire tearing at her.

Songan's hold let up a little. Freeing her arms, she wrapped them around his neck. No doubt about it, being in rut added bulk and muscle to his human form. As a wildlife biologist, she was familiar with the creatures that inhabited the Northwest forests. Songan was at his sexual peak. Depending on how well he took care of himself and how many bull-to-bull battles he got into, he could stay like this for years. Be everything she wanted in a man.

In a distracted way, she knew she had no business letting his body take control of hers, but she'd been fantasizing about this moment for too long, when she could be free of grief.

Needed it too much. She'd gone looking for him because she wanted justice for her mother, but even that would have to wait.

First and maybe always came feeding this awesome hunger.

A low whimper escaped her as she stood on her toes, tilted her head and raked her teeth over the side of his neck. Grunting, he lifted her off her feet. Since moving away from Forestville, she'd engaged in rough sex with two men, but they hadn't outweighed her by over a hundred pounds and weren't more than a foot taller.

They weren't half animal.

"What's this?" Smiling slightly, he turned his head so she could see the red marks she'd left on him. "Some point you're trying to make?"

"Impulse. Craziness."

"Caused by what?"

My mother's murder. "It's not like we've ever set any limits set on what happens between us. Let me down."

Smiling, he shook both his head and her. "Like you said, no limits or boundaries."

He's in his prime, dangerously so. Don't do something stupid. Despite her warning, however, she lightly pressed a knee to his groin. "Things haven't changed with you. You still insist on being in control."

"Human nature." Giving her a look she couldn't fathom, he lowered her to the ground but kept his hands on her waist. Her fingers dragged over his neck.

"You aren't human, not all the way."

"And you can't handle it. That's why you left."

"That wasn't the only reason, and you know it. It was time for me to find out who I was. In part to break the addiction between us." Any other woman would probably be too intimidated to say what she just had, but Songan brought out something strong and wild in her, something she didn't understand or trust.

"You also wanted more than any elk shifter can give," he said. "Me being there all the time."

"Not now. That's not what I—"

"What then?" he demanded. "Damn it, Rane. I am what I am, just as you are."

"What are you saying?" Lightning hadn't struck. Songan and Songan alone was responsible for what raged through her. "That I don't live up to your expectations because I'm not a shifter?"

"I've always accepted you. I just wish you felt the same way."

"It's easier for you. You don't have to deal with human emotions all the time." The words weren't out before she wished she could take them back. "Look, I'm sorry. This is hardly the time to—what brought you here?" She nodded in the direction of the dead elk. "Did you sense—maybe you heard shots."

"I don't know." Letting up on the pressure around her waist, he started stroking her there. Her nerves jumped. "Maybe you're responsible."

He was talking about the powerful connection that had once existed between them, a connection she'd believed she had to sever if she was ever going to live her own life.

These mountains had once been part of her world, but they no longer were. She had to remind herself of that, somehow.

But later. When her body no longer cried out for him.

She'd intended to beg for his help in finding out who had murdered her mother, not beg him for sex. As early as this morning, she'd believed, or told herself she believed, that her need for justice would see her through seeing Songan but not wanting to fuck him.

What a damnable liar she'd been.

Feeling as if she was drowning and flying at the same time, she yanked her flannel shirt hem out of her jeans waistband. Her fingers jabbed at the buttons, and she fumbled repeatedly before she managed to free all of them. An insistent inner voice cried *hurry, hurry, hurry* as she attacked her jeans fastening. To hell with that broken nail. She'd never cared about how her hands looked anyway.

Grabbing her shirt, Songan pulled it as far off her shoulders as he could, given her determination to get out of her jeans.

She felt no need to speak. Action said everything. Obviously Songan felt the same, because the moment she'd finished her task, he spun her away from him. Not asking permission, he tore off her top and hauled her jeans down over her hips.

Despite the hindrance, she crouched and clawed at her boots' lacing. Songan unhooked her bra and started to pull it off her, causing her to stumble. Muttering something unintelligible, he gave her his legs to brace against. Once she'd succeeded in loosening the boots, she lifted a foot and tried to shake off her footwear.

Something moved in the nearby woods. Tense, she clutched Songan's arm with both hands. With the veins at her temples pulsing, her ability to hear was compromised, but her sight was still sharp, wasn't it? A little more time and she'd know who or what was out there.

"What?" Songan muttered.

"I'm not sure. Something."

Chapter Three

Motionless, Songan looked in the same direction she was. The clouds were still darkening, but that wasn't the only reason she was having trouble making out details. Being around Songan had always made her stupid. Stupid and horny. Maybe dangerously so today.

He tensed and let out a long, slow breath. Then he inhaled, and she guessed he was searching for telling smells. She tried to do the same, but Songan's earthy scent was so strong.

"Bear," he whispered.

Of course. Now that Songan had pointed out the obvious, she made out the large, dusky form among the equally dark tree trunks. The creature was down on all fours with his head high and nose up, looking at them.

"He didn't leave." She winced at having voiced something so obvious. Then because it was driving her crazy dangling from her shoulders, and certainly the creature didn't care, she finished pulling off her bra. If this turned into a footrace, she didn't stand a chance.

What was she thinking? Songan would protect her.

Except he was now in human form, naked and unarmed.

"My rifle." She tried to determine how far away it was, but Songan's form was in the way.

"You won't need it."

A shiver that might or might not be a reaction to the wind struck her. Still studying the bear, Songan drew her against his warm, strong chest. "You can't know that," she told him.

"He's content to watch."

Her lips went numb. "Watch?"

"Us having sex."

The world suddenly became even less comprehensible than it had the day she'd learned her mother was missing, but as much as she needed Songan to explain how he could be so sure about the bear, she knew better than to ask because he understood the other creatures that called the forest home.

"We're going to fuck," he said. "Now."

He was right. Until mutual need had been fed, nothing else mattered, not even justice for her mother. Thinking to hide her wanton response, she started to sigh, then swallowed the lying sound. Songan knew her too well for anything except honesty on her part. Her leaving hadn't changed that.

Besides, Songan knew her body as intimately as she did, maybe more.

"Watch, then," she silently told the distant bear. *"You'll do what you want, same as us."*

Relegating the grizzly to a quiet part of her mind, she watched and waited and trembled as Songan crouched and placed her left boot on his thigh. Running her fingers into his tangled hair, she balanced herself. He wasted no time pulling off her footwear, followed by her jeans, but left her practical panties untouched.

Palms together, Songan slid his hands between her thighs. Believing he intended to head for her pussy, she closed her eyes and held her breath. Her heart raced. His hands didn't move.

"Songan?"

"I'm still elk." The words came out low and rushed. "In rut. Don't forget that."

"I won't." Could she fully comprehend what that meant?

"I have needs."

Leaning into him, she rubbed her breasts against his face. Her nipples were already hard, but they tightened even more, almost painfully so. Seeking both distraction and a way of responding to what he'd just said, she hooked her thumbs over the elastic in her panties and began a downward journey. Much as she wanted to go slow, she couldn't. When her buttocks were exposed, she was forced to stop because his hands were in the way. Trusting him to finish what she'd begun, she straightened. As she did, she admired the strength in his legs that allowed him to crouch for so long.

Leaving the garment he must know she had no use for in place, he exhaled. His breath floated over her naked belly. Eyes unfocused and breathing ragged, she followed the warmth into her pubic hair and between her legs.

"Foreplay?" she managed. "I like. Oh damn, I like."

He leaned into her and raked her belly much as she'd done to his neck earlier. Swaying, she clamped her fingers over his shoulders. The moment she did, she realized she'd set the stage for what she knew was going to happen next. Foreplay was for civilized men and women, not a half man/half elk and a wild woman who had spent much of her life outdoors.

Songan surged to his feet, lifting her and heaving her over his shoulder as he did.

"What the—" she started.

"Putting distance between us and the dead elk."

Lost in conflicting thoughts, she waited as Songan walked

them away from the body. "Thank you," she said at length.

"Don't talk." He slapped her bare ass.

"Hey, that hurts."

"No, it doesn't."

Planting her hands against his back to brace her upper body, she lifted her head and looked around. There the bear was, a large shadow barely distinguishable from other shadows and thinking thoughts she couldn't comprehend.

Thoughts? Yes.

Songan stood with one arm looped around her middle. The other stroked her buttocks. No way could she call his touch anything except firm, hard almost. The pressure ate into her, going steadily deeper, claiming her. Caught in sensation, she let her head drop and pulled his scent deep into her. Running her nails over his back, she noted his spine, ribs and muscle.

When he slid his hand between her legs and ran a finger along her wet, hot sex, a mewling sound rolled out of her. Her breasts slid over his shoulder blades, prompting her to rear away and then fall back down, twisting her upper body as she did so her nipples stroked his flesh. There. Let him try to ignore that.

Perhaps he knew what she had in mind but was determined to stay in charge when he made a return trip to her pussy. This intimate exploration lasted longer and went deeper.

"Damn you." Why did she have to sound so delighted?

"No talking. The only thing you need to do is experience." With that, he lightly thumped her clit.

A hot wave rolled through her. With it came surrender. Everything else could wait, even vengeance and justice. What did she care whether the clouds continued to gather, at whose hands the young elk had met its death, why the bear was still around? The world beyond her body didn't exist.

"My head—the blood's rushing to it."

"I like you this way."

What way? Before she could pull the words together, he rolled her clit. She moaned like a bitch in heat. He liked her helpless and undone, down on his animal level, which was one of the reasons she'd convinced herself she needed to break free. Her pussy wept, and her nails left thin white lines on his flesh. Her panties were still around her thighs, holding her legs together and digging into her. Pleasure mixed with pain, confusing her and taking her even farther from reality. Her world blurred and swirled, colors melting into something indescribable. She was dizzy and half sick, helpless and lost.

Moaning and mewling, she fought the iron grip around her waist. Her nails plowed deeper, and she tried to kick him but was forced to stop thanks to the nylon around her thighs. He didn't give up, damn him, continued his wonderfully wild assault.

"Damn, damn, damn," she chanted. The next time he stroked her opening, she tried to pull him into her.

"Not yet." He punctuated his order by trapping her clit under a rough, slick forefinger.

"Knock it off! Songan, this isn't funny."

"I'm not laughing. Neither are you."

Shifting her higher on his shoulder, he gave up his claim on her clit and turned his full attention to her sopping channel. Over and over he fucked her with a thick finger. The sucking sound both embarrassed her and brought her even closer to the jagged cliff.

She didn't want to reach the edge this fast! At the same time, she could hardly wait to catapult out into space.

"I shouldn't—damn you, I shouldn't…"

"Shouldn't have come looking for me," he finished. "Maybe, but it's too late."

Too late, all right. The point of no return was so far behind she was no longer sure it ever existed. Done in, she stopped fighting. Her spent and ready body sagged, and she tried to time her breathing with his finger's long, slow invasion and retreat. She dimly comprehended that he knew how close she was to climaxing and was deliberately holding her back. Much as his power unnerved her, she gloried in it.

Songan knew her in ways no other man ever could. He'd awakened her virginal body, and together they'd explored the height and breadth of what sex could be.

And today he was using his knowledge against her.

For her.

"Songan, please. I'm going to be sick." Had she really meant to say that?

On the heels of a sound she couldn't comprehend, he leaned forward, and she slid off his shoulder. Her ribs and belly ached from bearing her weight while all but upside down. Her stomach was a little queasy all right, but that was inconsequential in the wake of the molten, melting sensation throughout her.

Looking down at her with a wary expression and wide-legged stance that seemed to be daring her to try to make a break for it, Songan folded his arms across his chest. Strange how she could both dismiss his nudity and be possessed by it at the same time.

"What is it?" she asked as she ran her less than steady fingers over the nylon roping her legs. "You think I'm going to run?"

He didn't answer, but his gaze remained steady and alert on her. "I would," she admitted. Pull her briefs back into place or rip them off? The choice she made would determine today's direction. More than that, this single decision could impact the rest of her life.

"But I won't," she admitted.

"You know how I am." Unfolding his arms, he held up a glistening finger. "Nothing subtle about that."

Another woman might be embarrassed, but their relationship went too deep. She indicated the erect male flesh aimed at her. "You're right, nothing subtle." Feeling disconnected from her body, she stepped into his space and placed a hand over his cock. Blood pulsed against her palm, and her mouth filled with saliva. "That's what's in charge." She stroked him. "For both of us."

When he gave her a puzzled look, she said, "Every time your cock speaks, you heed it. If I so much as see a bulge under your jeans, I have to have you."

The skin under her fingers was like silk. Beneath that lay strength and the essence of what made him a man. No matter how many times he'd filled her over the years, she always lost her mind. Her body. Sex between them tore her apart and glued her together. And climaxing—oh God, that was like dying and being reborn in the same breath.

Trembling, she ran her hand around his cock. At the same time, she tugged one-handed on her panties and brought them down to her knees. Several shakes of her lower body had them down around her ankles. Still holding on to Songan, she stepped free.

Placing his hands under her breasts, he slid his big, workman's fingers around and down them so his thumbs and forefingers gripped her taut nipples. The unspoken message was clear. No matter what happened today, he was in control.

"What now?" She hoped she sounded lighthearted. "Standoff?"

"I don't think so."

A sudden shockwave in her breasts brought her onto her toes. What she could see of her nipples was turning white. Distracted, she let go of his cock.

"Hands behind you," he said.

They'd done this before. Rough was nothing new. Unless she protested, which she almost never did, he took her hard. Hard and mind-stripping. Off-the-chart explosions.

He'd backed the pressure off a little, but her nipples were getting numb. No way could she get free if he didn't want her to. Despite the months since they'd last done this, she knew what was going to happen. He'd order her down on her knees. She'd obey, not because she was afraid but because she wasn't the feminist the world believed she was. In her heart of hearts, she wasn't so different from the female elk he and his fellow shifters forcefully mounted each fall.

"You know how it's going to be." His every word was clipped. "How I want you."

Staring down at her trapped breasts, she spoke through clenched teeth. "Yeah. Like I'm an animal."

She'd said what she had in an attempt to reach the compassionate and caring man who sometimes emerged from the beast, but when he gave no indication he'd heard, let alone cared, she leaned away so her breasts stretched out. A burning sensation ripped through her; then suddenly she was free. Newly restored circulation made her nipples pulse, and she lightly rubbed them. Songan watched.

"Tell me something," she said. "Have you had sex with any

women since the last time between us?"

"No."

No? Thank you. She nearly shook her head at the double standard she'd set up. Yes, she'd been celibate since her last visit, but she could hardly expect that of him. It wasn't as if they'd promised themselves to each other. Still, knowing he'd mounted only female elk helped. Instead of telling him that, she looked around for a spot where the grass was particularly dense. Getting in position should be simple, right? Her pussy throbbed in anticipation, and her legs were losing strength by the moment. But—

A chuffing sound shattered her disjointed thoughts. The bear. "Make him leave! Who or whatever he is, I want him gone."

"Who?"

"Maybe I don't know what I'm saying, but there's something about him."

"What is it?"

Facing Songan was easier than acknowledging the grizzly right now. The creature's behavior unnerved her more than she wanted to admit. "I don't want him here."

It doesn't matter.

Shocked by the words inside her head, she pressed herself against Songan and wrapped her arms around him. His cock served as a reminder of what had nearly happened and what she still needed from him with every fiber in her.

"Did you hear that?" she asked. "You—you didn't just say something did you?"

Songan's arms against her shoulders and back felt like life. "What something?"

"I heard—I thought I heard someone say, 'It doesn't matter.'

I...ah...I'd just said I didn't want the bear here."

Songan hadn't changed his mind about fucking. As long as their bodies spoke to each other this way, sex was going to happen. She'd become one with him.

Gathering her courage, she turned from Songan until she glimpsed the bear out of the corner of her eye. She couldn't be sure but thought he was closer than earlier, and yet there wasn't anything aggressive about his stance. He was part of his surroundings, simple as that. Waiting. Watching.

"What do you want?" she asked the bear.

Chapter Four

The beast didn't answer. She heard no response in her head. Despite that, she had the unnerving sense that the bear was trying to communicate with her.

"I want to leave," she told Songan.

"I don't."

"Oh? And if that thing attacks, you'll throw me at it? Protect yourself?"

"That won't happen."

"How can you be sure?"

"How?" Songan pushed her back so she had no choice but to look into his eyes. "I'm as much of an animal as it is."

She couldn't argue with that. Hell, she couldn't do anything except press herself against his cock.

"Down," Songan commanded her. "Now."

Feeling disconnected from everything—including their silent audience—except for Songan, she sank to her knees. Her hands and cheek slid over the elk shifter's athletic form as she did, and once she was in place, she parted her lips and brushed them over his cock. His taste and texture flooded her. Moaning, she wrapped her arms around his legs. "I've waited so long. Wanted this so much."

"Rane, now."

Just like her, Songan was trembling. She didn't think he had since they were teenagers. Did that mean she'd weakened this man who ruled the forest when he was in elk form? Admitting vulnerability was beyond him, not that she'd try to force the words from him, and yet seeing the mortal beneath the potent exterior made her fall in love with him.

Just for now, she told herself. Only until we've had sex.

Biting down on a weak and helpless cry, she planted her hands in front of her with her fingers spread and palms against the ground. Dampness seeped up from the earth to coat her hands, knees and feet. She felt deeply connected to her surroundings.

She wouldn't tell Songan she loved him. The emotion had never lasted once they'd had sex, and she remembered how little she'd have of him. But her body, oh God, her body!

"Now!" she commanded with her head low and eyes closed. A few tears leaked out to dampen her lashes.

Songan dropped to his knees behind her, making the ground shake a little. She knew he was going to touch her, had forgotten nothing about the ways he'd handled her. Just the same, she flinched when he ran his thumbs between her ass cheeks. His short nails pressed against her rear opening. Excited and unnerved, she shivered.

"Legs apart."

She thought she'd already adequately spread them, but today she'd give this man everything he needed. Tomorrow, hopefully, belonged to her and her mission.

If there was a way for them to remain together.

When her legs were so far apart she felt the strain in her back and buttocks, Songan slowly ran his hands under her, coming closer to her dripping opening. Lifting her head, she stared at the closest treetops. She'd been wrong when she told herself today was for him. She needed to be mounted as much as he needed to mount.

Human forms, animal mating.

That was what they'd told each other back when they first realized that switching from elk to man didn't change Songan's base nature. She'd said she accepted his need to do it doggy style, and she did, most of the time. Except for when she longed to look into his eyes as they climaxed.

Even as his fingers tested her labia, clit and opening, Songan kept moving about. She should try to see what he was doing, but his fingers, his glorious and knowing fingers, owned her. Her pussy twitched. The familiar hot wanting seized her, promising relief, threatening loss of control.

"Songan, Songan!"

Moist warmth slipped over her inner thighs and along her channel. She was still trying to put the pieces of what he was doing together when he lapped at her. His tongue slipped light and electric over her pussy, causing her to mew like some lost kitten. Strength melted from her, and she started to collapse but forced her elbows to lock. She shook.

He licked her sex again. Bowing her back, she dug her nails into the earth. A long, low moan pressed past her clenched teeth.

"You're making me crazy."

"Not close. Not close."

Despite the havoc to her nervous system, she managed to stay in place as Songan fed from her liquid offering. She floated someplace between this world and a space bright with hot colors. Maybe she was climaxing. Maybe she'd gone beyond that and was caving in. Repeatedly dying and being reborn.

The thought of reincarnation briefly distracted her. Then

suddenly everything centered on her. On Songan. Mindlessly giving herself to him, she dropped onto her elbows and lifted her ass as high as possible. She swayed from side to side in invitation, but maybe he didn't notice, because he was now trying to suck her labia between his lips. Ropes couldn't imprison her any more than this did. At the same time, she felt free and wild, a winged beast.

Songan might have been born to live in both human and animal worlds, but he wasn't the only one torn between two existences. Most of the time, she willingly abided by society's rules. But nothing else mattered during those times when Songan and she shared the same air. She flew then.

Lost in thoughts that swirled over her, exploded or evaporated, she lowered her upper body even farther and rested her forehead on her forearms. There. A cunt offered up to a cock.

Crisp air raked her hot, wet labia where his breath and tongue had been. If this hadn't happened before, she might believe Songan had abandoned her, but she knew what was coming. The knowing made her both patient and half crazed with anticipation.

Still panting, she pushed herself back up and locked her elbows. She saw only browns and greens bleeding together.

Then Songan spread his hands over her ass cheeks and pulled them apart. Knowing he was staring at her rear opening didn't embarrass her. She just needed him to hurry. To spear her.

All at once her face felt as if it was on fire, prompting her to stretch her neck and stare upward. The wind had grown teeth, which only excited her more.

"I wish it wasn't like this," he muttered from above and behind her. "Just once I wish we could take it slow."

"We tried, remember? Do it, Songan. Now."

Cursing, he closed his hands around her hips. In her mind's eye, she saw him rock toward her with his cock between her legs. Determined to make the alignment perfect, she bowed her back and set herself.

The first touch—that whispered moment when he was gentle—was over too soon. What began with his cockhead light against her entrance slipped away, ended abruptly, really. Pressure built against her sex. He drove into her and relentlessly claimed her.

They'd fused. Become one.

Tears bled and tracked down her cheeks. She couldn't say whether she truly wanted to have sex with Songan. It simply was. They simply were. Like winter following fall, this moment was destined to happen.

Her contours no longer existed. Only her pussy mattered. That and her dangling breasts. The elk shifter pushed deeper so his groin pressed against her buttocks. It felt as if they shared the same thigh muscles. Her hair was plastered to her cheeks. A strand tickled her nose. She tried to bite on what had never been permed or colored, then forgot what she was doing.

Songan demanded ownership of her body. She gave it to him, all of it. Crying but not knowing why, she held herself steady. One second and then another passed. This hesitation, she understood, was Songan's attempt to rein in his savage nature. He'd never told her he wanted some measure of self-control during the act of fucking, but she'd long sensed his battle.

"It's all right. I'm ready. I want."

Songan's breath whistled, and she imagined his nostrils flaring. His cock and her cunt were locked in on each other. The rest of their bodies be damned.

His hands tightened, no doubt leaving fingerprints on her buttocks. Damn it, she didn't want him to be at war with himself. They were having sex, and that was enough.

They also had an audience of one.

Something about acknowledging the bear allowed her to relax. She again stopped thinking, tapped into her nerves. The breeze was sandpapering her skin and heightening her awareness of herself. She'd offered her body up to Songan, and he'd taken the gift. She was his, body and heart.

Her face flushed. Even her eyelids burned. Heat claimed her chest and ran over her unrestrained breasts. Songan repeatedly buried himself in her, rocking her forward with each thrust. She gasped, then stopped so she could concentrate on pushing back against him. Reaching under her, he grabbed a breast and pressed it against her chest wall. The trapped heat there built. She was catching fire! Alarmed, she tried to shake him off.

"I wanted to be there for you after your mom, you know." His voice was clipped, even angry.

"Not now. Later."

He still had hold of her breast. Between that and his hard, harsh thrusts, she didn't know where he ended and she began. She met him strength for strength. Need for need. Flames continued to slip through her veins and center in her pussy.

Yes! What she wanted! What no other man had been able to give her. Her thoughts died, to be replaced by the crazy rapid-fire whimpering coming from her throat.

Songan cried out. The hand not on her breast landed on the small of her back, and he pressed down. His hot, sticky come filled her channel.

The second time he cried out, she climaxed.

Chapter Five

Rane hadn't yet recovered her strength. She wanted nothing more than to curl up on the ground where she'd collapsed and fall asleep. However, she was already getting cold, which left her with no choice but to stand and put back on her clothes. Songan had remained on his knees watching while she did. As she knelt one-legged so she could tie her boots, he stood.

They'd never been any good at finding things to say post-fuck. Any other time she'd hide behind the silence she'd become good at, but today was different. Standing, she faced the big, naked man.

"I didn't thank you for calling when Mom first went missing." She made a point of meeting his gaze. "Deputy Gannon kept me informed until I could get here but—anyway, thank you."

He shrugged, causing his limp but still considerable cock to bounce. "I wanted it to be more. To have a role in the search."

He hadn't, because much as Forestville residents accepted the elk shifters in their midst, certain things like search and rescue were dependent on year-round, dependable help, not someone who might be a man one day and an elk another.

This was her mother, she'd told Gannon when Forestville's lone county deputy tried to discourage her from joining those who'd been looking for Jacki for two days before she arrived. Gannon, who'd worked with her mother for years, had eventually agreed, but she hadn't been with those who found her mother's body east of the remote Forest Service cabin known as Wolverine.

By then, rut had claimed Songan.

"Look." Shaken by the wash of memories, Rane tried to push her loose hair behind her ears. "The investigation—they've been all over the Wolverine area, but not even the tracking dog found a clue about who shot Mom."

"It's been raining."

"I know. The storm started before they found her. It's a wonder—"

"A wonder they found her. She wasn't that close to the cabin."

"You know that?"

"I came back once." He frowned. "I can't remember when—a few days ago. It didn't last long, just long enough for me to talk to the deputy."

"He didn't tell me that."

"I asked him not to."

"Why?"

"Because I couldn't be there for you. I hated—damn it, this is so powerful." He fingered his cock.

"Resisting rut is hard today, isn't it?"

He nodded. "I'm fighting, but between you and that"—he indicated the mutilated elk carcass—"it happened."

She hadn't intended for things to get complicated so soon after letting him into her body. Damn it, his gift was still leaking from her and staining her panties. "I'm glad you were able to resist nature."

"I should have tried harder to break free."

Even though it had been long-distance, he'd helped her hold it together the nightmare day she'd learned that her mother, a Forest Service ranger assigned to the Chinook Mountains, was missing. Songan had helped her make the decision to drive instead of fly so she could bring many of her belongings with her. By the time she'd gotten in touch with Gannon, Songan had stopped answering his cell phone. She'd known what had happened to him, where he'd gone.

"She'd been shot." The words tore at Rane's throat. "That's what destroys me. I know it wasn't an accident. Someone deliberately—"

Before she could finish, Songan grabbed her and pulled her into him. "Don't," he insisted. "Thinking like that will only make you sick."

"I'm already sick." With her face against his chest, her voice sounded muffled. She wouldn't cry! The endless hours of fear and tears were behind her. It was time for action. Maybe redemption for her.

After filling her lungs with Songan's scent, she pushed back, but only a little because she wasn't yet strong enough to ask him to release her. "There are signs she was dragged," she managed. "That means she was killed somewhere else. If I knew where it happened, maybe I could figure out why."

"Let law enforcement do their job."

"The bullets went through her. They didn't find any shells." Exhaustion clawed at her. "All that rain... If Gannon knows something, he isn't telling me. I can't just sit in her house, blaming myself, feeling worthless."

"Blaming yourself?"

Yes. "I don't know what I'm thinking." Not trusting herself to say what she most needed to, she ran her knuckles over

Songan's breastbone. His skin was sticky from fucking her and cool from the worsening weather.

"Maybe it was hunters. She was in the wrong place at the wrong time, an accident, not murder."

"If that's it, they were poaching. Just like what happened today with the young elk. Songan, what if she came across something *they* didn't want her to see? She was killed to silence her." She shuddered.

"Don't go there. That's for law enforcement to determine."

"This isn't a city," she snapped. "There's no CSI here, just one deputy. And a whole damn forest to search for—for something." Right after climaxing, she'd told herself to look to see if the bear was still there, but things had gotten away from her. Now she studied her surroundings.

"He isn't here," Songan told her.

"You saw him leave?"

"I know."

Believing him, she picked up the thread of what they'd been talking about. "I'm supposed to go back to a career that suddenly means nothing to me? Leave flowers on my mother's grave, put her house on the market, do what has to be done to her possessions and wrap up her finances? I can't. It isn't enough."

Songan lightly ran his rough hand over her neck and cheek. "No. I guess it isn't."

She didn't want to hear him say *guess*. The word served as a reminder of the missing parts to him. His human body couldn't be more perfect. In contrast, his emotions didn't seem to be fully developed. Something had alerted him to the dead elk, but if he mourned the loss, he gave no sign. No anger over the sexual mutilation.

Taking a deep breath, she clamped both hands around his wrist. "I need something from you. That's why I'm here."

A barely perceptible shudder rolled through him. He glanced around at the forest, then looked at her. Obviously he wanted to become an elk again and not have to deal with human concerns, even hers.

"What?" he asked after too long.

Even though she'd mentally rehearsed the words for days, she had to gather herself before continuing. "This is your land. I know it as well as any man or woman can, but you're at another level."

"I taught you all I know."

And she'd always be grateful for his patience and willingness. "But the wilderness doesn't speak to me the way it does to you. No matter what I do, I'll never hear certain things."

A simple nod made her believe Songan understood what she was trying to say.

"I want your help," she blurted. "I need it. She was my mother, the only parent I ever had. She deserves justice, and you..."

"*You* need closure. And you're afraid that'll never happen."

"Not just closure. Justice. You've seen elk that have been shot before. Maybe you can simply accept it. I can't. Please understand, I can't." *I owe Mom that and more.*

Rane knew how vital it was to be prepared when in the forest, which accounted for the rain jacket she'd pulled out of her backpack and put on before heading back the way she'd come. She was sore between her legs and hadn't put back on her bra because her breasts were still sensitive.

Head low to protect her face from the rain, she replayed the last things she and Songan had talked about. To her relief, he'd agreed to go to Wolverine. When he could.

He'd ask questions of his surroundings and listen to whatever the wilderness might tell him. He'd use his keen senses in an attempt to uncover what law enforcement had been unable to. If he found nothing, which she feared he wouldn't, she'd have no choice but to let law enforcement continue to investigate, but if he learned more than the searchers had about the identity of Jacki's killer or killers, she'd do everything within her power to find that man or men.

Her throat dried, forcing her to swallow repeatedly. She'd carried a knife since Mom gave her one for her eighth birthday. To mother and daughter, a knife represented a wilderness insurance policy. They could cut branches for a fire with it, dig roots to eat, gut any fish they'd caught. And, if necessary, a knife might keep them alive.

Jacki's knife had been found near her remains, and it now hung from Rane's backpack. If she had her way, she'd slit her mother's killer's throat with it.

Accepting what she was capable of, she took comfort in the last things Songan had said to her. After reassuring her that whoever had poached the young elk had left the area, he'd added what she'd already known. He had to return to the herd, but as soon as rut was over, he'd come for her. Together they'd go to Wolverine.

Pushing her pack higher on her shoulders, she picked up her pace. Breeding season was nearing its end. Just before he'd turned back into an elk, they'd touched on what hiking to Wolverine entailed, but their eyes and body language had acknowledged what would happen the moment they again laid eyes on each other.

They'd fuck.

As always, feeling Songan's flesh and not a condom inside her had contributed to her pleasure. For generations, elk shifters had sought out women to have sex with when they were in human form. Never once had a union resulted in a pregnancy. An elk shifter—and only bulls could shift—could have sex no matter which form he was in, but his sperm only took root inside a cow elk. In addition, shifters didn't carry sexual diseases and were immune to anything a woman might have.

In other words, when she and Songan wanted to fuck, there was never a reason to say no.

Looking up, she noticed a few snowflakes in with the rain. Unless the weather changed for the better in the next few days, the trip to Wolverine might be futile. Wishing she could change nature, she made a mental calculation. If she kept up her present pace—and she intended to—she'd reach her truck in about an hour and a half. Good. Fine. A relief. Getting stuck out in a snowstorm was the last thing she wanted to have happen today.

Catching a glimpse of something to her left, she swiveled in that direction. She was back on the deer trail she'd taken earlier. How then was this dark shadow able to keep pace with her despite being in the trees?

Telling herself not to jump to conclusions, she reached behind her and pulled her mother's knife from its sheath.

"Who is it?"

She heard no answer. Determined not to telegraph her unease any more than she already had, she continued walking. If this was her mother's killer or the elk poacher—no damn it, she wouldn't panic!

Wouldn't let her imagination get away from her.

The substantial shape continued to match her pace. At times she lost sight of it and surmised it had stepped behind a tree or trees. Other times nothing of any significance stood between her and her shadowy *stalker*. The creature occasionally came within about fifty feet but no closer, even though it had opportunity. She wasn't foolish enough to tell herself she had nothing to worry about.

Still clutching the all but worthless knife and struggling to see despite the downpour, she did what she should have when she'd first spotted the shape.

"What do you want?" she asked the grizzly.

"You."

No, she couldn't have possibly heard that! Her imagination had taken hold, that's all. Between everything she'd gone through with her mother, reconnecting with Songan, and the lousy weather, having her hearing suddenly go bad shouldn't surprise her. As soon as she got back to the house, she'd pour herself a tall glass of wine. Maybe drink the whole damn bottle.

"I need you."

"Stop it!" Her knuckles turned white from gripping the knife handle. "Go away."

"I can't."

Cursing herself for having stopped walking, she started plowing ahead again. Her boots were covered in mud and pine needles, and she risked a broken ankle or two if she tried to run. The great bear continued to match her stride, prompting her to send a silent message to Songan. If the elk shifter was still around, he'd charge the grizzly and skewer it with his antlers. Maybe. Hopefully.

Unless the grizzly overpowered him.

The mental image of a battle between the two powerful

creatures made her heart pound. Because of their different body structure, she wasn't sure which weighed the most. Unfortunately, elks were prey animals, while a grizzly's teeth and claws had been designed for killing.

"This isn't happening," she said, then clenched her jaw because of course it was. Still, she fought to keep the lie going. "You're an animal. I can't possibly hear you."

"Am I?"

Nearly choking on a cry, she forced herself to stop again. The rain had turned what she could see of his coat so dark it made her think of a moonless night. He was motionless and achingly awesome in his power.

"What are you? There aren't any grizzlies in this part of the country."

"I am what I am."

"What's that supposed to mean?" When Songan took on an elk's shape, he was no longer capable of communicating with her. In contrast, the bear seemed capable of reasoning and responding intelligently.

"I'm different from anything you've ever known."

No way was she going to continue this so-called conversation. If his intention had been to kill her, he would have already attacked. Just the same, the last thing she wanted to do was sit down for a chat. Trying to convince herself that the beast couldn't break down her truck door, she started walking again. Even with her raincoat on, she was cold and getting colder. If she dared take the time, she'd stop and haul her sweatshirt out of her pack to put on under her jacket. However, as long as her blood kept pumping, she'd reach where she'd left her vehicle. There wasn't much she could do about her chattering teeth and sluggish mind.

That's it. Right now she'd walk. Later she'd put the pieces

together. Try to, anyway.

Despite her chilled and numb skin, her nerve endings told her when the bear stopped following. Step by step, the distance between them increased, and his impact lessened. She wasn't going to look around for it. No way was she going to risk a panic attack.

During storms, rodents took shelter underground or in downed trees. Birds huddled under large branches, while deer and elk tended to gather in thick groves. As a result, right now it felt as if she had the forest to herself. Because this wasn't the first time she'd been out in inclement weather, she simply accepted the change. Just the same, she would give a lot to see a chipmunk or jay. She'd chatter back when they scolded her, maybe pull out a granola bar and offer it to them.

Alone.

Except for the bear.

Wherever it had gone.

At nearly a thousand pounds, the grizzly knew he couldn't fit into the hollow log he'd spotted, but even if he'd been able to squeeze in, he wouldn't have. Granted, he had no doubt he could find the woman again, but he wanted to go on watching her. Rain had washed away some of the sex smell after the man she'd mated with had changed into an elk. He wanted to get closer, to bring her aroma into his body, only she wasn't ready. He'd done enough for now. Made his presence known. Later he'd make her face reality—his reality.

Rivulets ran between his eyes and down his nose. Occasionally hard-pressed to see anything, he'd stop and shake his head. The easy solution would be to move onto the deer trail, but if he did, she'd know he hadn't left after all. And she would look. Unlike other humans he'd watched over the years, she gave no indication her surroundings made her uneasy. He'd alarmed her, but the forest itself comforted and sustained her.

That was why he'd been drawn to her.

His cock tightened, and his heart rate kicked up. Faced with those realities, he admitted that familiarity with the wilderness was only part of her appeal. She was young and healthy, with curving hips, full breasts, narrow waist and long, strong legs. A sexual creature.

A few snowflakes brushed his forehead and chilled him there, but elsewhere his thick fur kept him warm. If it continued to snow, he'd feel compelled to wrap his front legs around the woman and thus shelter her.

A near laugh put an end to his crazy thoughts. The moment he had her under his control, he'd want to fuck her. Warming her might become the last thing on his mind.

Picking up his pace, he gave a fantasy born of years spent emotionally alone free rein. Mindless to the nameless female's resistance, he'd rip off her clothing and throw her to the ground. Part of him hating what he was doing, he'd force his bulk between her legs and his cock into her core.

His massive paws left indentations in the ground that would alarm anyone who came across them, but thanks to the rain and remote location, he doubted that would happen. The wildlife was preparing for a heavy, early winter, but he and the others like him had grown up where winter meant shards of ice crystals capable of cutting flesh and ground that froze solid for much of the year.

That, in part, was why he'd come to these mountains. As a prime male, his task was to find a new place for his kind to live. Coming across the dead and savaged young elk had given him pause. Then the human female had discovered him.

The way she handled her weapon said she was comfortable

with it but didn't want to use it. She carried herself as deer did, confident in her body's ability to react to any and all situations. She was leery yet prepared, curious and cautious. And beautiful.

He'd still been trying to make sense of her impact on him when the big bull elk had arrived. To his surprise, the female had eagerly approached the newcomer. Moments later, beast became human, and man and woman had had sex.

Turning his head to the side to escape the wind, the bear planted his legs and stopped. His body trembled, and his penis extended from its furred protection. Oblivious to the cold, the organ reached full length and breadth.

He hadn't had sex since summer when the last clan-sow had come into heat. Like the other males of his kind, he wished it was otherwise, but once a sow became pregnant, she wanted nothing more to do with mating. Watching today's humans fuck had stirred his blood. He wasn't sure when, or if, he'd return to acceptance and resignation. That, he told himself, was why he had to stop following her. He didn't trust himself the way he was. Later, once he was back under control.

But soon. Soon.

Chapter Six

Rane needed to run into the small, family-run grocery that served the entire town. However, she decided to stop at the Sawmill Bar first. Thanks to her relentless pace, she'd reached her pickup before the sun, such as it was, had set.

Fortunately, she'd been able to get her cell phone to connect and had called both the sheriff's deputy and Chinook Forest Supervisor Donald Cushing to let them know about the poached elk. Both men had promised to investigate the illegal killing. However, manpower was in short supply.

After parking in the gravel lot behind the Sawmill, she pulled her key out of the ignition. Instead of immediately grabbing her steaming rain jacket, she studied the back of the bar with its trio of garbage cans, a motorcycle with two flat tires propped against a wall, and a frayed blue tarp over a truck engine on the ground. A single yellow light bulb did a poor job of illuminating the rear door only employees were supposed to use. The bar's exterior hadn't been painted in years. Because it was night, she couldn't see the roof but doubted the original metal had been replaced.

In part, the Sawmill represented why she'd moved away. She'd been afraid she'd turn out like it if she didn't experience the world beyond this backwater town. More to the point, she'd sensed she'd become a mountain woman like her mother.

So much for taking off for parts unknown. She was back.

Throwing the damp jacket over her head, she got out and jogged around to the front. Smoking in bars had been banned, and she imagined Joe and Deana Thetford, who'd owned the place forever, had done what they could to get rid of the stale stink. Unless things had picked up for them financially, that might be the only improvement.

Despite the dim lighting, it was brighter in here than outside, which made taking her measure of the place relatively easy. All but one stool at the bar was occupied, as were four of the five tables. The two women at the bar were regulars and qualified as the town's hookers, for lack of a better term. She couldn't wrap her mind around the idea of spending her adult life putting out for the same tired, unwashed men over and over again.

Three middle-aged women sat at one of the tables. Two worked at the grocery store, while Alice owned the gas station/repair shop with her husband. Again Rane pondered having little choice but to talk to and drink with the same women for years. Alice, who worked more hours at the gas station than her husband Dave did, had long insisted she was going to move to Hawaii when she retired, but no one believed her.

Alice's friends acknowledged Rane with nods and noncommittal smiles. In contrast, a sober-faced Alice continued to study her after the other women returned to their conversation. Her mother and Alice had been casual friends for years. Despite the difference in their education level—her mother had a college degree, while Alice had dropped out her senior year of high school when she got pregnant—their freedom didn't surprise her. After all, there weren't that many women in and around Forestville. Men either. The town was slowly dying.

If Alice had been alone, she might have spoken to her. Instead, feeling a little uneasy because of the other woman's scrutiny, she continued toward the bar.

Male heads swiveled toward her, and although she recognized most of them, she didn't say anything. Obviously she needed to spend more time in here if she was going to fit in, like that was ever going to happen. Like her mother had told her, getting hit on in here was a given. A quality pickup was another story. Besides, after what had taken place between Songan and her, all of Rane's itches still felt scratched.

Except when her thoughts snagged on the grizzly, if that's what the creature was.

"Move over, boys," Joe said from his station behind the bar. "The lady looks wet and thirsty. What'll it be, Rane? Your first drink's on the house."

Joe was a good fifteen years older than her mother had been and from all indications happily married. Just the same, he'd flirted openly with Jacki. That was just his way. Still, Rane considered Joe and Deana people she could count on. They'd come over with a casserole right after she'd arrived, and their mentally challenged daughter had drained the water pipes in Jacki's house before that in case temperatures fell below freezing at night. If Deana was here, she'd thank her.

"Wine," she said. "House red."

"You've got it."

Rane sat as Joe wiped water off a wineglass. Once she was settled, she glanced at the men on either side of her. Harry Schneider was on her right, what was left of his left hand around a beer bottle. Harry had lost three fingers to a table saw while doing some remodeling around his place. Word was he got some kind of disability and still did occasional long-distance trucking. He also collected firearms. Divorced with grown children, he could have gone wherever he wanted. Apparently he hadn't wanted.

Nodding at and then dismissing Harry was easier than doing the same to the man who'd already twice bumped her left elbow.

"I heard you've been riding the deputy's ass," Clifford Jones said by way of hello. "What is it, you think he should bring in the FBI?"

Forestville couldn't afford its own police department and contracted with the county's sheriff's department to have a deputy assigned part-time. Gannon gave Forestville more than twenty hours a week, but that left a lot of time with no law enforcement. As far as she knew, the FBI didn't know Forestville existed. Even though her mother had been a federal employee, she couldn't imagine them sending anyone here, because the entire sheriff's department had initially been involved in the investigation. What more could the FBI do?

"I've talked to Gannon a number of times." She had no intention of telling Clifford more than that, because several years ago her mother had helped arrest his and his older brother Chip's three cousins for hunting out of season. The trio had been convicted, which had stripped them of the right to hunt for five years. Needless to say, Andy, Aaron and Albert Jones hated her mother.

"Talk's cheap," Clifford said. "What about action?"

She accepted the full wineglass from Joe. "I trust Gannon. He and the rest of his department will get the job done."

Heavy hands landed on her shoulders. Instead of whirling and punching whoever had touched her as she wanted to, Rane willed herself to remain still.

"Hey Rane, good to see you."

For a moment, she couldn't put a name to the voice, but

the pleased look on Clifford's face helped. Little more than a year apart in age, Clifford and his younger brother had always been best friends, more like twins than siblings.

"Hello, Chip," she said. She noticed that Joe's lips had thinned a little. "You startled me."

"Sorry." Chip squeezed her shoulders. "I just didn't expect to run into you in here. Still staying at your mom's place, are you?"

Everyone around here knew what she was up to. There was no reason to read anything into what Chip had just said. Of course there was the memory of when Chip had tried to maul her behind the school gym when they were both in high school. She'd been shocked, but not so shocked she couldn't ram a knee between his legs. He'd later apologized.

After school, he'd spent a couple of years in the army and came back much more mature. To her way of thinking, Chip should have stayed away. There was no future here for either him or his brother.

To her relief, Chip let go of her. That done, he squeezed in between her and Harry.

"Harry, old man, how about you let me talk to my friend?" Chip didn't wait for Harry's response but hip-bumped the thin man off his stool. Grumbling, Harry backed away still holding on to his beer.

"Say Rane," Harry said. "If you've got no use for your ma's rifle, give me a call."

"What? That's the last thing on my mind right now."

"Of course, of course. I'm just offering to take it off your hands."

"You heard her," Chip said. "Bug off."

"That was rude," Rane said after Harry was out of earshot.

Just what she didn't need, being sandwiched between the Jones brothers.

"Was it? Sorry."

"No you're not." Glaring, Joe leaned across the bar. "I thought you were going to be at the logging site all week."

"I wish." Chip frowned and pointed at a refrigerator behind Joe. "The usual. Damn transmission on the loader's shot. I've got to go into the city for a replacement."

"It's shot?" Clifford asked from her other side. "I thought you said it could be repaired."

"I said I hoped it could. One damn thing after another."

As the brothers and Joe agreed that everything seemed to be against them when it came to the small Jones logging company fulfilling their contract with the Forest Service, Rane decided to cut Chip some slack. He and Clifford weren't as crude and uneducated as their cousins.

For generations men from the Jones and other local families had filled their freezers without governmental rules and regulations. In recent years, short hunting seasons and limits on how much game they could harvest had meant an end to a way of life they'd long taken for granted. In addition, Jones Logging was part of a dying industry thanks to more bureaucracy and decreased need for timber products. Chip, Clifford and their cousins knew how to fell timber and hunt. Unfortunately, that was basically the limit to their skills.

"I feel sorry for them," her mother had said more than once. "They represent what our pioneers were about. They should have been born decades ago. At least most are telling their children not to follow in their footsteps."

That, Rane had tried to tell her mother when Jacki asked why she was so dead set on building a life far from the Chinook Mountains, was why. There was an exciting world out there, new places to explore. No way was she going to spend hers stuck in Forestville the way her mother was.

Well, she was back. And it was too late to apologize to her mother.

"Where's your wife?" she asked Joe. "Isn't she always with you?"

"Deana's been sick. Well, not sick. She needs a knee replacement. That keeps her off her feet."

"I'm sorry. Will she be having surgery—"

"Not unless I win the lottery. We're self-employed, don't have insurance. Don't have anything except this." He indicated the bar.

After a minute, Joe left to tend to the needs of his other customers. Wishing she knew what to say to Joe, Rane continued to sip her wine. Even with the TV blaring, she could hear rain hitting the metal roof. No matter that she was tired and hungry, she couldn't quite talk herself into going home. If only the small, well-built place her mother had loved didn't feel so empty.

Sighing, she looked toward the front door, then shook her head. Surely she hadn't been hoping Songan would walk in, and even if she had, it wouldn't happen.

Enough with the sexual energy building at the base of her spine.

Enough with asking herself if the *grizzly* might be contributing to her mood.

"You didn't get married, did you?" Chip asked. "I thought for sure you would."

Chip's unexpected question accomplished what she'd been unable to do on her own, which was get her mind off sexual matters. She turned toward him, then was sorry because he hadn't brushed his teeth for a while. Apparently dental hygiene took a backseat to keeping one's work equipment running. But if the company was that important, shouldn't he be heading for Eagle Pass since the city was a good hour and a half away?

"I didn't realize my marital status mattered to you," she said.

Chip shrugged. The gesture sent his beer belly to jiggling beneath his padded flannel jacket. "Just making conversation, Rane. You were the best-looking girl to come out of these mountains. Too good for me, remember? I figured someone would have snagged you by now."

"Guess I didn't take the bait. Mom told me you married Kathy Framer."

"Had to," Chip muttered. "Got me two sons and a daughter, not that I see much of them since the divorce."

Another wave of sympathy for Chip caught her by surprise. Maybe he could have done a better job of planning his life, but this was what he was stuck with. Logging with his brother put food on the table and paid child support right now, but what about after the current government contract was over?

"I'm sorry," she said, feeling inadequate. Did everyone in town have financial problems? Enough to make them do reckless, crazy and illegal things? Enough to turn them into killers?

"Just like I'm sorry about what happened to Jacki," Chip said. "I thought I knew everything there was to about these mountains, but she... Just goes to show what an education will get you. She had a career, a damn secure one. Now she has nothing."

Much as she hated hearing that, Rane couldn't disagree with Chip. For all the bureaucracy that went with working for the Forest Service, it could turn out to be a life-long career.

Unless the employee was murdered.

Rane stayed at the Sawmill for the better part of an hour, sipping slowly and talking to several other people from the past. A couple of men offered to buy her drinks, then backed off when Joe gave them the evil eye. When Joe privately asked why she was putting up with this, she decided to tell him the truth, that she needed to learn as much as she could about the people who had made up her mother's world.

"I'm not a detective," she'd said unnecessarily. "I'm hoping someone will say something that, I don't know, will trigger something in my memory. Mom and I talked a lot, which means I got all the gossip."

She hadn't mentioned the possibility that her mother's killer might have been in the Sawmill.

Joe had hugged her to his sticky apron but hadn't added anything to what little she'd learned from those conversations. Either Joe tuned out the wagging tongues loosened by the liquor he sold, or he didn't want to encourage her poor excuse for an investigation. Or concern for his wife's health came before anything else.

Alice and her friends had left before she did, saving her from trying to decipher the older woman's expression. She couldn't imagine Alice approving of her coming alone to the bar and allowing herself to be surrounded by men who weren't the town's most upstanding citizens.

Fortunately the rain had let up. There wasn't much snow mixed in with it, but according to the news she caught on the truck radio, things were going to get colder in a few days. That coupled with the accompanying clouds added up to one thing: winter's first snowstorm.

Then what, she asked herself as she unlocked the door to what had been her mother's place. Should she stay here and risk not working for the Service in Alaska after all? Her supervisors were being understanding about her need to take some time off, but they could only leave that wildlife biologist position out of Homer vacant for so long.

She couldn't remember her or her mother ever locking themselves in while she was growing up, but she did so. After putting away her groceries, she started a toasted cheese sandwich. Then she went into what had been her childhood bedroom and took off all but her shirt and jeans. She put on slippers, turned on the TV in the living room and flipped her sandwich over.

A police investigation show was playing. She'd never understood the appeal of graphic crime scenes but stared at the screen until she smelled something burning. After scraping off the burned parts, she plunked herself on the couch in front of the TV with her dinner and a glass of milk on the coffee table. Tonight she wasn't going to think about the nights her mother had spent doing the same thing; she wasn't!

Jacki had had at least two romantic relationships after her daughter moved away. The one she'd talked the most about had been with another ranger who'd been transferred up to Washington State. Instead of asking for a transfer herself as Jerry had wanted, she'd chosen local spotted owl research over him.

Prescott had entered the picture less than a year after the relationship with Jerry ended. He'd been and still was a Fish and Wildlife employee. Whenever Rane asked about him, Jacki had given her a brief answer and changed the subject. Finally her mother admitted that Prescott was married. Separated but not talking divorce.

A few awful times right after Jacki went missing and Rane was sick with fear, she'd wondered if her mother had decided she couldn't live without Prescott. By day's light, she'd acknowledged her mother was stronger than that. Her belief in her mother had been confirmed when Jacki's body was found. No way could the bullet that killed her have been self-inflicted.

An ad for a luxury car came on. As she watched beautiful people speeding along a deserted stretch of highway in a black convertible, she wondered what made advertising companies think that would sell cars. Her job paid relatively well, but she'd never be in that driver's seat. Besides, she didn't want to be.

That led to the question of what she was going to do with her life now that the most important person in it was dead. Murdered.

"Damn it, enough!" Upset and angry at herself, she extracted the knife her mother had given her from her backpack. Today had been full enough without throwing questions about life direction into the mix. Placing the knife on the couch next to her, she leaned back and closed her eyes.

Did she really want to see Songan again? He might be her only chance of learning the truth about her mother's death, but there was a lot of baggage where he was concerned.

He turned her sexual cranks. Absolutely no doubt about that. When he became human, he gave new meaning to the word hunk. Not only could he make professional athletes and bodybuilders wave the white flag of surrender, sex with him had always been wildly satisfying. For someone who spent only roughly half his time as a human, he sure as hell knew what a woman—this woman—needed.

Was sex enough?

Standing, she carried the dinner remains into the kitchen and returned to the living room. The crime show had started again, not that it mattered, because she had no idea what the plot was about. Her mother's house was about fifteen hundred square feet, which she figured was more than enough room for one person, so why did she feel as if the walls were squeezing her in? She'd spent the day outdoors. She'd had great sex. She should be tired and brain dead. Tomorrow was soon enough to revisit the awful questions surrounding her mother's death. Give it a rest for one night, all right. Find a spot of peace.

No longer listening to her self-directed argument, she paced from one end of the room to the other and turned around. Thinking to retrace her steps, she lifted her right leg. Her slipper hit the short brown carpet.

Jacki had bought tan drapes to cover the large living room window. Judging by the dust patterns in the fabric, she'd seldom used them. The window provided a view of the forest that grew nearly up to the house, but although Rane wished she was looking out at dripping tree branches, she hadn't opened the curtains she'd drawn before leaving this morning.

Damn it, death had changed so much.

Now, however, even with her heart hammering against her chest wall and her feet dragging, she headed toward the window. Something or someone was out there.

Chapter Seven

The child he'd met the first time he'd ventured out of the forest had called him Ber. Although the boy's father had apologized and explained that his small son was trying to say Bear, from then on he'd introduced himself as Ber. He might not know much about adult humans, but he'd never doubted the little boy's wisdom.

Tonight, standing outside the house of the woman he'd followed out of the mountains, Ber nodded in admiration of her ability to sense his presence. Until he'd heard her start toward the window, he hadn't been sure what he was going to do, whether tonight might change everything for both of them. But it had to be done. Why not now?

The drapes pulled back. Staring at the slender, strong woman from earlier today, he tried to put himself in her place. She was looking at a six and a half foot tall man with wavy, pure black hair that came to his shoulders. Maybe she couldn't tell that his eyes were equally black or that he hadn't shaved for the better part of a week, but hopefully his sheepskin jacket and worn jeans would keep the truth of his musculature from her for a while longer.

Her hand went to her throat, and she pulled back. Instead of screaming and shutting the curtain again, however, she stared. Her startled yet steady glare sliced into him, making him wonder if he'd ever felt this vulnerable.

Him, vulnerable? Shouldn't that be her?

"Let me in," he said loud enough to be heard through the glass. The request shocked him. He hadn't intended to move so fast, hadn't planned things out well enough.

"What? Who are you?"

"They call me Ber," he told the woman who probably saw him only as a shadow. "I need to talk to you."

About what? she mouthed.

My life and your role in it. "I'm not armed." Hoping she could read his lips, he spoke distinctly. "I won't hurt you."

Her eyes widened, but she dropped her hand from her throat and opened the window a crack. "You expect me to believe that? What are you doing here?"

I don't have a choice. "Looking for you."

"You know something?"

The instant the words were out of her mouth, the woman didn't look as sure of herself as she had moments ago. There was a melancholy about her that touched a part of him he barely comprehended. "Yes," he said, even though he didn't know what she was talking about. "Please, let me in."

Maybe his request made the difference, but then he might never know why she stepped away from the window. Several seconds passed before he heard a clicking at the door, and it opened. When he walked over to where she stood in the doorway, warm air reached out to caress him.

She smelled of soap and woman.

"Ber," she said, looking up at him. "Is that what you said your name is?"

He'd told her it was what people called him. "Yes."

"I don't recognize you, and I know just about everyone who lives here."

"I'm new to the area." *In ways you can't comprehend.*

"Look, I'm reluctant to let you in. I think you understand why. Why don't you tell me what this is about. If you know something about my mother—"

"I do," he lied.

The sorrowful look returned, and he understood that taking advantage of her grief was the opening he needed.

"What is it?" she asked.

"The house is getting cold." Even before he'd finished, he acknowledged how much he was risking for both of them if she let him in. "I saw you at the bar earlier."

"Did you? I didn't see you."

Because he'd been outside. "Oh."

"Look," she said, "I don't want to have to pull things out of you. If you think you can get me to pay you for—"

"I don't think that."

"Why are you coming to me instead of the sheriff's deputy?"

Her left arm remained down by her side, while she occasionally rubbed her right hip. Accustomed to studying all movement, he wondered what that said about her. If only he knew more about what went on inside women's minds. "You have more at stake."

"Yes, I do. All right, come in. Wait. There's something you need to know. A lot of people are keeping an eye on me these days. If something happens to me, the investigation will start with who was at the Sawmill."

Only they couldn't, because he hadn't been among the drinkers. Also, her house was set back from the road, and except for him, no one was out tonight. No wonder she was leery about letting him in. As he closed the door behind him, the sense that he'd made the right choice grew. This woman lived alone.

Not taking her gaze off him, she backed toward the couch and indicated he could take a chair at the other end of the room. She slowly sat. Her straight and alert body had him comparing her to a deer. He wanted to see her run, to watch the long slender legs propel her through the forest. In his fantasy, he'd be running behind her. Moving swift and sure, he'd overtake her. When he caught up to her, he'd bring her down, trap her under his greater weight.

No! He wasn't a beast tonight. Would never be, around her.

"I lied," he said, done with pretense. Either she'd accept him for what he was or—what?

Her nostrils flared, and she started to stand, stopped. "About what?"

Surprised by the lack of panic in her voice, he continued. "I don't know anything about your mother. That's not why I'm here."

Chocolate eyes widened. "Then you have thirty seconds to explain. Otherwise, I'll make you leave."

How, he came close to asking but didn't.

"We met earlier today. In the meadow where the young elk had been killed."

"No way." She shook her head. "There wasn't—oh shit."

Understanding spread over her and took her from beautiful to exquisite. She might be the only woman on earth capable of fully comprehending what he'd said.

"Ber," she whispered. "Bear. That's what you are."

"Yes."

"A shape-shifter." Her mouth barely moved.

"Like your *elk*, yes."

"He isn't mine. He—you saw him change."

"Yes."

Looking resigned, she nodded. "And what took place between us."

From the moment responsibility for his kind's future had fallen on his shoulders, he'd worried that no woman would be able to comprehend what he needed from her. He'd be forced to give up too many secrets in his attempts to get through to her. Even if she finally accepted the truth, she'd remain horrified. She'd reject him. Now, however, he'd found a human who understood what it meant to inhabit two bodies. Everything had changed.

But was it enough?

"You had sex."

"So?" She sounded defensive. "We're consenting adults. We—what does this have to do with you being here?"

Surprised by her reaction, he stared back at her. Instead of being shocked and angry, she'd gone straight to the heart of what tonight was about for him.

"You accept one shifter," he told her. "I need you to accept another—me."

"Oh crap." She raked her fingers through windblown hair. "Let me get this straight. You're not just a human being, you're also a bear. A grizzly."

"Yes."

"Yes, just like that. Look, I'm trying to wrap my mind about this. Elk shifters have lived in the Chinook Forest for generations. I guess there can be other kinds of shifters. Just because I've never seen or heard—but you're a grizzly, not a black like we have around here." Her breath whistled as she exhaled. "It's overwhelming. More than I want to try to handle."

"It doesn't matter."

"Easy for you to say." Leaning forward, she stared at him. "You're big. The whole grizzly thing—in a weird way, that fits." She again ran her hand through her hair. "I don't want to be having this conversation. You knocked on the wrong door. Whatever you were thinking when—my mind's already on overload from dealing with what happened to my mother. I don't need—"

"What happened to her?"

"You really don't know."

"No, I don't."

"She was murdered."

"Murdered?" *Like today's elk?* "What's your name?"

"My name?" A little of the color drained from her cheeks. "What are you doing here if you don't even know that? I'm nothing to you. Just get out."

The weight already pressing down on him increased. "It isn't that simple. I told you my name. What's yours?"

She looked all around the cozy room, then back at him. If only he could tap in to what she was thinking.

"Rane." She sighed. "Rane Haller. Mom named me for what was happening the day I was born and because nature means—meant a lot to her." Her gaze narrowed. "You said you watched Songan and me have sex. He and I talked about Mom. Surely you heard that."

"I didn't care what you were saying."

"Damn you." She glanced at her slippered feet and then up at him. "Mom didn't like to hear me curse, but she did it herself. I've done more of that since she went missing than all the years before that."

She shifted position so she was now angled toward him instead of straight on. Watching her move was like studying the rising sun touch dew. Like watching water run clean and wild over rocks and past moss and ferns. At the same time, his reaction to her was different from his appreciation for nature's beauty. The woman was innately, deeply sexual, with a fluid way of moving her body that told him she was proud of what it was capable of. No matter what was going on in her life and world, at her core she was female. Everything else came after that.

And tonight he was a man. Not a shifter with his kind's future at stake—a man.

He spoke through a throat that didn't want to work. "I saw you and the elk shifter go at each other, the way he took you. I heard you climax. Wanting the same thing became all-important to me. For a while, only that mattered."

Eyes darkening, she sprang to her feet. "I don't like the way this conversation is going. What happened between Songan and me is none of your business, and I want you gone. Now."

He might have laughed if she hadn't reached behind her while she was speaking. Looking grim and determined, she produced a knife that went from broad and thick to razor sharp. The way she held it, he knew she'd done so many times. Still, even with it pointing toward his throat, he couldn't stop focusing on her slender wrist. If he wanted or if instinct got the better of him, he could easily snap the bones there.

When he looked back up at her, her expression told him she knew what he'd been thinking. "I have quick reflexes," she said. "And I know where to bury this. You'd be bleeding out before you knew what happened."

Much as he wanted to stand, he wouldn't take the chance of further alarming her. Too much was at stake. "Have you ever stabbed anyone?"

"Mom and I practiced. We got damn good at it."

"Why?"

"Self-preservation. Better than a gun at close quarters. I'm done talking, Ber. I want you out of here."

Her tone gave her away. She was still wary but no longer determined to immediately get rid of him. He'd like to believe his hard body beneath the coat he'd kept with the rest of his clothes near town was responsible. She'd seen through the layers to a chest too broad for most shirts and legs meant for embracing a woman's body.

"Sit down, please," he said. "Keep the knife out. I won't move, I promise."

She didn't believe him, not that he blamed her. At least she lowered the knife to her side. Watching her get to her feet had been all he needed to know she hadn't been lying about how quickly she could move. It might be interesting to pit their speed against each other, someday.

"I need to tell you some things," he said. "Things you'll understand at least in part because you know what it is to be a shifter."

"What if I don't want to hear this?"

Her wishes weren't important. One way or the other, he'd force her to comprehend. If necessary, he'd launch himself at her and wrestle her onto the floor. He'd force her onto her belly and yank her arms behind her. Then he'd straddle her, clamp a hand over her mouth, and speak slowly and deliberately. In time she'd stop struggling.

His cock would press against her buttocks, yet, somehow, he'd ignore its command until he'd told her everything. Then he'd turn her over and reach for her jeans zipper.

"That's it," Rane said and jerked her head at the door. "I've had enough of whatever it is you think you're doing."

Instead of taking her not so subtle hint to leave, he leveled a steady gaze at her. "I'm still getting used to these mountains. I don't understand them the way I need to. The way you obviously do."

She touched her chest with a fist. "Yes, I do. All right, damn it. What brought you here?"

Was it possible she'd tapped into his mental images of capturing her? Was that why she'd agreed to hear him out?

"This time last year I was far from here with the rest of my kind. You call the place Alaska."

"Your kind?"

Her whisper was like a warm breeze on his flesh. Beneath the layers of human clothing, his cock stirred. Watching her have sex had jolted him to his core. If he hadn't been concerned that her fuck partner might turn back into an elk and battle him, he would have forced himself between them and finished what the human she called Songan had begun.

Now, in contrast to his earlier reaction, he simply accepted the feminine touch on his senses. For as long as necessary, he'd drift in her presence.

"Shape-shifters. Not so different from your Songan."

"He isn't mine." Eyes wide, she shook her head. "You, a shifter. This is so much to absorb. I always thought only elk—and not all of them. Only the males."

He could tell her that one of the reasons his kind were considering moving here was because they'd heard about the elk shifters who lived peacefully in the Chinook Mountains. He'd been sent here to check further into the situation. That would have to wait, however, because he first needed to tell her something more vital. Something that might end what had barely begun between them.

"I was born a human," he began. "As a small boy, I believed my parents had died."

"Believed? You mean it wasn't true?"

"No. An elderly woman who I assumed was my grandmother raised me."

"She lied to you?"

Much as he wanted to believe Rane felt sorry for the child he'd once been, he didn't dare let that distract him.

"That was to protect me from saying things I shouldn't to outsiders, to protect my true identity. A child accepts the world he finds himself in. Then *they* came for me. Said it was time for me to embrace my destiny." He hated revisiting the emotions that had overwhelmed him that fateful day and had no doubt they showed in the way he held himself and how the words came out.

"They?"

"Bear shifters. We call ourselves Enyeto."

"Enyeto?"

"Eskimo for walks as a bear. My *grandmother* and I lived in a small, remote village. I was too young to wonder how someone who didn't work was able to keep a roof over our heads. A few weeks before I was taken away, she started acting different. Distancing herself from me. I thought I'd done something wrong, but we'd never been good at communicating, so I didn't know how to ask. The day the Enyeto came, she told me she'd been trying to make things easier for me."

"I don't understand," Rane said and sank back onto the couch. "You were doing whatever it was little boys in the middle of nowhere do. Living an ordinary life when suddenly these strange people—were they in human form?"

"Yes."

She looked relieved. "Okay. So these men and women showed up and—"

"Only men."

"Only men." Her fingers trailed over the knife handle. "They knocked on the door and said pack your things, you're coming with us."

"In essence." The truth was, the moment he'd looked into coal eyes much like his own, he'd known he belonged with them.

"I don't understand." Rubbing her thighs, she leaned toward him. Just like that, her impact doubled.

"You will in time. Because you fuck an elk shifter, you must know how it is for them."

"How what is?"

"The way they are at birth. What are they, elk or human?"

Her hesitancy said she wasn't sure she should answer. "Elk."

"Tell me, please."

"I, ah, guess. Every one comes from a cow elk. The females don't shift. From everything I've been able to determine, they're one hundred percent animal. For the first year, all calves are nurtured by the cows. Then they push the yearlings away to make room for the next year's calves. The bulls move into the male society, where they're guided into life as shifters."

Her features sobered. "It's always bothered me that after the first year, the males never have anything more to do with their mothers, and their mothers, because they're what they are, forget who they gave birth to."

"Oh."

"You're right, oh. Different strokes for different folks."

What she'd just said made little sense, but then maybe he'd never understand the nuances of human speech. He often felt like an outsider during human conversations. Maybe, if things turned out the way they needed to between this mountain woman and himself, she'd guide him toward greater comprehension.

"When does a bull elk learn he's more than an animal?" he asked.

She rubbed the bridge of her nose. "It's different for each one but basically when adolescence begins. Songan told me it's tied into sexual maturation. Older males are always there to insure that the youngsters understand what's happening to them."

"That's good."

"More than good—essential. There's so much that needs to be learned. When does a boy start to become a bear shifter?"

Heartened by her curiosity, he granted himself a slight smile. "The process, which takes the better part of a year, begins before adolescence. I wasn't yet nine when it started. I've sometimes wondered if that's so an Enyeto grows up accepting his existence."

"Wait." She pressed her hand to her forehead. "Male bear shifters are born to human mothers, only somehow the Enyeto know which infants belong to them? They what, harvest them? My God, that has to be devastating to their human parents."

"No, it isn't."

Looking as if she'd forgotten she had hold of it, Rane stared at her knife. He wondered if she still believed herself capable of using it on him, or if she had at the beginning. "What then?"

Getting her to fully comprehend might be easier if she was

in his arms, but maybe if their bodies so much as touched, they'd never get around to words. And maybe his touch would repel her.

Chapter Eight

"Shifters are born to sows," Ber explained. Saying the words made him feel as if he'd come to the end of a long search. Finally, he'd found a woman he trusted with the truth. "The male newborns, which are identical to human infants, are taken from the sows—I've done that—and placed with humans to raise for the first few years."

"No way! How—damn, I don't know what I'm saying—how do you get some woman to nurture a baby knowing she'd have to give it up?" She flattened her hand over her heart. "The vast majority of women aren't made that way, and those who are shouldn't have children."

Knowing they'd eventually get to this point didn't make it any easier. "We carefully select the surrogates."

"Do you? Or do you rip little boys from the only mothers—or grandmothers, as in your case—they've ever known?"

"No." He'd been sitting too long and needed movement, but the only place he wanted to go was toward her. "Rane, the Enyeto kind have always lived in Alaska. Near the Inuit."

"Which is Eskimo for The People. Are you saying you have some kind of arrangement with them?"

"No matter how much whites study and think they know about Alaska's indigenous people, they'll never be privy to certain things."

"Ber, I'm a wildlife biologist working for the Forest Service. Before my mom—I'd just accepted a transfer to Alaska. I know more than a lot of people about that incredible wild country, and yet I never—what kind of things?"

He had to tell her. Otherwise, they'd never move beyond this point. "A heritage that goes back to when the land bridge connecting Siberia to America existed. Tradition. Cultures people like you believe no longer exists."

"Too much." Mouth open, she pushed herself to her feet, plodded over to the window and looked out with the knife dangling at her side. She seemed to have forgotten he was there. "I can't absorb all this."

Aware of every heartbeat, he waited her out. If necessary, he'd continue the explanation but hoped she would start to put things together on her own.

Arms still dragging at her side and knife appearing too heavy to hold, she faced him. "What are you doing here? I don't mean tonight. I'm talking about being in Oregon. Did you come alone or are others with you? Maybe they're out there, closing in, taking over."

"I'm alone."

Closing her eyes, she started to lean back against the window. Straightening, she stared at him. "Why?"

"I was chosen to determine if this is where some of us will relocate to."

"Go on."

Her lips had barely moved. Despite that and her clenched teeth, her mouth was soft. If he pressed his to hers, she'd respond. Their tongues would dance, their breaths meet.

"We knew this would eventually happen," he explained. "That eventually there'd be too many of us in one place."

"Too many? You're talking about Alaska."

"Only a small part of it. A safe region where we're accepted."

"Which is where?"

"I can't tell you, yet."

"Oh."

She'd better not say the word again because if she did and her lips softened as they just had, he'd be on her. Over her. In her.

Willing his thoughts to return to what needed to be said, he took a deep breath. "The Inuit there embrace us. We're part of their culture and belief system. With their help, we've thrived. Too much so."

"Overpopulation?"

Amusement looked good on her, but then her every emotion, even sorrow for her mother, captivated him.

"Yes."

"So some of you are looking to, ah, move elsewhere?"

She was trying to put what was happening to the Enyeto in terms she understood. He just hoped he could deal with her sensuality and the effort wouldn't make him lose sight of how vital she was to his kind's survival.

"We need a safe place to live."

"Why here?"

If he pointed at the couch, would she sit back down? He doubted it. "I told you. The humans who live in or near the Chinook Mountains accept elk shifters."

"Yes." She made the word last a long time. "We do. Most of us anyway."

"Most?"

"It's complicated. Do you really care?"

"I must."

"Of course. That was stupid for me to say. Sorry. I'm still trying to wrap my mind around the fact that we're having this conversation."

"So am I."

"I, ah, didn't think about that. All right, when the elk shifters are in human form, they're strong, hard workers. Not a single *man* is motivated by money. They simply need to be doing something physical. Only this area doesn't need any more strong backs. Men like some of those who were in the Sawmill resent having to compete with shifters for the few timber jobs."

Much as he tried to comprehend what she'd just told him, human concerns mattered little. Physical activity was essential, being rewarded for that activity a foreign concept.

"A question," she said. "One I never in a million years thought I'd be asking. When the Enyeto have on their human skins, what do they do? I mean, how do you earn a living?"

He held up his big, scarred hands. "I build."

"Construction?"

"Because of the elements, road work never ends in Alaska."

"Okay. All right. No." Turning away a little, she pressed her hand against the windowpane. He imagined the night cold seeping into her flesh. "Not all right. Where do I fit into this?"

Much as he wanted to wait until there was more between them, he couldn't. Better, maybe, to say it now. "As my mate."

Shock transformed her, but even with the loss of color in her cheeks, she was still beautiful to him. Knife now clenched in both hands, she stalked toward him. "Get the hell out of here."

"Rane—"

"Listen to me, Ber." The knife tip touched the base of his throat. Her eyes raged. "I'm dealing with my mother's murder. I'm a strong woman, maybe stronger than any you've ever known. I want nothing to do with you, get it? Nothing!"

When this was all over, she was going to head for someplace warm and sit in the sun until her flesh shriveled like a forgotten piece of fruit. She'd chug fruity drinks with tiny umbrellas in them and flirt with shirtless hunks. Hopefully bed a few of them. Maybe, although she was a bit young for it, she'd pick up a toy boy and parade him around. Of course she'd have to become something resembling rich if she was going to attract them, but she could dream.

Mostly she wanted the sun on her back and no worries. No murder mystery and absolutely no shape-shifters. Positively no damnable bear-man wanting to hump her.

Rechecking the front lock, Rane admitted that her crazy thoughts were a temporary shield against reality, a damn ineffective shield. Cabanas and bikinis aside, she was heading for her bedroom, which happened to be at the back of a house stuck in the middle of a forest and maybe a grizzly waiting outside.

No more bear thoughts, she warned as she crawled between the sheets. And no thinking about what Songan was doing to what tonight.

Stretching out, she willed the homeopathic sleeping aid she'd taken to do its job. Any other woman in her position would be fighting sleep. That woman would be sitting in the lighted living room with a loaded gun sweeping from the door to window and back again.

Then again that decidedly more intelligent woman would

have already called 911 and be speeding away.

"Mom," she whispered, "would you be disappointed if I just let the sheriff's department do their job? I mean, what do I think I am, some psycho avenger?"

No, she wasn't. Even at her most insane right after she'd learned her mother had been murdered, she hadn't believed that of herself. She simply was someone who'd lost her mother in a way no *child* ever should.

To complicate her life, she sometimes had sex with a half elk, half human, and as of tonight a bear shifter was lusting after her and determined to return.

Lusting. Sex. Two conditions guaranteed to have her climbing the walls. Maybe not the wall thing. More like trying to ignore the hot fingers currently slipping over her body. Darn it, she'd had sex today. She shouldn't be sliding her hand between her legs and jumping when a practiced thumb touched her waiting and willing flesh.

Her nipples tightened, prompting her to work her free hand under her nightgown and finger her sensitive nubs. A little friction made them ache and quickened her breathing. The hand against her sex quieted. Moisture oozed over her fingers. Fighting to ignore her body's encouragement, she sighed and rolled onto her back. Bending her knees so she could play with herself seemed like too much work after the day she'd had. Besides, her nipples had started to soften.

She was exhausted, worn out physically and mentally and every other way. She hadn't become less of a sexual creature simply because she didn't feel like masturbating tonight. Tomorrow, if she lasted until then, was soon enough for…

Her breathing slowed, and the time between each inhale increased. At the back of her mind she wondered if falling asleep was the last thing she should be doing; still, it felt so good to let go.

At first, gray dominated. Then the fog thickened and was replaced by black. Night, probably. Night, and no moon and trees between her and the stars. Maybe clouds had gotten in the way of the sky.

Too much to think about. Drifting was better. Sinking into—into something.

She was walking, lightly stepping on packed ground and lifting one leg and then the other over random rotting logs. Being barefoot wasn't a problem, because nothing was there to poke the bottom of her feet. It was good to have tough feet. And strong legs. And no clothes between her and the warm breeze.

Ah yes, the temperature was just right. Maybe the most perfect she'd felt in her entire life. She couldn't see where she was going and yet wasn't concerned. She could, she guessed, stop and figure things out, but walking felt like floating, and that was awesome.

Wherever she was belonged to her, and yet she shared it with something living. Maybe a lot of somethings. Of course. Critters and creatures, birds and insects. Maybe frogs. Thinking she might step on something living if she wasn't careful, she looked down. As far as she could tell, which wasn't much, nothing was ahead of her, but maybe that was because her feet had never intrigued her as they did now.

Men would love her toes. She could tickle and stroke certain male body parts with them, but only if the man met certain criteria.

Intrigued by possibilities, she pondered how a man or men might please her. Having sex, of course, but not just getting it on and getting it over. She'd insist on variety, the unusual, the heretofore unknown.

The word unknown had her looking up and around. It might

be her imagination, but wasn't it getting warmer and wasn't night giving way to a soft, shadow-filled dawn?

Logic said that wasn't right. Night lasted longer than this. But she didn't complain since daylight was better. Once she could truly see, she might start to make sense of what was happening.

Determination lasted for as long as it took her to cover about a hundred feet. Then, maybe in response to the air's growing warmth, she contemplated her naked body. Movement rolled through her breasts to send sensation over her belly and from there to her pussy.

Not giving a damn what the resident creatures and critters might think, she cradled her breasts. The wavelike movement floated from her palms to her fingers. When the aftershocks tiptoed up her arms and claimed her shoulders, she shivered.

Interesting. Walking braless had turned her on.

Thinking to play things out to the fullest extent, she cupped her breasts and lengthened her stride. There still weren't any obstacles in the way, and morning was full upon her. A few shadows remained among the trees.

With each step, her thighs brushed. Each caress of flesh against flesh ignited her sex a little more. Sighing in pleasure, she ran her hands down her sides and spread them over her thighs.

Despite the unexpected thought that she should hurry away from wherever she was, she slowed. Every part of her was engaged in the act of walking, and yet it was more than that. Curious about what that more might be, she brought virgin air into her lungs. Oxygen fed her veins and heart and filled her muscles with warm energy. Something she couldn't see or touch started circling around her and brought her fully in touch with herself.

She was a sexual being, a woman who had sex with a man who felt most alive when he was impregnating one cow elk after another. She'd never carry his child, but that didn't mean she didn't worship his cock.

Oh yes, a cock, the organ that said everything about what made a man a man.

A moan pressed against her teeth and then escaped. Intrigued, she stopped and concentrated on the fading sound. When she could no longer hear it, she vigorously rubbed her thighs. The friction sent a hot rage between her legs. Her heartbeat doubled, and she nearly collapsed.

Too much time passed before she was strong enough to look around. Her body still felt sexually used up. No longer trusting herself or her surroundings, she lifted her hands off her thighs and wrapped them around her waist. If this was what touching an electric fence felt like, she'd do it again and again, later.

This wasn't happening. She was dreaming. No doubt about it, she'd never had a more vivid or sexually productive dream, but she hadn't lost contact with reality.

Reality? Where was it?

Still clutching her waist, she slowly turned in a circle. The tree shadows she'd dismissed earlier now seemed sinister, but that couldn't be right, because she'd never feared anything in the wilderness.

Only this wasn't the wilderness she knew. This terrain was the product of her imagination, wasn't it?

Growing more alarmed, she stared intently at the trail she'd been traveling on. Despite being well tended, it didn't seem to be heading anywhere. For all she knew, she was walking in a circle.

It was time to wake up. So what if she spent the rest of the night staring at the ceiling? At least she'd have control over—

Something to her left and slightly behind her whispered. Heart slamming, she started to turn toward it, only to stare disbelieving as a rope loop appeared over her head. It hovered there, tantalizing her. Then gravity claimed it, and it floated down to settle around her. Before she could think what she should do, the rope tightened, pinning her arms to her sides. She tried to shake it off but couldn't.

More confused than panicked, she stumbled backward, pulled about by tension on the rope. She'd been lassoed, but by who? And why?

The tension continued, compelling her to take several more steps. Someone was playing games with her! Treating her like some cow or bronc being readied for branding.

"Damn you!" she cried and dug her feet into the ground. Widening her stance, she leaned forward and braced herself. Two could play at this—this whatever it was.

At least the rope, although unforgiving, didn't abrade her flesh. In fact it was quite comfortable, all except for the unrelenting and inescapable part. Now that she'd had a few seconds in which to process things, she allowed as how she certainly wasn't a cow or wild horse, no one had any reason to want to slap a brand on her.

Determined to locate and hopefully identify the rope's owner, she looked back over her shoulder but couldn't see anything except the glimpse of a shadow directly behind her.

"Not funny. Whoever you are, knock it off."

To her shock, the shadow started circling, wrapping more rope around her as it did. No, she acknowledged when two white strands rendered her arms completely useless, this was no game. She'd been captured. By a man.

Chapter Nine

Rane's captor was at least six and a half feet tall with a warrior's body and the thickest, darkest hair she'd ever seen. He needed a shave. Like her, he wore nothing. Unlike her, he was in control. Overwhelmed by his greater size and the way his ebony eyes burned into her, she put up no resistance as he placed a third loop around her. She couldn't lift her arms and yet her circulation wasn't being cut off.

He stepped closer. She commanded herself to fight but didn't. Feeling stupid and trapped and excited, she watched as he did something to the rope in front. The backs and sides of his hands grazing her breasts confused and thrilled her. He was doing that on purpose, damn him, yet it felt so good.

When he stepped back, she realized he'd tied a knot in his handiwork, guaranteeing that the bonds would remain in place as long as he wanted them to. Dropping the loose end so it trailed over her belly and against her mons before hanging between her legs, he folded his arms over his chest and studied her.

Caught. His.

"I don't understand." She hated the squeak in her voice, but maybe it would keep him from figuring out she was more turned on than frightened. "What's this about?"

"About you learning what I'm capable of and you need. What I'll do to achieve what I must."

Ber's voice! Why hadn't she recognized him? "I told you to leave, that I want nothing to do with you. I meant it then, and I mean it now." All except for the pulsing in her pussy.

"No you don't, and even if you did, it wouldn't matter."

When he reached down, she thought he intended to snag the rope. Hoping to outmaneuver him, she whipped her body to the side. Gripping the loop closest to her breasts, he hauled her back in place. She was still struggling, stupidly so, when he took hold of the loose end and threaded it between her legs. That task completed, he turned her from him and pulled up so the cotton pressed against her sex and settled between her ass cheeks. All too soon, he'd tugged it tight and secured it to one of the damnable loops.

"There." He held up his hands much as a steer roper at a rodeo might. "You wanted me to let go. How does it feel?"

Like the world revolved around her body. She'd risen onto her toes in reaction to the pressure against her labia. Now she slowly lowered her weight onto the balls of her feet. It was just her imagination, her overloaded brain's attempt to hold it together, but she couldn't help but wonder if he'd chosen white rope because he knew it would contrast with her tanned flesh.

Her legs were free. She could take off, not that she stood a chance of outrunning those long, powerful limbs. Besides, every time she shifted, she became even more aware of the foreign object her sex juices were dampening.

She couldn't let him know that! Much better if he believed she loathed what he'd done to her.

He stood far enough away that she shouldn't be able to feel his presence, yet something reached toward her, calming and exciting her at the same time.

With minimal and undoubtedly pleasurable work on his part, he'd turned her body into a sex object. The rope under her heavy, *sensitive breasts lifted them and accentuated that part of her body. Her nipples had become tight nubs. Her arms were useless, the constant pressure against her pussy impossible to ignore. He could do anything he wanted to her, and she couldn't stop him, couldn't touch in return.*

Touch? Surely she didn't want to do that.

She always bought jeans that didn't bind at a strategic place. Otherwise, her sex had a disconcerting way of responding when she needed to concentrate on other things. So much for thoughtful purchases. The rope between her ass cheeks, against her rear opening and pressing on her slit owned her. She could barely think beyond the sensation.

Ber knew exactly what he'd done to her. He might be a bear with a man's body but undoubtedly he understood how hers was responding. What did it matter if she ignored him while taking a few experimental steps? Despite herself, she gave silent thanks for what felt more like soft cotton than a binding. If she tried to run, the strands would irritate certain sensitive places, but as long as she stood still or took slow, small steps, she felt no discomfort.

Discomfort? Hardly. More like hovering inches and moments away from losing control. Any other time, given the so-called assault on her sex, pleasure would have already swamped her. She'd have embraced her sexuality and leapt head and heart into a climax.

But this was here and now. Until Ber decided to end this—this whatever it was—she'd continue to dangle over the erotic cliff.

"What's this about?" *Teeth clenched and throat hot, she walked in a tentative circle. What might be endless moisture continued to soak the rope between her legs. Her juices tracked down the insides of her thighs. Her nipples ached deliciously,* and she didn't dare take a deep breath. "Why are you doing this?"

"Training you. Teaching you what we're both capable of."

Confused, she rose onto her toes then dropped back down when her experiment offered no relief. Her fingers had been clenched so long they threatened to cramp, and she wished she could think how to stop her nostrils from flaring. Except for Ber, her world had become hazy. Only he was important.

"What am I?" she demanded. "Some wild horse you roped for the hell of it?"

"You're wild, all right."

When he started toward her, she shied just as a nervous horse would. Stopping, she bit down a gasp as he slid a hand between her belly and the rope. He hadn't pulled or tugged, but he could.

"It doesn't have to be this way." She hoped she sounded calmer than she felt. "You're a man and I'm a woman. We could—"

"Am I a man?"

"All right," she amended with her attention on what was happening. She prayed he wouldn't do anything she couldn't handle. "You're a shifter. I get that. What makes you think you have to"—she nodded at his hand—"do it this way?"

"You kicked me out, remember."

"Me, kick you out? Like I could pull that off. Besides, you went willingly."

"I had my reasons."

Later she might be interested in what those reasons were. "And after you did, you decided to do this why?"

For the few seconds his smile lasted, she fell in love with what it did to his features. Then he turned sober, and in his eyes, she found his grizzly half.

"Because I can. Because we both want this."

Like she'd ever admit that to him! It was safer if he believed she was furious and repulsed. Of course, if he reached between her legs... "Where are we?" she asked in an attempt to turn the conversation in another direction.

"It doesn't matter."

It might be her imagination or reaction to the hint of a growl in his deep voice, but his outline seemed to be becoming less defined. Because she'd seen the same thing happen to Songan, she wondered if Ber was about to shift from human to animal. The thought of what he might do to her once he had alarmed her.

"I was wrong." She stumbled over the words. "I should have heard you out earlier. I'll listen now, I promise I will."

"It doesn't matter." He pulled up on the rope just enough for her to take note. "I'm not interested in talking."

"Then what?" She had to keep him calm, somehow.

His slow, searching gaze took her in from neck to feet and back up again. The pressure against her sex increased. Even with the growing tension, she wasn't sure she'd ever felt more of a woman. More wanted or wanting.

"You're after sex," she whispered. "Sex with me. I get it."

"Do you?"

Her teeth clenched against a whimper, she stood as straight and tall as possible. Goose bumps chased over her shoulders, and her stomach muscles tightened. Even as she strained to lift her arms, she wasn't sure what she'd do with them. Loss of control meant turning everything over to this big, strong man. He wouldn't hurt her. She had to believe that.

"This isn't a game for you," she managed to get out. "It's not some kinky sex play."

Releasing the rope, he ran his nails over her belly. "No."

Gasping, she looked down at herself. Her nerves threatened to explode. Still, she noted that their surroundings were becoming darker. Was night returning?

"What?" she managed, thinking he'd just said something. "I, ah, didn't hear you."

"You're essential to my future and the future of others like me." His nails made another pass.

Half out of her mind, she sucked in a breath and stepped backward. His features neutral, he kept pace.

"You heard what I just said," he said. "I know you did."

Praying she could regain control over her body and mind, she squared and looked up at him. "What I did or didn't hear isn't the point. Ber, this is insane." She made a show of trying to move her arms. "As long as you treat me like this, you can't expect me to give a damn what happens to the Enyeto."

He lightly flicked her right breast. "You don't like this?"

"Stop it!"

"I asked you something. Go on, tell me you hate what I'm doing."

Much as she wanted to lie and tell him she loathed everything about what was happening, she couldn't force the words. "Let me go. Then we'll talk."

She watched, alarmed and shivering in anticipation, as he slowly extended a hand toward her. Taking hold of her chin, he lifted her head a little. "I love seeing you like this—mine."

"Everything done your way and me having no say?" she threw back at him to keep his words from making too much of an impact. "That's not how it happens in the human world, don't you get it?"

Waiting for his response exhausted her. Either that or her system had had all it could handle of his presence. The strange thing was that for a moment she thought she was looking at Songan. Did she need any more proof of how overwhelming this was?

"I'm not human," he said after too long. "Not in ways you comprehend."

Suddenly she knew what she needed to do to get through to him, at least a little. Turning her head to the side, she slipped out of his hold. Instead of trying to escape, she leaned into him so her breasts grazed his bare middle. His cock shuddered and jerked.

"So you're more bear than man, are you? Tell me, how would an Enyeto react to this?" She rolled a little one way and then the other, keeping her breasts with their taut nipples against him. The nonstop electrical charges going off throughout her short-circuited her mind.

Ber or Songan and what did it matter? Bear or elk, both dominated their world—and her, if she wasn't careful.

"Enough, damn it!" Rough fingers gripped her arms, and Ber pushed her back as far as he could without letting go, shaking her as he did.

Feeling as if she was melting, she sank to her knees. Even with him guiding her journey, she started to tip forward. She rested her cheek against his leg until she regained her balance and a measure of self-control. Only then did she acknowledge his cock.

"Didn't expect that, did you?" she asked, hoping to convince him she'd landed where she had on purpose.

On the tail of a deep breath, he ran his fingers into her hair. His fingertips against her scalp tore into her. She could remain on her knees before him forever, his prisoner and sex slave, bound and willing.

But if that's all she did, he'd never understand her, and he'd remain a stranger to her.

"I take your silence as a no," she said. "You figured you had to rope and tie me in order to get me to listen. What you didn't count on is how I'd react, the whole female response thing."

"Go on."

"My reactions, damn it. I'm not some sow bear in heat. I'm not going to stick my rump in your face."

"I didn't say you would."

"You're sure as hell acting like it. But you're wrong. For one, I'm not in heat. There's a lot more to me than the instinct to procreate."

"I know that."

Maybe, maybe not. The only thing she was sure of was that she was no longer interested in what he was thinking. How could that matter with his feet, legs, hips and cock scant inches away? Licking her lips, she touched them to his erection. He rocked back on his heels but didn't shove her away. God, but he was beautiful! Sexy in a rough, untamed way. Stimulating parts of her that hated the word no.

Filling her lungs, she opened her mouth, leaned forward and brought him into her. She made no comparisons, lived fully in the moment. Ber tasted like the wilderness and more, the more beyond her ability to find words for. His veins were so swollen she wondered if they might burst, prompting her to bathe them in warm saliva. Dizzy and light-headed, she withdrew. Then, moving so fast her head didn't stand a chance of clearing, she again housed him. Laid claim to him much as he'd done to her.

His hold on her hair tightened. Beyond caring what he might do, she turned her head to the side, taking him with her via the strength in her lips.

Groaning, he relaxed his hold. She did the same. Then, propelled by her clenching sex muscles, she worked more of his length into her until his tip pressed against the back of her throat. Gagging, she paused before coming at him again. She'd swallow him, that's what she'd do, take him so far into her that he'd never find his way out.

As for why she wanted to do this—no, she wouldn't go there!

Light-headed was good. Light-headed made mouth-fucking Ber easy. Her thoughts swimming, she worshipped his width and length, smelled him, tasted him.

He started working with her, arching into her and pulling back, guiding her head one way or the other by his hold on her hair. Her belly tightened and stayed that way as she pummeled and was pummeled. Moisture dribbled from the corners of her mouth. Wet heat flowed from her pussy. His harsh, erratic breathing pounded through her.

A gust of cold air struck her right side. She went still.

"Winter's coming," Ber said. "That's all. Nothing to concern ourselves with."

How right he was. Nothing and no one else mattered. Dismissing the chill, she pushed his foreskin back with her tongue.

He might be saying or trying to say something, but as long as his balls pressed against her chin and her teeth lightly raked his length, she didn't care. Unfortunately, bobbing about with her jaws wide open was getting to her. Not sure where the idea had come from, she turned her head to the side so his tip pressed against her cheek.

Feeling like a dog with a bone, she growled. Releasing her hair, Ber clamped his hands over the sides of her face. Once more his tip grazed her throat.

Was the crotch rope getting tighter? Maybe her sex juices were making it shrink. No matter. She loved having her body's heat trapped inside her. Determined to increase the sensation, she pressed her thighs together. The soft fibers against her labial lips belonged there.

Tightening his hold, Ber pushed her back a few inches. Holding on with all the strength left in her aching jaw, she met his gaze.

"Damn you," he muttered. "Damn you."

Sensing the truth behind the curse, she pushed him out and licked his balls and cock. Moisture beaded on his tip. Thirsty, she lapped. She'd become a cat, an insistent, rough-tongued cat.

Ber groaned. The pressure against her cheeks abruptly ended. Eyes closing, she once more claimed his cockhead and leaned back. A moment later, she rocked forward.

It didn't matter who or what he was, what name, if any, he went by. His agenda.

Back. Forward. Back once more. Her pussy hot and tight.

"Ah! Ah!" *he bellowed.* "Shit, yes!"

Sticky heat filled her mouth. Unexpected tears burned behind her lids. Crazed, she stayed with him.

"Ah yes!" *His fingers pressed against her temples.* "Oh shit, yes!"

Her mind spinning and vaginal muscles twitching, she swallowed what she could of his discharge. The rest ran down the sides of her mouth. When he'd given her all he had, she slowly freed him. Remained drunk on his taste.

She wouldn't open her eyes, not yet! Not until—

Whining low and desperate, she rocked her hips from side to side so the rope rubbed against her hot flesh. Still whining, she twisted about while lifting and lowering her body. A flame licked.

Ber's come was inside her, sliding down her throat and reaching her stomach. He'd taken ownership of her arms and declared mastery over her sex.

Damn him!

On the heels of her oath, she climaxed. Shaking, she slumped over and onto the ground.

When, finally, she could, she looked up at him. Night had taken another forward step. She could no longer see her captor and lover's features. Shadows clung to his limbs and torso, rendering them indistinct. Now they could belong to any man.

Chapter Ten

Because of space limitations, the hot water heater held only twenty gallons, but as she stood in the steaming spray, Rane wasn't sure she could make herself get out of the shower even after the water turned cold. A few minutes ago, she'd been asleep; at least she thought she had been. As dreams went, the one she'd just wakened from was above the top of the chart.

Dream, yes, damn it!

Maybe.

Turning her back to the water, she ran a washcloth over her face and opened her eyes. She hadn't bothered with lights until she'd made her way from her bedroom to the one bathroom and deliberately hadn't looked at herself in the mirror while waiting for the water to heat. Her arms burned, but when she looked at them, she saw no sign of rope marks. There was also no evidence that a rope had pressed against her belly.

Doing what she needed to, she reached behind her and hesitantly ran her hand between her ass cheeks. Nope, no overly sensitive skin there. After hanging the washcloth over the cold water handle, she leaned forward, spreading her legs as she did. Leery of her reaction to touching herself there, she experimentally fingered her labial lips and clit. They were responsive, all right, but then they always were.

More to the point, they weren't swollen or sore.

Groaning, she straightened and rubbed her mouth. No soreness there either, and she didn't taste anything except toothpaste residue.

So Ber hadn't captured her? There'd been no less than intelligent conversation between them? He hadn't forced her to endure a crotch rope, and she hadn't given him head?

The bathroom was cold, prompting her to back into the spray so it caressed her shoulders and spine. By morning, she told herself, she'd have everything pulled together. No wonder she was confused right now—she was half asleep.

Except for one little item, she had nothing to worry about.

By the time the water started to cool, she still hadn't managed to convince herself to face that item. Turning the faucet all the way on gave her another minute of comfort, but long before she was ready to leave the wet cocoon, she started shivering. Stepping out, she wrapped a towel around herself. Then, although a niggling voice warned that she didn't want to do that, she grabbed the hand towel and wiped steam from the mirror.

The face waiting for her belonged on a woman who'd been through a hell of a lot. Her eyes blatantly said she was exhausted. Her skin seemed to droop a bit, which reminded her of her mother.

"All right!" she snapped. "I should look hot and bothered and in need of some serious masturbation. Instead, I feel not satisfied but damn close."

And confused, she silently added.

More than a little lost.

After drying off and applying moisturizer, Rane had put back on her nightgown, but despite the weariness tugging at her, she knew she wouldn't be falling asleep anytime soon, so she went into the living room. After grabbing a throw to put over her legs, she curled up in the recliner and turned the TV on. She found an all-night news station but paid little attention to what the two overly chipper anchors were saying. Ber had been the last person to sit in this chair, and she caught hints of the essence he'd left behind. Just like Songan, the bear shifter was too large to comfortably fit in the recliner. If she was going to have a couple of mountain men for gentlemen callers, she needed to buy appropriate furniture.

A burst of pain between her eyes distracted her. Much as she hated facing the cause, hiding from it would only delay the inevitable. Bottom line, at the end of the *dream*, she'd been unsure whether she was with Ber or Songan. Okay, so it was a dream, maybe. Okay, so she had no control over whatever had or hadn't taken place, but what if there was meaning behind the confusion?

A shiver had her pulling the throw up around her neck. Leaning forward, she tried to concentrate on the weather report, but what was the use? Not only did the recliner smell of Ber, Songan had left something of himself in the fabric and padding.

No woman needed two shape-shifters in her life.

She certainly didn't.

However...

Songan had told Rane he wasn't sure when he'd next see her, but three days after leaving her in the forest, he stepped onto her porch and knocked on the door. Her truck was in the driveway, which meant he hadn't come in vain. When after maybe a half minute, she hadn't opened the door, he tried the knob. To his surprise, he discovered she'd locked it.

Things change, he acknowledged as he knocked again. He didn't fully comprehend how much and in how many ways her mother's murder had altered her life and probably should ask, but she had a way of looking disappointed and a little sad when he pumped her for personal information. Apparently she expected him to already know what she was thinking and feeling. However, he seldom did. Truth be told, he didn't know why what she called human intuition was so important. Her mother's violent death upset and saddened her. He understood that. Wasn't that enough?

"Who is it?" she asked from behind the door.

"Me, Songan." Strange, he hadn't heard her approaching. Had she tiptoed?

"What are you doing here? I thought—"

"Are you going to let me in?"

The old lock gave a rusty groan, and he found himself looking at her. Seeing her hair down and drifting around her face instead of corralled like usual knocked him off balance. Given what he'd decided to tell her, he'd nearly convinced himself he could concentrate on passing on certain information without sexual attraction getting in the way. Obviously, he was wrong.

She was staring at him as if she didn't quite recognize him, so he stepped in. The way she backed away instead of reaching for him surprised him, not that he'd say anything. Turning his back to her, he walked into the living room. It smelled of her and the several plants she'd brought with her from wherever she'd been living. Why she wanted growing things inside when there was so much vegetation around was another mystery he might never fathom.

"I didn't expect to see you so soon," she said. "Figured you'd be otherwise occupied."

So had he, he acknowledged as he settled himself in his usual chair. A faint male scent lingered in it.

"I was at Wolverine this morning," he said.

The way she reared back told him he probably shouldn't have been so direct. Was there no end to the things he needed to be aware of around her? If only sensitivity came easier, or she didn't matter so much.

"Why?" she asked and sat on the couch across from him.

"It seemed like something I should do."

"Without me and before the end of rut?"

"It's close enough to the end."

She nodded. "What you're trying to say is you've mounted everything that can be mounted."

"It's more than that. Rane, I don't want you going to Wolverine if there's a possibility of danger."

Her mouth tightened. "It can't be any worse than what happened to Mom. I'm sorry." She ran her ringless hand into her hair. "I didn't mean—did you see anything?"

"No. There are so many smells, it's impossible to separate them."

"Human smells, you mean?"

Now it was his turn to nod. Rane had on jeans and a too-big flannel shirt he concluded had belonged to her mother. Even with the extra fabric, he saw enough of her body that his responded. The bull elk in him might be satiated, the man not at all.

"Nothing fresh," he told her. "That's what I wanted you to know, that I'm not sure we're going to find anything."

"Don't say that."

"You needed to—"

"What I need is the truth." She leaned back, only to straighten and rest her elbows on her knees. "And to connect with her one last time."

"What do you mean?"

Suddenly pale, Rane held up a hand as if to ward him off. "Never mind. That's between Mom and me."

"Is it?"

"Yes." The word sounded fierce, angry and defensive. Even he got that. "Back to what you just said, between the searchers who found her body and law enforcement, a lot of people have tromped all over the area. And it's rained. I get that." Her gaze stayed on him as she gnawed her lower lip. "Oh yes, let's don't forget that whoever killed her was also there."

Still watching him, she began rubbing her knees. "Songan, are you telling me you've changed your mind about going there with me? Maybe you think the only way to insure I won't fall apart is by keeping me here."

"If I could, I would. There was frost when I got there. If there's a storm between now and when we reach—"

"What if we go today?" Eyes bright, she stood. "How'd you get here? I didn't hear a vehicle."

"I ran."

Her nod said she understood he hadn't changed into human form until he'd reached where he kept his clothes.

"We'll take my rig. It'll get us within about five miles of the Wolverine cabin. I have enough food here to hold us in case we have to stay overnight. I'm not sure my mother's sleeping bag is long enough for you. You might—what am I saying, you can switch to elk."

Watching her, he knew he'd never be able to talk her out of this. The weather had concerned him, not for himself, of course, but a decent storm could blanket Wolverine in snow all winter. This might be her last chance, her one opportunity to make good on her promise to her mother.

The area known as Wolverine had felt of death. That's what he should be telling her.

"You don't want to do this," he said, feeling inadequate.

Walking over to where he sat, she placed her hands on the armrests and stared at him. No matter that his strength far outstripped hers, he'd never doubt her determination. "If you don't go with me, I know someone who will."

Anger momentarily rendered him mute. He couldn't remember when he'd last experienced the emotion and didn't know how to handle it. "Who? The other man to sit in this chair?"

Disbelief followed by acceptance transformed her expression. "I should have known you'd sense—"

"Not sense—smell." Taking hold of her wrists, he pulled her onto his lap.

"Let me go!" She tried to slap him. "I hate being manhandled."

"No, you don't."

"This time I do. I mean it, let me go."

The bull elk who'd spent the summer bulking up pressed against Songan's skin. If he wasn't careful, the animal would break through. That, more than Rane's insistence, made him release her. The moment he did, she scrambled to her feet, but instead of running out of the room or ordering him to leave, she stared at him while rubbing her arms.

"What?" he asked at length.

"I'm trying to make sense of something. A lot of somethings." Her voice dropped to a whisper. "Never mind.

What's it going to be? Will you go with me, or do I ask him?"

Him had a name, not that he wanted to know it. "I'll go."

"But you don't want to."

"No."

"Why not?"

"It doesn't matter," he said, when of course it did. Watching her rub her arms with her eyes big and vulnerable, he vowed to do whatever it took to keep her alive. To make a lie of the aura of death deep in the mountains.

"I appreciate you telling me," Deputy Gannon told Rane when she called him after deciding to take both her pistol and her mother's rifle. Eager as she was to start what she'd been wanting to do for too long, she also needed to get out of the house. To put distance between herself and the nightly erotic Ber-filled dreams. "And I understand what's driving you, but I wish I could stop you."

"If you're thinking about the weather, why do you think I'm in a hurry? For the record, Songan is going with me."

Gannon didn't immediately respond, making her wonder if he disapproved. "I guess better a shifter than some of Forestville's residents. I just don't want you forgetting he's half animal."

"I'm aware of that."

"Are you?"

Sometimes, she decided, two words had more impact than an entire speech. "Songan and I have known each other for years," she said unnecessarily. "I understand him as well as any human can."

"Yeah, maybe. Look, those shifters never lose all the elk in them. He's a male in his prime. Instinct drives a lot of what he does."

"I've noticed that."

"Yeah?"

"Yeah," she said. Better to be honest.

"That's your business, but no matter how devoted to you you might think he is, he and his kind don't value life in the same way you and I do. They're wired different."

"What are you saying?"

"Just that I don't see him risking his life for yours if it comes to that."

Now it was her turn to wait a beat before responding. "You think that's a possibility?"

Gannon sighed. "Rane, there's something you need to know. Hell, maybe you already do. Did your mom talk to you about what she'd been up to near the end?"

A too-familiar stab of grief had her slumping into the nearest chair. Was she going to spend the rest of her life regretting putting her mother on the back burner while she did everything possible to put her isolated and limiting Forestville upbringing behind her? "Such as?" she asked.

"Are you alone?"

"Songan's here."

"Hmm. Rane, your mother and I suspected illegal activity was going on in the woods. She was trying to convince her superior to assign someone to work with her so the bulk of the investigation didn't fall on her shoulders, but you know how it is with a federal agency. Everything moves slow, and there are other priorities."

"Wait. I don't—what investigation?"

"You don't know? I'm sorry. Maybe she didn't want you

worrying."

Teeth clenched, she said, "It's too late for worry. Gannon, please."

"This isn't for the public to know, but I feel safe telling you. I'm sure you've come across the same thing in your work."

Chilled, she waited Gannon out.

"It started this spring. A couple of hikers following the Chinook River came across a bear carcass with bullet holes in it."

"Spring. It wasn't hunting season then."

"No, it wasn't. I'm not sure who the hikers called initially, but things were routed to your mom, who immediately went out. Only one organ had been taken. The rest of the bear was left to rot."

"The gall bladder, right?"

"Then your mom told—"

"We've talked about this insanity, of course." No matter how much evidence there was to the contrary, some people, traditional Chinese in particular, believed bear gall bladders were effective in treating heart disease, diabetes, liver disease, even obesity. A single gall could net a bear poacher several thousand dollars.

"Only one bear has been wasted?" she asked.

"No, unfortunately. Four other carcasses have shown up since then, and who knows how many others might be out there."

An image of an enraged Ber standing over a slaughtered bear momentarily came between her and the ability to speak. "Are you saying Mom was working on this alone?"

"Essentially yes, unfortunately. Several environmental groups were up in arms, and at least two politicians are trying to get funds earmarked to bring Forest Service investigators to the area. Your mother and I had reservations about how effective that would be. Having some strangers show up around here would tip our hands and maybe drive the poachers elsewhere."

I wish she'd told me. "What happens now?" she made herself ask. "With Mom dead, is whoever's responsible free to..."

"You don't want to talk about this. I understand." Even with the distance between them, she heard Gannon's compassion. "The Service hasn't yet chosen someone to replace your mother. Once that person has been selected, I intend to meet with the new guy and press to make apprehending the poachers a priority."

"They're more than that." Her throat burned, forcing her to swallow repeatedly. "The bastards murdered my mother."

"We don't know for sure. It could be—"

"What does your gut reaction say?"

"You don't dance around, do you?"

"Jacki was my mother." *I owe her this.*

"Yes, she was. Rane, my gut says that when or if we determine who's selling black market bear galls, we'll know who to look at for her killing."

Thinking Gannon couldn't have anything more to say, she looked at but didn't really see her mother's living room. Songan had come inside and was watching her with his wary animal eyes. If only life was simple and ruled by sex.

"Rane," Gannon said, "your mom and I were pretty convinced the poacher is a local. Someone we maybe see every day, a neighbor even."

Suddenly numb, she shivered. "Because of how many area bears have been taken?"

"Exactly." Gannon sighed. "The poacher—I'm thinking it's one person, because there's less chance of loose lips talking—knows these mountains as well as the bears themselves."

"A neighbor," Rane repeated. "A so-called friend."

"Maybe someone your mother's known for years."

"She arrested several locals for illegal hunting. Andy, Aaron and Albert Jones blamed her for their convictions."

"Now there's siblings without a spare brain cell for the bunch. They've caused me trouble for years."

She struggled to think of something to say. Given Songan's keen hearing, she had no doubt he'd heard the deputy's side of the conversation. Compassion and concern weren't Songan's strong suits, and yet she took comfort from his unwavering gaze.

"Gannon, I was in the Sawmill the other night. I talked to their cousins Clifford and Chip. I'm not—not pointing fingers at them in particular, just thinking they're probably barely holding it together financially."

"You're asking me if they're on my suspect list, aren't you. I haven't eliminated them, but they aren't as high as the A brothers."

"Why's that?"

"Clifford and Chip's logging operation won one of the few harvesting contracts to come around in recent years. They're busy and making money for a change."

"I went to school with Andy and Aaron. Albert's younger. Like you said, they aren't the sharpest knives in the drawer. What are they up to these days?"

"Don't go there, Rane. You aren't a detective."

"What are they up to?"

"Not working for Chip and Clifford and that's caused some

tension in the bunch. From what I hear, the A brothers figure their cousins should have put them on the payroll because they're blood."

"I'm trying to remember whether I've seen them since I got back."

"No, you don't. I've already told you more than I wish I had. Let it go. Let me do my job."

She said something about him already saying that. He asked whether she'd changed her mind about going to Wolverine. Telling him no, she hung up.

Chapter Eleven

"Let Gannon and the rest of the sheriff's department do their job," Songan said. Pushing away from the wall he'd been leaning against, he started toward her. "You can't bring her back."

But maybe her spirit will find me once I'm where she died. "I know."

Songan stood leaning down a little as if trying to blanket her body with his. Every night since she'd met Ber, his spirit or something had laid claim to her mind and body in what was unlike any dream she'd ever had. Now Songan was here, and even with her thoughts on the conversation with the deputy, she gave silent thanks to Songan's strength.

She suspected she'd need it to get through the next few days.

"I'm glad I'm here," Songan said as he brushed her cheek. "You shouldn't be alone."

She leaned into his touch. "It's a natural state for you. What makes you think it's different for me?"

"Instinct."

Placing his hand under her chin, he guided her face upward and lightly covered her mouth with his. Warmth stole through her as she returned his kiss. Unexpected dizziness prompted her to wrap her arms around his waist. Anchored, she parted her lips.

At his core, Songan was a good man. Single-minded when it came to sex and sometimes rough—not that she minded. Their limited time together had revolved around satisfying their physical needs, but even when his powerful grip left her bruised, she never doubted his heart.

"I want this," she muttered. "God, how I want."

His hand slid over her neck, over her collarbone, reached her breast. He started to rub it through the layers of clothing, then stopped. Pulling back a little, he stared down at her. "Do you?"

Warned by his tone, she struggled to meet his somber gaze. "What are you talking about?"

"You tell me."

What was that she'd just thought of Songan, that he could be rough? What did she expect of someone who could never take survival for granted? Perhaps that's why he believed in seizing every moment.

Today, dreading what she might find at Wolverine, she longed to live in the present. Songan's erection had bloomed the instant they touched. He could, they could— "How's this for your answer?" Sliding her hand between their bodies, she rubbed her knuckles against the familiar and always exciting bulge. "Hell yes, I want." *I need.*

To her surprise, Songan didn't respond as she believed he would. Instead of increasing his hold on her breast, he gently but firmly pushed her away from him.

"Songan?"

"Daylight isn't going to last. We need to get up there."

Five minutes later, Songan and she had packed and placed everything they'd need on the front porch. Like ninety-nine percent of the people who lived in the Chinook Mountains, Songan knew how to handle a weapon. So did she. Fortunately the Forest Service-built cabin at Wolverine meant they wouldn't need to carry a tent. Still shaken by what had happened between them, she patted her pocket to reassure herself that, yes, her cell phone was there. She reached for the handle. Songan stopped her.

"I can't do it."

"Can't do what?" She felt sick. "Have you changed your mind about—"

"Not that. Damn it, Rane, who'd you have sex with?"

She stared at what she could see of her wrist under the man's fingers. "What?"

His grip tightened. "Don't do that. I hate being lied to."

"All I did was ask a question." From the beginning, Songan's skin touching hers had turned her on. Something as simple as his elbow brushing her had her wanting to see him naked. After what had happened between them a few minutes ago, having him hold her in place with his legs, both barriers and potential stripped her mind and filled her body with heat.

"There are certain scents a shower can't get rid of. Arousal. Who turned you on?"

"No one. I've been having dreams. Explicit ones." *Didn't I?* "I can't help how my body responds. And even if a man spent the night, you don't own me."

But he wanted to. The harsh intensity in his eyes left her with no doubt of that. Dream-Ber had acted the same way.

"I don't want to get into this," she told Songan with the

need for something she refused to name arcing through her. "There's only one thing I'm interested in right now. If you can't handle that, I'll go alone."

"No, you won't."

He'd cut off the circulation in her wrist, but he probably wasn't aware of how much pressure he was exerting.

"I mean it, Rane," he continued. "Gannon's right. It isn't safe for you to be alone up there."

"I'm aware of that. No way I couldn't be." Later, maybe, she'd ask why he was being so insistent but not now with desire strong and dangerous between them. Either they get underway, or they'd tear off each other's clothes.

Songan hoisted one of the two backpacks off the floor before releasing her. Instead of descending the porch steps and heading for her truck, however, he stood motionless. On edge, she picked up her pack.

Because the big elk shifter still hadn't moved, she slipped around him. That's when she spotted what had captured his attention. Ber stood with his back to the truck's driver's side door, and his deep black eyes slowly moved from her to Songan and back again.

The men were pit bulls, two potent males taking their measure of each other. Willing and ready to fight. A lightning strike couldn't have made more of an impact.

"What are you doing here?" she asked Ber.

Despite the biting wind, he wore only jeans, hiking boots and an unzipped denim jacket over a muscle-hugging white T-shirt. He seemed oblivious to the way the jacket slapped at his chest and airborne leaves and other debris swirled around him. Behind him the gray-black sky promised winter.

"Waiting for you," he said.

"Who the hell is he?" Songan demanded.

Even though doing so left her even more off-balance, Rane took her time studying the two men. Given how they were positioned, she couldn't say which was taller, not that it mattered. Both were densely muscled and carried themselves in ways that said they were aware of their bodies' full potential. Ber's hair seemed a little darker and longer, while Songan's eyebrows were bushier. Neither had shaved recently. Their clothing was made for a physical life.

Because he was so close, Songan's warmth didn't surprise her. At the same time, she swore Ber's heat was reaching her. The bear shifter gave every appearance of being impervious to the weather, but then she could say the same of Songan.

Two shape-shifters meeting for the first time. Challenging each other for supremacy and without moving a muscle, yet. Both men determined to lay claim to her.

Feeling weightless and disconnected from everything, she hoisted her pack over her shoulder and started down the stairs. She half expected Songan to stop her, and when he didn't, she looked back at him. He continued to glare at Ber, who was doing the same.

So this was what it was like to be desired and desirable, she distractedly mused as she reached the ground. Only, was she the prize or were the men more intent on proving themselves to each other?

"You said you were waiting for me. Why?" she asked Ber. Her lips felt numb, and looking up at him made her neck ache.

"I have no choice."

Was he referring to the crazy thing he'd said about her being a vital cog in the Enyeto's future? Hell of a time to bring it up if he was. "You ever hear of free will?" she threw at him, when the truth was, she longed to touch him. To explore the connection to her dreams. "It means I don't have to do anything I don't want to."

"It's not that simple."

Irritated and aware, she dropped her pack. Moments ago she'd touched Songan's cock. Now she wanted to do the same to Ber. She wouldn't, damn it! "Whatever. I need you to get out of the way."

Ber folded his arms across his chest. "You have to go there? Nothing can stop you."

There. Where my mother's life ended. "Yes."

"Then I'm going with you."

"The hell you are," Songan snapped from behind her. "That's what I'm doing."

Songan was right. The two of them had come to a reluctant decision about how today would play out. As exciting as the thought might be—and it was—she didn't need two bodyguards.

Only these men were far from bodyguards. They were, what, her lovers? But she hadn't had sex with Ber. Had she?

"I've been listening." Ber directed his comment at her. "Learning."

"Learning what?"

"There've been more deaths than just your mother's and the young elk. Bear."

"How do you know that?" Songan asked.

Struck by the lessening of macho in his tone, she studied Songan, who was studying Ber as if he'd never seen anything like him.

"Death stays in the air and on the ground," Ber said. "And in the hearts of those who witness it."

A cop like Gannon probably wouldn't have any idea what

Ber was talking about, but she'd spent enough time around Songan that she understood.

"What did they witness?" Songan asked.

"A rifle being fired in the middle of the night. A bear bellowing in pain, trying to bite where he'd been shot, falling to the ground, bleeding. Dying."

That could have been her mother! Some of it anyway.

"And they," Songan said, "whoever they were, told you those things?"

Alerted by Songan's challenge, she tried to divide her attention between the two men. Once again she was captivated by the similarities between them, the wildness in their harsh gazes. The pure sex flowing through their veins and reaching her.

"Yes," Ber answered Songan. "They did. And to answer the question you haven't yet asked, I learned what I needed to from deer. Owls. A young cougar."

Wondering if Songan would call Ber a liar, she readied herself for renewed hostility. Instead, Songan slowly relaxed. He no longer held himself as if he was about to attack.

"And you," Ber said.

"Me?"

"When we found the young elk with a bullet through its heart."

"You..."

"I was there."

Comprehension exploded in Songan's expression. "You're the grizzly."

Ber nodded. "I felt your grief as you stood over what could have been your offspring."

Songan slowly nodded. "You also watched Rane and me fuck."

"I'm more than a bear, not that I have to tell you that. Just as there's more to you than man."

"Elk."

Rane might be part of the conversation, but at the moment she felt as if she'd faded into the background. Songan probably had never suspected any creature except an elk could shift. Maybe the same held true for Ber. It certainly had been like that for her until Ber walked into her world.

This was magical, mystical and unbelievable all rolled up into a single moment. The truly incredible thing was, she was privy to it.

Ber jerked his head at her. "You were going to Wolverine with her?"

"Were? I still am." Dropping his pack, Songan draped a possessive arm over her shoulder. "A bear shifter isn't the only creature who senses death."

"What are you saying?" she demanded.

Before Songan could answer, if he was going to, a growl so low that for an instant Rane thought it was thunder rolled out of Ber. Grabbing her arm, he pulled her away from Songan and shoved so her back was against the truck. He kept her there via a hand against her shoulder. Even with the wind beating at her, she felt herself drifting back to her *dreams*. She wouldn't be surprised to see rope appear.

"Don't go." Ber's breath warmed the top of her head. "There's no reason for you to risk—"

"It's my decision!" She surged forward then sunk against the truck again when he continued to hold on to her. To her shock, hot need slammed at her. She fought it the only way she could think of, with words.

"No one's holding a gun to either of your heads. I've been there any number of times. Obviously neither of you has enough human in you to understand. I'm not going to waste my breath trying to explain why I have to do this."

Ber wasn't the only one who growled when he was agitated. So did Songan, as witnessed by the low, sharp note erupting from deep in his chest. Grabbing Ber's arm, Songan spun the bear shifter away from her. Thank goodness Ber had the presence of mind to let go of her. The instant she was free, she shoved herself between the two would-be fighters.

"Stop it! You're acting like animals!"

"We are," the men replied almost as one.

"Whatever. Look, arguing like this isn't going to get us anywhere. If you two draw blood, I'm not going to bandage you."

"Won't you?" Ber challenged. The way he was looking at her, she wondered if he knew about her dreams. Was responsible for them.

"Look." She stumbled over the word. "The last thing I want to do is deal with a couple of oversize egos and even more oversize muscles. If I don't get to Wolverine today, it might not make any difference until spring. What I said about going alone isn't—Songan, I need your hearing and sight."

"And mine," Ber said.

"Why?" Songan asked when she thought he'd tell the bear shifter to leave them the hell alone.

"I have my reasons."

"Which are?" she blurted, still trying to absorb everything that was happening.

"You don't need to ask."

No, she didn't, did she? He was hung up on his belief that

she was vital to the Enyeto's future. She wasn't about to try to explain that to Songan. Let Ber do it.

"You learned about the bear deaths," she said, hoping to change the subject. "I'm sorry. That must have hurt."

"The blacks here are a kind of kin, part of me."

Ber's eloquent words made her heart ache. "Do you know why they were killed?"

As he shook his head, she acknowledged that, despite his human form today, Ber didn't fully understand what it meant to be one. Like Songan, he existed on the fringes of modern society and maybe didn't fully comprehend what humans were capable of. The evil in some of them.

Trying to keep the telling as basic as possible, she relayed the conversation she'd had with Gannon. Even before she finished, Ber's confusion turned into barely contained rage. He paced from the truck to her porch step and back again. Watching him, she concluded that, as Songan had done, he'd come to her place as a beast. Not only didn't he have any transportation, he didn't have a decent winter coat.

He frightened her. No way could or should she deny that. At the same time, watching his effortless movements thrilled her. He was perfect, raw and proud, savage beneath the surface.

Damn him, he didn't need to throw ropes on her. She'd come to him of her own free and hungry will. If he didn't make the first move, she'd rip off his minimal clothes, launch herself at him and beg him to bury his cock in her sex. They'd fuck standing up, him holding her in place while her nails clawed at his shoulders and he bit at the side of her neck.

They'd climax in the same heartbeat. Scream their shared pleasure.

"I'll find whoever has been doing this. Tear them apart."

Ber's hate-filled voice yanked her back to reality, but even as she threw her pack into her truck bed, she knew she'd eventually have to ask Ber whether he'd deliberately planted the edgy dreams in her.

Dreams?

"I don't have a coat that'll fit you," she told Ber. "And even if he had an extra"—she jerked her head at Songan—"I doubt if he'd lend it to you. You can throw my sleeping bag over your shoulders if—"

"I'm fine. Not cold."

"And if you get chilled, you'll turn into a grizzly, is that what you're saying?"

He nodded.

"Fine. Whatever. My truck. My keys. And my gas after I've gone to the station. My plans haven't changed. I'm still going to drive as far as the road will let us before taking off on foot. Look at the weather. It has to be done today."

As if reinforcing her words, the wind slammed into her. She should have gone on this have-to trip earlier. Before the weather became her enemy. Alone, if necessary.

"There's barely enough room for the three of us in the cab," she pointed out unnecessarily. "I wouldn't want to be the one sitting in back, so I won't suggest it for either of you. As I see it, the only other option is for one of you to shift now and join us at the start of the trail."

Despite the sudden tension, she nearly laughed at how Ber and Songan stared at each other. Obviously neither man was willing to let the other be alone with her. Two suitors? Yeah, right. More like two wild stallions.

Chapter Twelve

The mile long drive from her mother's place outside the town limits to the gas station Alice ran with her husband Dave seemed to take forever. Despite their attempts to maintain their own space, Songan and Ber's wide shoulders were jammed together, while she had a little more room behind the wheel. Like it or not, and she wasn't sure how she felt about it, it made more sense for her to sit in the middle when they got underway.

Between two men whose presence redefined the word male.

With her libido ratcheted up so high she was hard-pressed to think of anything else.

Chances were they would spend the night in a small cabin designed for hikers. The night. With the woodstove for warmth and mood, a single bed, hours of darkness with nothing to do and thoughts—damn it, the thoughts!

She'd never slept with more than one man at a time. Multiple sex partners weren't her style. Well, not in the real world. There was nothing wrong with a little fantasy, right? And threesomes, or more, had been a sometimes fantasy, an exciting way of passing a solitary night.

Except she wouldn't be alone tonight. Both men wanted her, and she wanted—damn it, she was losing her mind!

The problem was too much male in an enclosed space and entirely too much testosterone coating the air. As soon as they started hiking, she'd stop imagining two naked bodies and her smaller, equally naked one between theirs. Touching and being touched.

No other customers were at the station when they pulled up. The moment she turned off the engine, silence enveloped her. As far as she knew, neither man had looked at each other during the short drive, and she didn't trust herself to meet their gazes. What if her expression gave away what she'd been thinking?

Because self-serve gas was illegal in Oregon, she got out, made her way to the weathered building adjacent to the pumps and opened the door to where Dave did occasional mechanical work. Fortunately it was warmer in the small shop than outside. She spotted Alice doing something with the brakes of an old Chevy up on portable jacks. What was it Gannon had pointed out, that her mother's killer likely was someone who lived in the area?

But not Alice! No more crazy thinking.

"Sorry to disturb you," Rane said, "but I'm nearly on fumes."

Alice, who'd been kneeling, slowly got to her feet. Watching her, Rane recalled the other night in the Sawmill when the older woman kept studying her.

"Going somewhere, are you?" Alice asked.

"Yep." Because Alice and her mother had been friends, she was tempted to explain, but she couldn't fully shake off Gannon's warning. Right now, the less she said, the better.

Alice wiped her hands on a dirty towel she'd had in her back pocket. "Shitty day for it. Your mom was one of the good people; I hope you know that."

"I do. I'm having a hard time dealing with how she died. I don't think I'll ever get used to it." There. She'd said what she needed to.

"Neither will I." Alice made no move toward the door. "Your mom was one of my best friends. I used to think she was slumming when we hung out, her being college educated and all, while I—" She held up grease-stained fingers. "But we were both into the area's history. Digging through records at the county historical society was what first brought us together. After awhile, it was like there was nothing we couldn't share. That's why…"

Rane placed her hand on Alice's shoulder. The older woman didn't have any extra weight on her. Everything was pure muscle forged from hard work. "Don't hold back, please. Whatever you're thinking, I need to hear it."

"Maybe you do, maybe not. She changed near the end. Kind of closed herself off. I knew she had something on her mind, but she wouldn't tell me what it was."

So much for thinking she'd cried herself out. Just like that, tears started to flow. Rane clutched Alice to her, and Alice did the same. The older woman's arms felt like vises around her waist.

Ber and Songan were waiting for her. They expected her to be in a hurry, not to stand inside a small repair shop holding on to a woman old enough to be her mother and crying.

But she had to be strong around the two shifters. She didn't have to with Alice. Couldn't be.

Several seconds passed before Rane felt composed enough to speak. She stepped back, taking hold of Alice's rough, grease-stained hands as she did.

"I didn't mean to upset you." Alice sniffed. Turning her head, she wiped her nose on her coveralls.

"You didn't. I loved hearing what you said about Mom being a good person."

"I meant every word of it."

"I know you did. About her having a lot on her mind—was it because of me?"

"You?"

It was too late to try to cover her tracks. Besides, dangerous or safe, she needed to ask her mother's friend certain things.

"I asked for a transfer to Alaska. After a couple of years in Utah, I wanted a change of scene. Again. Mom didn't want me going that far away. We didn't exactly argue. It was more like a standoff." *Her asking why I kept running away from here.* "After that I, ah, I didn't stay in touch the way I should have." *The way I always had.*

"Why'd you want to move clear up there?"

"Lots of reasons," she said, even though right now she wasn't sure what they were. "Growing up here, I needed to see what the rest of the world was like. At least more of the United States. I couldn't understand why she was content staying in one place. Don't get me wrong. I enjoyed visiting." *Seeing Songan.* "But Alaska's incredible. Beautiful. Wide open. The first time I went there, I fell in love with the scenery."

"I have two kids. Boys. You know them."

She nodded. James and Mike hadn't been the sharpest students and had joined the military right after graduating. They'd both done a stint in Afghanistan but were stateside now, one in Virginia, the other living in the next county. Her mom had told her that one was married, but she couldn't remember which it was. She'd also mentioned that the one who'd come back to Oregon was having trouble making ends meet.

"When they were little, Dave and I thought they'd be taking over the business, but they never showed much interest. I miss having them around all the time, but Dave—he still blames them."

"For what?"

"Leaving us with this." Alice jerked her head at the cramped space. "We're barely keeping our heads above water. It'd be different if they were here to work on the big stuff. People wouldn't care about bringing their rigs up to Forestville if they got good service. James learned how to be a diesel mechanic in the military, but does he ever think of using his skill to help his old man? No. And Mike, well, all he thinks of is himself, not that he's doing that good a job of it. That's what has Dave bitter."

Not sure how the conversation had taken this turn, she released Alice's hand and turned toward the door, hoping to get Alice going in that direction.

"Children disappoint their parents, just like parents disappoint their kids," Alice said. "Your mom was hurt about the Alaska thing."

"Oh." She couldn't think of anything else to say.

"But that wasn't the only thing that was eating at her. I just wish she'd confided in me. It might have made a difference. Kept her alive."

Cold, Rane stared at Alice. "What are you talking about?"

"Maybe nothing, but I can't help thinking she wasn't paying attention the way she should have been when she got herself shot."

Got herself shot? Like it was something she should feel guilty for? "She was investigating something serious. Right now I can't tell you more than that."

Alice shrugged her bony shoulders. "Same as your mom."

As she watched Alice pump gas a few minutes later, Rane pondered something. Maybe her mother had had no idea who the bear poacher was. But what if she'd suspected a specific someone? If that was the case, she might have decided not to say anything to anyone, not even one of her closest friends. Her mother hadn't dared let anything slip, because the suspect was someone both women knew.

Was that the only reason her mother had retreated into herself? Or was her daughter's latest career decision responsible for the loss of concentration that had gotten her killed?

Mom, we used to be able to talk about everything. I need that now, more than ever. I'm coming for—I'm coming to where...

Ber and Songan had exited the cab and were standing at a telling distance from each other. Songan watched Alice while Ber's attention was on the sky. She might be fooling herself, but the clouds didn't appear to be as dark as they'd been a little while ago. According to the weather report, the storm out in the Pacific wasn't due to hit for some twenty-four hours. Considerable rain was forecast for the valley and snow in the mountains.

Well, it wasn't as if she'd never spent a night in the mountains in winter.

And it wasn't as if she'd be alone.

"That's it," Alice said as she hung up the nozzle. "If you can leave your *friends,* come inside and we'll handle the finances."

Shaking her head, Rane reminded herself that she shouldn't be surprised by Alice's comment. Songan or Ber weren't the kind of men who'd fade into the woodwork.

"Who's the stranger?" Alice asked when she and Rane were in the closet-size office. "I recognize Songan, all right. Long as the shifters have been around, you'd think I'd be used to them, but they're damn big. Too big for me, if you know what I'm getting at."

Rane worked at keeping her features neutral. "I've known him for years. I guess I'm used to his size."

"Whatever. Some folks here will always resent the jobs shifters have taken from them. Others point out they're bringing much-needed money into the area, which is what I tried to tell my son Mike. Me, I'm just glad they pay their bills. Who's the other guy, another shifter?"

Ber was, just not an elk like Alice surely believed. Instead of going into an explanation that really wasn't hers to give, she said she hoped Alice and she could catch up before long.

"I'd like that. It gets lonesome here for me." Alice gave the space a dismissive shrug. "When a couple's been married a long time like Dave and I have, they pursue their own interests. They no longer want to spend all their time together."

A sudden smile highlighted Alice's countless wrinkles. "You wouldn't happen to want some female company today, would you? Those men might be industrial-size and more than I can handle, but I'm not opposed to spending a little time around some of their energy."

"I, ah—"

"I'm joking." Just like that, the grin was gone. "An old woman full of wishful thinking. You sure you're going to be okay with them? I get the feeling they aren't exactly best friends."

Rane couldn't disagree.

The elk shifter was a good driver, not that Ber could imagine himself telling Songan that. Rane sitting between

Songan and him made for more shoulder room, all right, and he loved the feel of her body against his, but he hadn't yet resigned himself to having to be around the other shifter. He didn't see that happening any time soon, if ever.

Songan made no secret that he felt the same way.

Rane had turned on the radio, and although the reception was getting worse the farther they went into the mountains, he figured she preferred that to silence.

Shifting position a little so his right side wasn't jammed so tight against the armrest, he looked over at Rane. The wind had made a mess of her braid, not that he was opposed to the way the loose chocolate hairs tangled around her prominent cheekbones. He felt the same way about her lack of makeup, hip-following jeans, slim waist over childbearing hips, and firm breasts her flannel shirt couldn't hide. Long, rich brown lashes framed her gray-green eyes. From the looks of them, she didn't pluck her thick brows. He approved.

Maybe she sensed his scrutiny, because she glanced at him but went back to staring out the windshield before he could read her expression. He should be studying their surroundings, but as more and more trees closed in around the narrowing road, his thoughts went back to the last few nights.

He'd spent them curled in a hollowed tree trunk, not sleeping much and thinking a hell of a lot about Rane. Somehow he had to get her to listen to him, convince her to accept him in her world, embrace him and the rest of the Enyeto.

Unfortunately, he didn't know how to make that happen. Maybe if he'd spent more time among humans, he'd better understand what went on inside women's minds. But maybe, even if he wasn't a shifter, that might not make a difference.

Because he was who he was, he'd spent hours imagining

doing whatever he wanted to her. To hell with what civilization said was allowed. No more worrying about slowly introducing her to his world followed by subtle persuasion and the risk of being rejected.

None of that. Instead, he'd step onto her property, break down her door, back her into a corner and throw her over his shoulder. Ignoring her futile and arousing struggles, he'd carry her into her bedroom and throw her onto the bed. Not giving her time to recover, he'd climb next to her, rip open her blouse, and lift out one ripe breast and then the other.

If she fought, he'd tie her to the bed. Then he'd sit back and watch her eyes flash. Moving slow and deliberate, he'd unzip her jeans and tug them off her hips and legs. Desire would heat her. Heat him too. He'd slip a large, rough hand between her legs. Groaning, she'd open herself to him. Beg him to take her.

And he would. Repeatedly.

The pickup hit one pothole and almost immediately bounced over another. Rane leaned into him, jerked away, smacked his arm again.

"Sorry," she muttered.

"I'm not."

Staring straight ahead, she jammed her hands between her thighs. "No, I don't suppose you are."

Songan started to look their way. Just then the driver-side tires dipped. Cursing, the elk shifter yanked on the steering wheel.

Every time Rane's shoulder brushed his, Ber lost more of today. The past few nights closed back down around him, and he willingly returned to the fantasy that had sustained, aroused and ultimately frustrated him.

She wasn't in her house, after all. He found her in a

meadow next to a stream. Instead of approaching her slow and calm as he should, the grizzly in him ruled.

Each year when breeding season arrived, he ceased caring whether a sow was in heat. Lunging at whichever one he'd been stalking, he brought her to the ground under his greater weight. If the sow was ripe, she'd open herself to him. If not, they'd growl and wrestle and bite until he quit and took his frustration elsewhere.

Watching the Rane who existed only in his fantasy, he decided he wouldn't force himself on her after all. No, he'd do something else. Use something else.

A soft, strong white rope appeared in his hand. At nearly the same moment, she became aware of his presence. Instead of welcoming him, she bolted. Her pumping legs, gyrating hips and quickened breaths were like fire to his veins. Growling in excitement, he took off after her. The rope snaked out and settled over her, seeming to caress her flesh even as he jerked her to a stop.

His blood racing, he tied her up, restrained her, rendered her his. And when he'd taken the fight from her and tuned her in to her sexuality, they fucked.

Hard and loud.

"I'm yours," she said afterward.

Windblown pine needles struck the windshield and slid over the truck's hood. Just like that, Ber again lost his hold on make-believe. Even as the fantasy faded, he acknowledged that the Rane he barely knew would never utter the cliché words he'd put in her mouth.

"There." Leaning forward, she pointed at something ahead. "If you turn there, we can go a little farther."

Songan slowed from maybe fifteen miles an hour to about half of that and eased onto a long unused logging road. Within a couple of minutes, it gave out. Songan turned off the engine, acknowledged Rane and then looked past her at Ber.

"What?" Rane asked Songan. "If you're thinking you can still get rid of Ber—"

"I'm not. We need him."

"For what?" Ber demanded.

Songan's gaze hardened. "Keeping her safe. Alive."

Not replying, Ber opened the door and stepped out. The cold air smelled of snow and pine. When he'd first accepted that he'd be leaving Alaska, he'd never imagined he'd feel at ease anywhere else, but from the beginning, Oregon's mountains had embraced him. Even before he'd familiarized himself with the Chinook area, he'd felt secure here. Winter might be showing its teeth, but he loved that season as much as the others.

Rane joined him as Songan came around the truck. The elk shifter turned his head into the wind.

"I know," Rane said. "Not the world's best timing."

Songan shook his head. "No, it isn't."

Only a few minutes ago, Ber would have given a great deal to make Songan disappear. He still didn't like feeling as if he was competing for Rane with him, but he couldn't discount Songan's commitment to her. What was it he'd said earlier, that it might take both of them to keep her alive? Was he talking about the storm or something more dangerous?

Looking at Songan out of the corner of his eye, he placed his hand on Rane's shoulder. She tensed.

"Don't," he said. "Please."

She remained on alert but didn't try to move away. "I wish I could relax around you. I want to. But I can't stop thinking of what you said."

"What was it?" Ber demanded.

Rane lifted his hand off her. For a moment, he was positive he saw his fantasies in her eyes. Was it possible his desire to control her had reached her? Wanting the answer, he slowly lowered his gaze from her face to her breasts and then the join between her legs. Despite her layered clothing, he sensed her arousal. A like emotion gripped him as his cock strained against his jeans.

"What's this?" Songan pointed at his bulge.

"He thinks I'm going to raise his male offspring and then give that little boy or boys up," Rane blurted. "Go on, Ber, tell him. Explain all about how the Enyeto need human foster parents to care for your children on until they're old enough to be useful. I'm sure that won't bother him at all."

"What are you talking about?" Songan asked.

"What must be," Ber said. Rane gaped at him.

"No, never," Songan insisted. "You can't force her—"

"Can't I?"

"Stop it!" Balling her fist, Rane shook it at him and then Songan. "I'm not going to have this conversation, understand? We're going to where my mother was murdered. Do you think anything else matters?"

If not for the smell of wet female heat emanating from her, Ber would have believed her. She was trying to divide her attention between him and Songan, leaning toward one and then the other.

"Yes," he said, "I do."

Songan nodded. "So do I."

Chapter Thirteen

Get a grip! Please, get a grip.

Songan, who'd most recently been to Wolverine, led the way, while Ber brought up the rear. Watching the powerful elk shifter's legs work and aware of Ber's attention on her ass, Rane walked in the middle. Reality was, she could practically find Wolverine in her sleep, but the more time the three of them spent on the trail, the more grateful she was for the company.

From the moment her mother's body had been found, she'd known she had to come here. Back then having Songan accompany her had made the most sense, but that was before Ber had, what, become part of her life?

It was so complicated. Excitingly so. More and more arousing by the moment.

Two men. Two virile men. Every step she took pounded the reality deeper into her soul and pussy.

They both wanted her. Songan took having sex with her again for granted, while Ber—what had taken place between them?

Goose bumps ran down her spine. Oh yes, Ber was studying her, all right, just as he'd done when they were in the truck. It could have been her imagination. It would be easier if it was, but she suspected that somehow he knew about the erotic bondage dreams. Damn it, he'd probably done more than that. Most likely he'd planted them in her. Was that his way of having sex with her?

Groaning under her breath, she shrugged her pack higher on her back, glad that she was carrying her pistol instead of the heavier rifle. Ber, who still looked impervious to the cold and wind despite his lightweight clothing, had offered to carry it. She'd stubbornly insisted she wanted to be responsible for her own belongings.

Songan's pack held her mother's rifle, which he knew how to use, most of the food, flashlights and extra blankets he wouldn't need if he decided to shift. She was the only one of the three who couldn't get along without what she saw as necessities.

What was she thinking? Songan wouldn't shift if Ber remained in human form. Either both of them would become animals, or both would—oh damn! She and two confident, competent, over-the-top sexy men in a small, isolated space…

The cabin had only a single bed.

Cheeks burning and lungs not providing all the oxygen she needed, she pressed her fingers to her forehead. Looking around and beyond Songan, she spotted a rocky outcropping which was less than a mile from the cabin where, according to her day planner, her mother had spent the last night of her life.

She didn't want to be here! God, what had she thought she'd prove by standing near where her mother's blood had stained the ground? She couldn't bring her back to life. She wasn't a detective or investigator, a vigilante.

She was a woman being torn apart by the two sexiest, most powerful men imaginable.

Songan stopped so abruptly she had to put her hand out to keep from running into him. His heat seeped into her fingertips and up her arm to her breasts. Words failed her, and her legs threatened to give way.

"I have a suggestion," Songan said, seemingly oblivious to her condition. "It's going to be dark in what, maybe three hours?"

Determined to regain her equilibrium, she'd dropped her arm to her side. Her chest felt as if it had caught fire.

"Rane," Songan continued, "I say we first go to the cabin and leave everything there."

"I agree." Ber's voice behind her made her think of a solitary drum. "You need to do this right."

Stepping back from the men, she tried to look at both at the same time. "Right?"

"Take as much of what's left of today and tomorrow as you need."

Tomorrow. Spending the night with Songan and Ber.

"We should have started earlier," she admitted. "I should have pressed—"

"It's too late for that," Ber said and glanced skyward.

Yes, it is. "But tomorrow—what about the storm?"

Ber shrugged. "What about it?"

"Look, I get why the weather isn't a concern for you. All you have to do is shift and crawl into some cave. Maybe not wake up until spring. What do you care whether I find peace?" *Or connect with my mother.*

His eyes sobering, Ber stepped toward her. "I care, damn it, I care."

He did. She had no doubt of that. She also was in no condition to ponder why that was. Things had always been simpler with Songan, who, as far as she knew, had never tried to tap into her emotions.

Desperate for Songan's simpler and less emotionally invasive view of life, she turned toward him. To her shock, his gaze was a twin of Ber's intensity.

She could love these men. Or if not love them, care for and about them in ways she'd never imagined possible. Studying them, she acknowledged that only her mother and the wilderness had brought out these emotions in her.

Songan and Ber had called this a place of death, but she'd never felt more alive.

"I'm a little crazy right now," she admitted. "But I want to thank both of you for keeping me from falling off the deep end."

Ber took another step toward her. When he held out his hand, she took it. Connected with his energy. "You're not alone. Don't forget that."

"I know."

Positioning himself behind her, Songan rested his large, heavy hands on her shoulders. She waited for him to say something, but all he gave her was his moist breath pushing through her braid and dampening the back of her neck.

Her legs again lost strength, causing her to grip Ber's hand with both of hers. If it wasn't beyond insane, she would have dropped to the ground and begged both men to join her on Mother Earth. Primitive creature that she'd become, she desperately needed a cock buried deep inside her and the taste of another in her mouth.

Songan's grip tightened. Wondering if he knew what she was thinking, she glanced over her shoulder at him, but he wasn't looking at her. Instead, he was gazing around with furrowed brows and lifted head. Having seen that intense expression on him before, she knew he was calling on his senses to assess his surroundings. Much as she wanted to ask what had caught his attention, she knew better than to interrupt him right now. Turning her attention to Ber, she wasn't surprised to see him doing the same.

"I'm not sure what it is." Ber directed his comment at Songan. "The wind isn't helping. But there's something."

"What did you hear?" Songan asked, still looking left and right.

"Maybe a voice."

"Maybe." Songan sounded doubtful.

"You think someone else might be around here?" Even though it was probably too late to matter, she kept her voice low and hopefully calm. Her heartbeat picked up.

"Someone or something," Ber replied.

"An animal?"

Instead of answering, Ber fixed his gaze on Songan. "What about elk? Your kind waiting for their chance to kill me."

"No!" Rane gasped, silence forgotten. "I can't believe—Songan, tell him he's wrong."

Songan's hands continued to press on her shoulders, making her wonder if he was trying to lay claim to her. "Maybe it's another bear shifter, Ber," he said. "Two against one is a battle I can't win."

"Stop it!" she insisted, even though she couldn't shake the possibility that one or both of them might be right. "Look, I can't make you two accept and trust each other, but there won't be any bloodshed in my presence. There won't!"

Neither man spoke.

"Are you laughing at me? Is that what this is about? Feeling sorry for the poor dumb human who thinks she can keep bears and elks from trying to kill each other? Maybe I can't, but there's one thing I do know—I'll never forgive you. Never speak to either of you again."

Done with her impassioned speech, she imagined the echo of her words swirling around Ber and Songan, maybe knocking sense into them. And maybe preventing them from hearing what they needed to.

Cursing herself, she withdrew her hand from Ber's and placed it over her mouth. "I'm sorry," she whispered.

"It doesn't matter." Ber faced the woods. "What's done is done."

Rane's mother's body had been found about a half mile south of the cabin that anchored the area known as Wolverine. The lack of blood on the ground plus a few faint drag marks led law enforcement to conclude that Jacki had been killed elsewhere and brought to what seemed like a random location. Going under the assumption that the killer or killers had deliberately removed her from the kill spot, searchers had tried to backtrack. Unfortunately, the rain that had fallen between the time she'd gone missing and her remains were located had made that impossible.

Rane had asked Gannon why less than a day had been spent at Wolverine once Jacki's body was located. Gannon explained, not to Rane's satisfaction, that priority had been given to looking at potential suspects, not running his department's only tracking dog into the ground.

The Wolverine cabin had been constructed more than forty years ago by jail prisoners under supervision of Forest Service personnel. Built without electricity and plumbing—there was a nearby outhouse—it had some insulation and a cast iron woodstove. Volunteers periodically replenished the wood supply, and plastic water containers were left outside near the door. When the water froze in winter, visitors brought the containers inside to thaw.

Watching Songan effortlessly carry a five gallon container into the cabin, she imagined her mother doing the same. Ber had a double armload of wood, something else her mother would have had to do.

After putting down the wood, Ber opened the stove and peered inside. "Hardly any ashes."

"Mother—" Her throat seized, forcing her to wait until her muscles relaxed. "Maybe she's responsible."

Memories of her mother's voice, smell and touch swamped her. Sighing, she sank into one of the two easy chairs in the compact space. A single bed was against the wall opposite the woodstove, and a small table had been placed under the only window. Thanks to the men's sizes, she felt cramped and claustrophobic, and yet that was better than being here alone.

"Donald Cushing—he was Mom's supervisor—told me she was a natural for her job, a true steward of the land. I loved hearing that."

Ber, who was crumpling up newspapers left by volunteers and placing it in the stove cavity, shook his head. "Don't do this to yourself."

He actually thought she could turn off her mind? But even as pain enveloped her, she noted the way his jeans strained over his muscles. Sexual attraction practically screamed at her. She had to get a handle on things, she had to!

Maybe oblivious to her scrutiny, Ber added kindling and lit a match. He waited until the flames licked upward before placing several sticks on top of the kindling. When they caught fire, he added two larger logs. That done, he closed the door and slowly, gracefully stood. She marveled at his ability to get to his feet without using his hands for support.

"Now what?" she asked, feeling tense and alive.

Ber and Songan exchanged looks. "What happens is you stay here," Songan ordered. He headed for the door. "We won't be gone long."

Ber started after him.

"Wait." She reached for them, then stopped because no way could she prevent the men from doing what they wanted to. "Where are you going and what—"

"Before you start wandering around, we need to make sure it's safe."

Any other time, she would have stood up for herself, insist they had no right ordering her about. But these men had survived years in the wilderness. No matter how comfortable she was out-of-doors, she couldn't hold a candle to them. Besides, they'd sensed *something*.

"How long are you going to be gone?"

Ber shrugged. "I don't know."

Thanks to the mountains, cell phones were useless here. Besides, neither Songan or Ber carried one. When she'd offered to get Songan one, he told her he'd bought a couple but they quit working in a few days. Apparently there was something about a shifter's makeup that interfered with the cells' inner workings. She'd be alone until they returned. *If* they returned.

"I hate this," she admitted. "If I'd thought I was putting either of you in danger, I'd have never—"

"You couldn't stop us," Songan said.

For a good minute after they closed the door behind them, she stared at it. Then, restless and uneasy, she added more wood to the fire. After she'd turned the damper to hold in as much heat as possible, she unpacked the foodstuffs, but finally there was nothing to do except gaze out the window. Trees grew to within a few feet of the cabin and were so tall she couldn't see the sky, not that there was anything except clouds to look at today.

As far as she knew, her mother had spent the last night of her life doing what her daughter was right now. Had Jacki been at peace or nervous, angry at her daughter or sad, resigned maybe?

Had Jacki had any hint she was in danger?

What was she thinking? Jacki had been working a bear poaching case at the time of her death. She hadn't come to Wolverine for a vacation or because she wanted an isolated place to cuss out her damn stubborn daughter.

Don't go there, Rane warned herself. She wasn't a detective. Any possibilities she came up with were nothing more than conjecture. Possibilities she needed to bounce off someone else. More than one someone.

Shuddering, she pressed her cheek against the glass. It was her damnable imagination, of course, but she half believed she could feel masculine heat on the glass. Hear low male voices respond to the craziness bouncing around in her mind.

Two men. One woman. An isolated cabin. A single bed.

Need crawling over her skin and making her feel as if she might split apart.

Come back, Songan. Please Ber, come back.

Chapter Fourteen

Songan debated turning into an elk, but not only hadn't he discussed that with Ber, he didn't want to lose the intellect that came with being human. Granted, as an elk his senses would be keener, but he'd no longer care about Rane in a meaningful way. Animal instinct was all about self-preservation, and today her life was more important than his own.

Ber and he had circled the cabin together. He started to look to the other man for direction before remembering his longer history with Rane. The sex. Their relationship. His feelings for her.

"You feel *it* too don't you?" Ber asked. "That's why you told her to stay inside."

"We aren't alone," he admitted. "Beyond that, I'm not sure."

"Yet."

"We need to split up. If humans are out there, they'll stay near the trail, because it's easy to get lost around here. But that's not what we need to do."

"They? You think there's more than one?"

He pondered that. "Humans find courage in numbers."

"Why? That's what I don't understand."

"Don't you?" He took notice of the difference between them. Ber was a good inch taller with broader shoulders, while his arms and legs were longer. "How much time do you spend around humans?"

"No more than I have to."

Maybe that meant he'd walk away from Rane when she rejected him, which she had to. "I've watched them for years," he explained. When there was time, he'd ask Ber what his life in Alaska had been like. "Occasionally competed with them for jobs. Humans like sharing everything that's involved in hunting."

"Hunt? Is that what you think they're doing?"

Time was passing. They shouldn't leave Rane alone any longer than necessary. "I'm not positive, but we need to think that way. I've survived many hunting seasons by going where they aren't."

"We can't do that today."

"No, we can't." Looking around, he acknowledged that the terrain in all directions looked the same. "Head into the woods left of the trail. I'll take the right. If you see anything, howl. I'll do the same. Something to confuse and alarm whoever's out there, if it is someone. You know how sound like a wolf, don't you?"

"Yes." Ber held out his hand, and Songan took it. "Be careful."

Be careful, Songan kept repeating to himself as he eased between towering trees and around thick bushes. He didn't want Ber saying that, didn't want to care about him. At the same time, knowing the bear shifter was concerned for his safety eased his mind a little.

Rane had insisted on bringing a rifle and pistol with them, but the weapons were still in the cabin. Truth was, he hated them. Rifles killed elk, and in his heart, he was an elk. Weapons also killed bears.

Years ago he'd witnessed a trio of hunters track and kill an aging bull. Later, when he'd told the then teenage Rane what he'd seen, her eyes had teared, and she'd said she sympathized with him. At the same time, she explained that not many years ago, it had taken a committed hunter to keep himself and his family fed. There'd been no sport to the effort back when this land was being settled, only determination and necessity. Times had changed, and although she acknowledged the need for animal population control, she'd never embraced the change from necessity to sport.

They'd been naked in her bedroom with him lying face up and her straddling him so her breasts pushed into his chest every time she breathed when she'd told him that. He'd tried to pay attention to what she was saying; he always did. But they'd just fucked, and every time he caressed her naked ass, his need to do so again had grown.

"You aren't listening to me, are you?" she'd teased. Before he could deny her accusation, she'd shifted position and reached between his legs. Claimed his cock. "No indeed, you aren't listening, because this has your full attention. Again."

A sudden sound stopped Songan in mid-thought. Cursing himself for letting memories of his times with Rane intrude, he peered into the shadows. A branch had broken off and landed on the ground, the pine needles still quivering. Any other time, he would have already processed that. Shoulders squared and head high, he started walking again. Told himself to say in the moment. To wait for the wilderness to give up its secrets for him.

Then the wind moaned like Rane at the end of a climax.

She was safer in the cabin than she'd be out here. Unlike he, who sometimes considered himself invincible, she was all soft body and knowing hands, a welcoming cunt. She understood him as he'd never believed any woman could, accepted him and everything he was.

Even his long absences.

Soon he'd return to her. Soon he'd walk into the heated cabin, lift her in his arms and deposit her on the bed. Silent and smiling, she'd reach up, unbutton his coat and slide it off his shoulders. Her eyes would burn hot with sex-light, and her smile would morph into a laugh as he unzipped her jeans and tugged them off her smooth, rounded hips. She'd moan—God, how she moaned when need rode her.

Embracing the sound, he'd spread her legs and bury his head between them. Suck her through her panties until her nails left grooves along his arms.

"Do me, do me, do me!" she'd beg.

Needing her to be as hungry and ready as he was, he'd rip off her panties and pin her arms to the bed. Watch her twitch, hear her desperate demands.

"Let me be a part of this!"

Shocked, Songan started to look around for whoever had spoken, only to realize it had been Ber, not human and in the flesh, but the grizzly in his imagination.

"Go ahead," he told the other shifter. *"Make her crazy. I'll hold her."*

The wind was wrestling with the trees, making the tops whip about. Studying the rhythm behind seemingly random movement separated him from the task that had brought him out here. Embracing what was forming in his mind, he built one image upon another.

Rane was naked. On the bed. Arms over her head and wrists tethered to the bedposts with white rope. A shifter standing on either side of her. Apprehension warred with anticipation as she looked from Ber to him. Bending her knees, she twisted her lower body about. Her nipples were so tight he knew they hurt. Wondering if it was possible to tap into what she was feeling, he bent over his captive—his and the other shifter's—and closed his lips around a hard nub.

"Oh shit. Shit!" Rane gasped.

"Quiet!" Ber planted his hand over her mouth. Bringing his face to within inches of hers, the bear shifter swiped a wet tongue along the side of her nose. She tried to turn her head aside, but Ber clamped onto her hair and stopped her. In contrast to her immobile upper body, her hips thrashed.

Taking his time, Songan released her nipple and straightened. Only then did he realize he was as naked as his prisoner. Ber also wore nothing.

Smelling Rane's arousal, he tested the limits of her self-restraint by lightly trailing his forefinger over both areolas. Eyes widening, she mumbled something into Ber's silencing hand.

Still circling her quivering flesh, he flicked a glance at Ber. The bear shifter met his hot gaze with a like one.

"She's ours," Ber muttered. "Ours to do what we want with her."

"Finally. I've waited so long for this." He'd had no idea he'd been going to say that.

But why not? Sex with Rane had always skated the edges of sanity. Somehow he'd kept himself in check. Denied the rutting beast. The effort had taken its toll, weakened him and left him vulnerable to the animal beneath the human surface.

Not caring what Ber did, he positioned himself at the end of the bed and captured Rane's ankles. Even before he started to draw her legs apart, her scent seeped into his veins. She didn't fight him. Neither did she try to speak around Ber's hand. Much as he needed to understand what lay behind her silence, that would have to wait.

Wait until he'd slid his hands under her buttocks and lifted her off the bed. Wait until after—long after—he'd leaned over her.

Her legs opened, knees bending out, sex exposed.

Crazed, he lapped at her there. Lapped again. Drunk on her offering, he slid his tongue into the heated cave. One hand pressed against her mons. He clutched his cock with the other. Couldn't see, couldn't hear.

His curled tongue touched the top of her sex, causing her to buck against him. Ber's growl was more vibration than sound. Yet even as own his body shuddered, he forced himself to lift his head and study the other man.

Ber's hand was no longer clamped over Rane's mouth. Instead, it now sheltered and hid a pale, full breast. Ber had claimed the nipple of her other breast and was drawing it away from her, stretching out the glorious flesh.

"Oh, oh, oh!" Rane moaned. Her lashes fluttered. She seemed to be staring at the ceiling but maybe not.

He could turn her moan into a scream simply by slamming his cock into her. Teach Ber how to truly pleasure their woman.

Instead of crawling onto the bed and turning two bodies into one, however, he lowered his head again. This time, instead of running his tongue deep and strong into her channel, he lightly closed his teeth around her sex lips.

Thrashing about like a wild thing, Rane screamed. Came.

Chapter Fifteen

"That's good," Rane told the two men.

It didn't feel like it to her, but she must have let the cabin get too warm, because Songan had peeled off his coat the moment he stepped inside, and Ber had placed his palms against the window as if trying to cool himself.

"Isn't it?" she asked when they didn't respond to her comment. "I mean, if anyone can thoroughly check out an area, it's you two. I'm glad you didn't find anything suspicious."

Songan didn't so much as acknowledge her. In fact he seemed to be going out of his way to avoid her, not that that was easy given the small space. Ber had turned his back to her almost as soon as he'd closed the door behind him. Studying his so-broad shoulders, she half expected him to become a bear right then and there.

Ber and Songan were tense, no doubt about it. Damn it, if they were keeping something from her— "Are you hungry?" she came up with.

"No."

Jolted by Ber's short response, she got out of the musty-smelling chair she'd been perched in. She'd intended to walk over to him and shake him if that's what it took to get his attention, but before she could take a step, he swung toward her.

Those eyes! Those huge, dark, expressive eyes. Speaking of arousal. Need. Determination. Strength.

Limp-muscled, she looked over at Songan. His expression mirrored the bear shifter's.

"What's this?" she managed. Damn her nerves! She could barely think. "What did the two of you talk about when you were out there?"

"Nothing."

"Not a word."

Maybe, but there was more than one way of communicating, especially between animals, which at their core they were. Had they sensed what the other was thinking? Maybe the same thought had struck each of them.

As for what was on their minds—she'd have to be dead and buried not to know the answer. The same thing that had dominated her thoughts while she was alone.

"Going to where Jacki's body was found will have to until tomorrow," Ber firmly told her.

"It's going to be dark soon," Songan added. "Not enough time for what you need to do."

Maybe. Probably. She licked her lips. "What about the storm?"

Sober-faced but with his eyes now flashing, Ber positioned himself in front of the door. "There's more than one kind of storm, Rane. And something I've needed to do since I first saw you."

Oh shit! Her nerves sparked like exposed electrical wire, and her sex muscles clenched. She felt dizzy and alive.

She swallowed. Swallowed again. "I don't want to hear it."

"Yes, you do."

He was right, damn him, so right. "I had a dream," she

admitted. "About you. Us." She started to wrap her arms around her waist but cupped her hands over her sex instead.

"In your dream," Ber said, "I took you. Claimed you."

"Yes."

"With rope," Songan added. "White against your flesh. Holding you down."

"How—"

"I *saw* it," Songan explained. "Saw myself sharing in the act. Made it what I needed."

"What is it you need?" Ber asked.

Songan nodded at the bed. "Her. On it. Naked. Wanting us. Us claiming her."

"Stop it!" she blurted. Ber was between her and the door. No way could she escape, even if she wanted to. But this was too much. Too everything. "I didn't come up here to fuck you two. That's not why—I don't want—"

"Yes, you do."

She didn't know which man had spoken—maybe both. Maybe the words had taken place in her mind, her body. The fire snapped and breathed. Outside the growing storm flexed its muscles.

Inside—hell, inside her world was falling apart.

Maybe coming together.

"What do you want me to say?" She shouldn't have put her hands where they were, but it was too late, and she was feeding off the heat radiating from her.

"Nothing," Songan told her. "Just do."

Do. Act. Take the first step. Neither man had so much as hinted at it, yet she knew they'd back off if she declared she didn't want sex. Despite talk of rope and restraints, they wouldn't force her. Despite the crazy size difference, she was in control.

Of everything except her body.

Hands shaking so she could barely make her fingers work, she tackled the top button on her flannel shirt. She'd always felt sexless when she wore the thick garment, but not this afternoon. Not with two pairs of hungry male eyes watching her every move.

Neither Songan or Ber were true predators. In bear form, Ber was capable of killing and undoubtedly had, but he wasn't a cougar or wolf. If he needed to be one, a bull elk could be a formidable opponent, but he didn't initiate attack, unless—

"A question," she said when she found her voice. "You both—you're both willing to—you're talking about the three of us?"

Ber's gaze settled on her exposed throat. "Same as you are."

Oh God. God. "What about you?" she asked Songan.

"I'm as much elk as I am human. Maybe more. During rut, I sometimes cover a cow another bull got to first. Or take the same cow repeatedly."

That wasn't exactly the answer she'd been looking for but probably was as honest and introspective as Songan could be. If there was such a thing as life after death or awareness after death, her mother might know what was about to happen.

You don't want me to die with you, I know you don't.

Every atom of her being aware, Rane waited for a response from the woman who'd given her life, but none came. Fighting tears, she again focused on the men. Just looking at them returned her to the here and now.

Feeling reborn, she went back to tackling her buttons. She

could ask the men to handle the monumental task, but that would mean choosing one over the other. It was easier, relatively, to complete her chore and toss the garment at the chair she'd been sitting in. Watching the flannel settle, she tried to recall what she'd been thinking just before the door opened.

She'd been listening to the forest sounds, of course, trying not to imagine anything bad happening to her companions, her thoughts split between Songan and Ber.

Two men. Two shifters. Hers for the taking.

Or was it she who was for the taking?

Overwhelmed by the complex question, she bent over and untied her boots. Her breasts spilled over the top of her bra, and her nipples ached.

Straightening, she lifted one leg and then the other so she could take off her boots. She didn't consider the task erotic—hell, she barely thought about what she was doing—until she caught the men's expressions. If seeing her socks turned them on so much, what would happen when she was no longer wearing anything?

Ber started toward her. "I want—"

"No." She held up her hand as if that could stop him. "I know what you want, but I need to do this." She didn't add that undressing on her own was her way of reminding herself that she was up for this.

Up for this. No, that term described the men, specifically the erections straining against their jeans.

Damn it! She'd turned them on! Okay, so she'd known how little it took to arouse Songan, but now the proof was in duplicate. Ber was the unknown, the wild card. When push came to shove, would he fight to keep her to himself? Stop Songan?

She unsnapped and unzipped her jeans before gathering the courage to face Ber. "I have to know what you're thinking. How much of the bear is beneath the surface? If it's about to break loose—"

"I'll keep it caged."

Caged. Tied up. Was there any difference?

She nodded at Songan. "What about you?"

"This thing with the three of us is going to happen, Rane. Live in the moment."

Songan, who was far from the most philosophical man, had just said what she needed to hear. In the moment. Now. All of them wanting sex.

It was still light outside, but the small window didn't let in much light, and she hadn't bothered with lighting the oil lantern or looking for candles. As a result, everything seemed muted. All except for her emotions and anticipation.

Still not quite believing what she was doing, she guided her jeans down over her hips and stepped out of them. The side seams had left impressions on the outsides of her thighs. Fascinated by the indentations, she slid her fingers down and then up.

The men watched in the single-minded way of hungry animals. Ber started massaging his erection, followed seconds later by Songan. They didn't seem to be aware of each other. Did either know the rules and rituals of threesomes? Did she? They'd experiment, try one thing and then the other until something worked.

Imagining how body parts might mesh confused her, so she quit. Besides, she wasn't naked yet. Hadn't done her part.

"What about you?" she asked with her hands behind her and reaching for the bra fastening. "I don't want to be the only one doing this."

"You first," Ber said. "Us watching."

Of course. Why hadn't she thought of it?

Even more weary of thinking than she'd been moments ago, she unhooked her bra. Let her arms drop to her sides. Her bra, still held up by the shoulder straps, hung off her, and her breasts drooped. She'd just turned twelve when her mother told her she needed to start wearing a bra, but she'd resisted. Bras meant growing up, and she wanted to remain a child, a free, forest-exploring child.

Finally, wanting to be done with the whole damn thing, she pushed the straps off her shoulders and let the garment fall. Practical woman that she was, she bought underpants that rode just below her navel and covered her buttocks. Mostly white.

Who the hell cared? Who the hell wanted the damn thing?

By the time the last deed was done, she felt as if she'd climbed a mountain.

"Next," she prompted.

Ber, damn him, still felt no need of a winter coat. She might have resented his disregard of cold if not for how his shirt clung to him. Probably static electricity was responsible, she concluded, although maybe the cotton couldn't get enough of him.

Watching her watching him, he discarded his denim jacket. Pulling his shirt out of his waistband, he hauled it up and over him. His hair stood up in places, while other strands caressed his forehead and cheeks. Between that and his stubble, he looked barely human. Dragging her gaze lower, she took in the curling, equally dark mat over his chest and funneling down into his low-slung jeans.

The man's belly button was exposed. Also the outline of his hip bones.

Ber came from Alaska, so what was he doing with what appeared to be an all-over tan? His coloring wasn't the result of sunlight or a tanning salon. Nature had done this to him, made him perfect in yet another way.

His shoulders, ah his damnable solid shoulders, were lightly hair-dusted to give off an air that practically shouted masculine. He was the opposite of a modern and well-manicured man. Civilization barely had a hold on him.

"Go on, please." She was out of breath and close to exploding.

Jeans. Simple things. The uniform of nearly every man she'd ever known. Nothing new. Nothing erotic.

Yeah, right, especially when the owner of said jeans had just unfastened and unzipped, allowing his erection to press through the opening. Instead of finishing the chore, he turned his attention and fingers to his boots. His socks, she noted, were white. Then he slipped them off, and she studied his broad feet and long, sturdy toes. If need be, he could walk or even run barefoot.

White briefs. Elastic kissing his belly and gripping his buttocks. Barely containing his cock.

"Do it. Please."

Despite her plea, he took half of forever getting rid of his jeans. Still moving achingly slow, he pulled his briefs over and then under his cock. Like Songan, he hadn't been circumcised.

Stepping out of his final garment, Ber jerked his head at Songan. "Now you."

She'd seen Songan naked before, nothing new there. Except either her memory had deserted her or her short-circuiting brain and body kept her in the moment. Like Ber, Songan did a decent striptease. There was no wasted movement, no taunting her with his form, and yet her breasts expanded and her pussy oozed. She didn't now and couldn't imagine ever comparing cock size. Both were perfect.

For her. Today at least.

Stay human. Please.

Killing the space between them, Ber placed his hand under her chin and lifted her head. "Do you have any idea how far I traveled to find you? How long I searched?"

His heat, his awesome heat, flowed through her. "You were in the Chinook before I returned, weren't you? I wouldn't be here if Mom—"

"Don't go there." Bending a little, he covered her mouth with his. He smelled of wind and wilderness, and she became instantly drunk. Whimpering under her breath, she started to wrap her arms around him. Grabbing her wrists, he worked her arms behind her back. Still kissing and being kissed, she arched her back so she could keep her balance. His cock touched her, possessed.

There might not be any rope today, but he'd still captured her and now held her where he wanted her. Drunk on the thought, she parted her lips. His tongue dove into the space she'd created. A shadow to her right and slightly behind distracted her. She was still trying to make sense of it when Songan lightly slipped his hands around her throat.

"I can feel your pulse." He pressed a little. "Is your heart racing?"

Before she could tell him yes, Ber kissed her again. Thrilled by the touch of mouth against mouth, she closed her eyes. Songan's body heat claimed her spine, buttocks and legs. Ber's body was like fire against her breasts and belly. Opening her mouth even more, she went in search of everything the bear shifter chose to give her. Their tongues danced, first one and then the other invading, exploring, igniting. If Ber wanted her all to himself, he gave no indication, and if Songan resented the newcomer, he kept that to himself.

Right now at least, they were content to share her.

Drive her insane.

Songan pressed into her. She felt truly trapped between him and Ber. The elk shifter's hand remained on her throat while the other reached around her and began a maddening and exciting journey toward her breast. Crazed, she struggled to offer it to him. Her lips started to slide off Ber's mouth.

Muttering something she couldn't understand, Ber caught her lower lip with his teeth. His hold on her wrists tightened, and his cock pressed against her middle.

This wasn't happening! Two men at once was beyond anything she'd ever imagined, and yet, oh God, and yet—

Her mind whirling, she relaxed. A moment later, Ber's hold relaxed, and her lip slid out. Before she could comprehend the loss, Songan found her breast. A hand made for wielding logging equipment swallowed her mound. Opening her eyes again, she tried to blink her world into focus. Ber's form dominated.

All except for Songan behind her.

Flesh against flesh, not just hers against male, but male touching male. Those realities and more separated themselves out in her mind then fell apart. In contrast to the shifters, she was small and slight, her strength laughable. Yet these naked giants couldn't get enough of her. Wanted her. Owned her.

The heated blanket of Songan's other hand now covered the breast that had brushed against Ber. No longer having fingers against her throat should allow her to relax, shouldn't it?

Didn't matter.

"Me first," she heard Ber say. "Then you."

"Maybe."

"What about me?" she demanded. "Don't I get a say?"

Ber answered, if that was his intention, by crossing one of her wrists over the other and pressing them against the base of her spine so he could effortlessly keep her in place. That done, he gathered up her left ass cheek and squeezed it.

Startled, she tried to pull free. "Oh that's funny! Think you're a comedian do you?"

His hold on her buttock increased. She imagined his knuckles sliding over Songan's cock.

"What about this?" Songan roughly massaged her breasts. "Is it something you like?"

Truth was she loved everything they were doing to her; she just wasn't ready to admit it. Maybe she would once she didn't feel so overwhelmed or possessed.

Maybe.

"No major complaints," she belatedly came up with. "But Ber, an ass isn't the erotic equivalent to a breast." Hoping to prove her point, she gave it as much of a shake as she could. "Grab and grope is juvenile."

He didn't say anything, not this man who hadn't shaved for the better part of a week and had traveled hundreds of miles to reach this part of the country. Freeing her buttock, he began stroking it with calloused fingertips. She melted a little.

"Your turn," Songan said. "For now."

Chapter Sixteen

Just like that, the elk shifter was gone, taking his life-warmth with him and leaving Rane's breasts exposed and lonely. When her arms dropped to her sides, she dimly realized Ber had let go of them as well. She now stood before the bear shifter with the tip of his cock kissing her belly every time she exhaled and his breath showering heat over her.

She wanted to know what Ber had in mind, and yet she didn't. Needed to anticipate and lived for every breath the two of them took. This wasn't about shared or not shared bondage dreams, the past or future. Everything was now. Him. Her.

Taking her hand, Ber walked her over to the bed. Instead of climbing onto it and telling or asking her to join him as she thought he would, he turned her so her back was to him and her knees against the mattress. She hadn't noted where Songan was but felt his eyes on her. Watching. An audience of one. Next in line.

Ber ran something, a knuckle maybe, up from the base of her spine to her nape. Gripping the bedspread so hard she risked bending her short nails, she stared up at where wall and ceiling met. Ber's touch was so light, an exploration maybe, a half man testing both their boundaries.

Another knuckle joined the first. The second journey was firmer, slower, deeper, touching her core and making her shudder. Looking down, she fixed on her loose breasts and whitened fingers half buried in the spread. His fingers slid over each vertebra, caressing them. Outside, wind and rain slapped at the cabin, but it didn't matter.

"You'd make a good deer," he muttered. "You're sleek and beautiful."

Beautiful. "I'm not prey."

"Aren't you?"

He should have given her time to answer, not that she had any idea what her response would be. But suddenly she was on her stomach on the bed, and she realized he'd effortlessly lifted her. Positioned her for sex?

"How do you want it?" he asked, joining her.

He was on his knees beside her, prompting her to roll onto her side so she could study him. Weighing twice as much as she did, he flat out dominated her world, and yet she didn't feel intimidated. Much.

Risking losing her balance, she cupped a hand around his cock and absorbed heat and strength. His eyes took on the look of a man on alert. Thank goodness he and Songan hadn't found anything to concern them during their study of the area. If they had, they wouldn't be here with her. *This* wouldn't be about to begin.

Studying his cock and her hold on it, Ber drew back a little. As she increased her hold, it occurred to her that the shifters might not have had their full attention on what they should have been doing outside, but it was too late for that to matter.

The three of them were here.

"How do I want it?" She repeated his question. "Deep. As deep as you can go."

He frowned. "I might be too much for you."

"Let me make that decision," she said, instead of reminding him of the times she'd welcomed Songan into her.

"I might lose control. You need to know that."

"I do."

Despite his warning, she trusted him not to forget his length and breadth or the strength difference between them. Letting him go, she rolled over onto her back and bent her knees, opening her legs as she did. So much for self-restraint and decorum. She needed it all, now!

Songan stood at the foot of the bed. Cradling his cock, his gaze burning into her. She sensed the man was reaching his own limits.

Both at once?

Satisfying and being satisfied by two at the same time?

Too much to think about.

Instead of accepting the invitation she'd offered Ber with her *take me, big boy* position, Ber slipped his hands under her buttocks and lifted her lower body. Once her ass was off the mattress and the back of her shoulders pressed into it, he repositioned himself between her legs and pulled her toward him. She had no leverage, could barely move on her own.

Bottom line, Ber could do anything he wanted to her.

His cock touched her entrance. Grabbing his forearms and straightening her knees, she let her feet reach for the ceiling. Opened herself to him. Turned her body over to this man. Needing to simply experience the ultimate loss of control, she once more closed her eyes.

There, his tip pressing against her wet, swollen and sensitive labia. She could barely think how to swallow. Gripping her by her waist, Ber drew her even closer and brought her into his space. His cock slipped into her. Claimed her. Limp with anticipation, she rested the backs of her calves against his shoulders and willed herself to relax.

"All right?" he asked.

"All right." Her mouth felt dry.

"Good."

Breathing fast and deep, he continued to pull until her ass jammed against his knees. Instead of leaving her there, he guided her up and closer yet so her buttocks rested on his thighs. His cock dove deeper, filled her. Laid claim to her stretched channel.

Opening her eyes, she tried to study his expression, but damn it, having him inside her felt so good! Her recently freed breasts splayed outward. When he lightly squeezed them, she thanked him by closing her thighs and gripping his cock.

Satisfying! Her pussy weeping.

"Don't need to ask, do I?" he said. His palms pressed against her nipples. "It's still good for you."

"Don't talk. Just, please, do."

Between the storm sounds and her heart hammering in her temples, she lost touch with everything except fucking and being fucked. The bear shifter's expression said everything and nothing. One moment she caught flashes of pleasure and determination in him. The next, a guarded shadow slipped over his features. Should she try to do the same instead of letting him know how ripped and raw she'd become?

Too late. Nothing mattered except this complex man looming over her with his hands once more against her ribs and their bodies locked together. She was helpless, couldn't escape!

Didn't want to.

Ber's hip bones ground against her ass as he worked her lower body even higher until her back arched and her fingers dug into his forearms. When he pulled back, she struggled to find a way to join him in the coupling, to be his partner, his equal, but maybe she existed simply to pleasure him—and be pleasured.

Ber hadn't lost any strength during his journey from Alaska to Oregon, as witnessed by thundering thrust after thundering thrust. Her channel stretched and stretched again. With each *attack* she felt as if she was racing down a mountain, falling out of an airplane, running class five rapids.

Heat bloomed everywhere on her. Her lungs strained to bring in enough air, and she could no longer see. Years ago she'd left these mountains because their hold on her had frightened her. Now she was back and lost. Lost and dying. Being reborn.

No matter that her only anchor came from her hold on Ber's forearms. No matter that he'd found a way to reduce her strength to nothing. She'd get back in touch with herself, ride the storm. Mouth open and eyes still unfocused, she chewed on the insides of her cheeks. The pain barely registered. Her head thrashed. Leaning down and over her, Ber pushed. Relaxed. Pushed again.

"Can't—" she started. What had she been going to say?

"Yes, you can!"

Distracted by Songan's unexpected voice, she tried to look back at the elk shifter. Just then Ber hammered himself at and into her. Branded her. Even with him anchoring her, she slid about a little. If she continued to move like this, he might lose his tempo and desperate strength.

Before she could think what to do, something clamped down on her shoulders and held her in place.

Songan's hands! Songan helping Ber fuck her!

She even more trapped and helpless.

Was that an earthquake, maybe a hurricane, perhaps a blizzard? No matter. She'd become a feather tossed about by nature's strength.

No, not tossed. Barely moving now. A home for Ber's cock. Receiving his gift. Every time the man threw himself at her, a little more sanity bled from her. Trusting Songan to keep her in place, she repeatedly clamped her inner muscles around the life pulsing inside her.

Pressure here. And here. Her nipples knotted, and the blood drained from her uplifted legs. Feeling foolish and wonderful. Sensation increased, screamed at her. Something both familiar and overwhelming hurried her to the edge.

"Oh God! God oh God!" Gripping her breasts, she held on to herself with all her strength.

Ber let go, flooding her. His cock jerked again inside her while his fingers ran hard and fast over her thighs.

The bear shifter grunted and then snarled. Rising up off his haunches, he took her with him. Filled her until she swore she could taste him.

A threatened cramp in her left calf distanced her from her own nearly there release. Ber was leaning away from her and allowing her heels to slide off his shoulders. He was done, no longer needed her. Had better things to do.

Before she could accuse him of being more animal than human, he planted a hand over her mons and pressed down, massaging her there at the same time. Rough yet magical fingers glided over her clit. They retreated, then returned. Toyed. Rotated.

Screaming her delight, she climaxed. Ber kept after her with his all-knowing hands. Under his tutelage, her body jolted, spasmed.

At length, when there was nothing left of her except the

need to breathe, she struggled to face the overwhelming task of trying to put herself back together. Ber's now diminished cock remained in her. Their sweat-sticky bodies had fused, and her fingers pressed against his thighs. Songan had taken hold of her breasts while she was otherwise occupied. Massaging them, the elk shifter kept the nipples hard.

She looked up at Songan, stared out at Ber.

"Don't talk," Ber told her. "Just be."

Songan hadn't thought he'd ever envy the bear shifter, but that was before he compared Ber's limp cock with his own aching one. He'd been able to ignore his painful erection while Rane and Ber had had sex. Anchoring Rane in place had made him feel as if he was a participant, but no matter how much he'd loved studying her writhing body and hearing her cries, those things were only substitutes for the act itself.

"So fast," Ber muttered from where he lay on his side. Rane too was still on the bed but sitting with her knees folded in front of her while she lightly touched her reddened sex. "I didn't think I'd come that fast," Ber admitted.

"It usually takes you longer?" Rane asked.

"There hasn't been a *usual* for months." Ber rubbed his hand over his face. "All that need built up."

"And soon you'll be hibernating?" Leaving off with what she'd been doing, Rane studied Ber. She seemed to have forgotten Songan's presence.

"Maybe," Ber answered. "Maybe not. I haven't decided."

Moments ago Songan had acknowledged his resentment because Ber and not he had been the first to mount Rane. Now envy reared its head, because the bear shifter could make a decision that had never been his. Like it or not, his existence was dictated by the elk half of his nature. These days the need to pack back on the weight he'd lost during rut nagged at him. The herd had headed for lower elevations. He should be with them.

No! He couldn't.

"Songan, you're quiet," Rane whispered. "What do you want me to say? Do?"

Studying her, he remembered the hours and nights they'd spent together. He hadn't taken those nights—and occasional days—for granted, and yet he'd always felt as if he'd been standing back a bit, not quite connecting with her.

He didn't want it like that now.

Sliding off the bed, she came over to where he was leaning against a wall with his heavy cock trying to rip free of his body, making him wonder what she might say if she knew what he was thinking. The things he wanted to change about himself.

"You're having trouble expressing yourself. Again." Moving to the side and avoiding his cock, Rane rose onto her toes. She kissed his chin. "Maybe you'll never have the words, but that's all right. I'll take you the way you are."

A sigh compelled him to look past Rane at the bear shifter. Ber no longer looked as satiated as he had just moments ago.

"What is it?" Songan demanded. Too bad if it bothered Ber that Rane had a history with him.

Frowning, Ber stood and looked toward the window. "I'm not sure."

"You hear something?" Rane asked.

Ber's frown deepened. "I'm not sure."

"It's probably the wind," Rane said. "It's pretty intense."

"Maybe."

Propelled by Ber's expression, Songan turned his ear to the

wall. The wind sang to him, and he heard occasional raindrops. Dismissing the other shifter's concern, he wrapped his arms around Rane and turned her so his erection prodded her naked belly.

"Words don't matter to us," he told her. "We have other ways of communicating."

"Yes, we do."

She sounded what, disappointed? He ran his hand down her right arm until he reached her hand. His first thought was that he wanted her to take hold of his cock and acknowledge it even more. Instead, he wound up drawing her arm behind her and pressing it against the small of her back much as Ber had done.

"You like to do that, don't you," she said, amusement and something else in her tone. "Exerting control over me."

"You've never complained." *Had she?*

"No, I haven't." Arching her back, she looked up at him so her breasts grazed the base of his chest. "You can't force a cow elk to do something she isn't ready for. Try and you risk getting kicked where no male of any species wants to be kicked. Getting yours during that brief window of opportunity is a hell of a lot of work. Frustrating too."

He didn't care what she was talking about but wouldn't tell her, yet.

"So," she said, "it leads to this." She halfheartedly struggled to free herself. "Where are we going with *this* today, Songan? What do you want from me?"

Before he could point out the obvious, a twitch at the corner of her mouth told him she was teasing.

"Sorry." Tilting her head, she raked her teeth over his collarbone. "I know you don't always get my sense of humor, but I had to say that. Confession time, big man. Right now I feel more than a little as if I've been hung out to dry. Wiped out. It might take me a few minutes to get back on track."

Rane had a habit of using figures of speech he didn't fully understand. Fortunately, many times they had no need to talk. Drawing her captured arm in front of her, he pushed her back toward the middle of the room while still holding on to her wrist. Just like that, she no longer looked as if she found what was happening amusing.

"I know you pretty damn well," he said. "Maybe more than you realize."

Eyes smoking, she ran her tongue over her upper lip. "Is that so?"

"Yeah. Needing sex has a way of sneaking up and biting you. You want people to think you're collected and professional, but beneath the surface, you're as much an animal as I am."

Lowering her lids so he could barely see her eyes, she grunted. "Just because I have a healthy sexual appetite doesn't mean—"

"Yes, it does."

Not waiting for her response, he hoisted her over his shoulder and carried her to the bed. Instead of planting her in the middle of it as Ber had done, he lowered her so her buttocks were barely on the mattress and her feet on the floor. When he let go of her, she tried to balance herself by grabbing hold of him.

"No." He pushed her arms aside, then planted a hand between her breasts and shoved. She fell back onto the bed, angling her body to the side so she could look at him.

With a *this is how I do it* look at Ber, he folded his arms over his chest. Nudging her legs apart, he settled himself into the space he'd created. Bending his knee, he placed it against her sex.

"Who's the animal here, Rane?"

"You tell me," she said.

Chapter Seventeen

Studying her, Songan increased the pressure a little. Her mouth sagged open. Amused and even more turned on, he watched as she pressed her heels against the floor and pushed, trying to increase the distance between them. All that accomplished was to bunch the bedspread under her back and buttocks. She dug her fingers into the fabric and tugged, but as far as he could see, that did nothing to straighten it under her. Then, as he knew would happen, he came to the end of his patience.

Wanting her to anticipate, he held up a hand while staring at her sex.

"Think you're pretty damn sure of yourself, don't you?" she challenged.

"More determined than sure, not that you mind."

Lowering his hand, he swiped two fingers over her pussy. Shuddering, she curled her body into itself a little more.

After dampening his fingers in her juices and what Ber had left in her, he coated his cock. Standing, he was too far above her for sex. Still, he loved the sight of her helplessly waiting for him. Waiting and maybe wanting as much as he did.

Maybe?

Jaw clenched, he turned his attention to Ber. The shifter

had left his discharge inside Rane and satisfied her. Not needing him.

No! Rane had always wanted him.

Reassured, he rewetted his fingers and deposited the mix of come and her sex juices on his erection. Lifting her ass off the bed in what he had no doubt was invitation, Rane stared at him.

Bull elks sometimes fought each other for control of a harem. He couldn't fight Ber today, not while they were in human form, but he could take the woman they shared and make her scream.

Glad Ber was watching, he eased a finger into Rane's opening. She'd started to lower herself back onto the bed, but the invasion had her rising up again. Her sweet sex smell filled his nostrils. Judging by his expression, Songan had no doubt the bear shifter was inhaling the same scent.

Ber took a step that brought him within two feet of the head of the bed, then stopped. Keeping his finger in Rane, Songan met the other man's stare. No words passed between them. Maybe Rane wasn't aware of what was going on.

I'm watching, Ber's expression said. *Just watching, same as you did when it was my turn.*

"I understand. She brings out the animal in both of us."

"Songan?"

Rane's sex muscles closed down around his finger, effectively ending the connection between him and Ber. Still, he no longer thought of the other man as competition. The enemy.

He wasn't sure whether he ever had.

"I'm here," he told Rane. He waited for her muscles to relax before pulling out, but only so he could place his middle finger next to the first and spread her even more. His cock throbbed and his balls ached. Damnation but waiting was going to kill him!

"I'm here," he repeated. "Doing what you love having done." Turning his hand so his palm faced up, he reached for the spot that, when stroked, made her crazy. Placing his thumb against her groin, he pressed.

"Shit!" Planting her elbows against the mattress, she lifted herself off it. Her pelvis tipped as if offering itself to him.

Another wave of sex-scent tore through him. Groaning, he clamped his free hand around his cock. Glorious agony blurred his vision. Determined to distract himself from the pressure so he wouldn't come right here and now, he ran a third finger into Rane's channel. Watching her twist about while sweat coated her throat, he let loose with a bugling sound.

"Don't change!" she gasped. "Damn it, don't!"

"Too late."

Barely recognizing his voice, he commanded the fingers within her to rest. That done, he forced himself to concentrate on the world beyond the cabin. Snow had started to fall, a few fat lazy flakes sliding down the window. What had taken place and was about to happen in here was separate from reality, a kind of collective madness. Acknowledging he could think like that surprised and pleased him, but now wasn't the time to share his insight.

Ber. Yes, he was part of this.

Standing on the edge of control, Songan concentrated on finger-fucking Rane. His fingers glided back and forth, never completely leaving her and hopefully suspending her in doubt. He rocked a little, which made his balls bounce, adding even more tension to wonderful pleasure. A sideways glance told him the bear shifter's erection was returning.

"Damn it, Songan, you're driving me out of my mind." Rane

reached for his arm but missed.

"Am I?" he teased.

Nostrils flared, she started to pant. Despite the throbbing weight of his cock, he studied her reaction to his renewed assault on her pussy. Rane would never be helpless. She was too liberated and self-assured for that, yet at times like this, she had no choice but to surrender to her body's sexual demands. Studying her expression for the battle he believed he'd find raging inside her, he was surprised to see only joy. Helpless joy.

"Pretty much love this, don't you?" He made his point by lifting his hand and bringing her pelvis up with him. A moment later he released the tension. He rubbed his forefinger over the top of her channel and was rewarded with a breathless squeal.

"What was that you said?" he demanded. "What was that agreement?"

Going by her contorted features, he surmised she was loath to admit anything. Much as he'd love forcing the admission from her, the top of his head was about to explode.

Dropping to his knees, he turned slightly so he could keep his fingers inside her. Her gaze followed him, yet he knew she was lost. Full of anticipation. Nipples looking like rocks and her sex lips red, swollen and wet.

Intent on economy of movement now, he drew his fingers out of her and wiped her juices and Ber's come on her belly.

"You're a river." He aimed his cock at her gaping opening.

"Do it!" She sounded as if she was drowning. "Just do it."

He did. Despite its size, he believed his cock had been created to fit inside her. The biting tension that had driven him half out of his mind eased as her hot, wet tissues stroked his length.

"Thank you," she muttered.

"No, thank you."

He thought she might have said something else but didn't care enough to ask her to repeat herself. Casting aside the question of whether she preferred his cock to Ber's—he hoped she was above making comparisons—he took hold of her hips and guided her to the edge of the bed. With the world outside darkening, he entered a world of shadow.

Nothing existed beyond this small place. Rane's mind had been stripped clear. She cared for nothing except pleasing and being pleased.

Still holding onto her, he looked into her eyes. They were at half mast, void of everything except the need for sex. Sex with him.

Fucking Rane would never become ordinary. Neither was it an instinctive act designed to insure that a species would continue to exist. He wasn't sure he loved Rane, not because of anything in her, but perhaps he hadn't been designed for the emotion. Still, these moments weren't only about spilling his seed inside her. There was also pleasuring her, hearing her cry out.

Bonding.

Strength flowed through his muscles and veins, yet he held back from climaxing as he rocked back and then forward, plowing into her. His balls slapped against her. Trembling from the jolt, he forced himself to retreat a little. Not waiting for his body to calm, he came at her again, maybe harder this time, certainly faster. His ass cheeks jiggled.

"Oh Jesus, Songan. Jesus!"

He tried to bring her features into focus, but the cabin was getting darker by the moment. No way could they find what she'd come to Wolverine for today. Better she stay in here. With him. With Ber.

Something hot and electric pressed against the base of his spine. Determined to ride the sensation, he thrust into Rane.

"Yes! God, yes."

She wanted this. Needed.

A sound like drums pulsed inside his head. Embracing the cadence, he repeatedly powered himself against her. Running his hands under her buttocks, he again lifted them off the mattress. Her fingers trailed over his forearms.

It didn't matter that he'd spent the last few weeks breeding. Today he was a man. A man having sex with the only woman who accepted him for what he was.

The bedsprings groaned. Ber was climbing onto the bed.

Unwilling and unable to slow let alone stop, Songan continued tunneling into Rane. Inches away, the bear shifter knelt beside her head, facing Rane. His cock jutted alive and full from his solid body, inches from her face.

He could touch Ber's cock. He'd have to stop fucking to do so, but maybe it was worth it. They had, after all, shared things he never had with another man.

No, not now. Maybe after he'd flooded Rane's channel and his terrible need had ended.

She lay on her back, her cheeks flushed, and her belly sucking in and out with each hurried breath. In contrast, a mix of peace, power and potential dominated her expression. Her total existence was locked on him. He'd become her reason for living, her escape from what had brought her here.

Wanting to deepen her escape, he struggled to slow down. That accomplished, he ran his fingers over her thighs, ribs and belly. She made a mewling sound that resonated throughout him.

Her mouth was still open when Ber rocked up and forward.

The bear shifter's cock touched her upper lip and then trailed over her mouth. Tilting her head upward, she closed her lips around the offering.

Songan waited for anger and jealousy to overtake him. Instead, his body's demands claimed him. He'd come too far, sweated and strained too much to back down now. To feel anything except the coming explosion.

"Do it!" Ber commanded. "Suck me."

Rane started shaking so violently Songan was afraid for her. Before he could decide what, if anything, he should do, he realized she wasn't trying to break free after all. Quite the opposite—she drew Ber's cock deep into her mouth. Closing her hot, strong fingers around Songan's wrists, she guided his hands toward her pussy.

Well-versed in what her body needed, he ran his fingers between their bodies and settled a forefinger over her clit. The tendons stood out on her neck, and he thought she might be trying to say something but couldn't, because Ber had started fucking her mouth.

Matching the bear shifter's rhythm, Songan slipped deep into Rane. He moved in slow motion with every muscle working smooth and sure and tirelessly. Her inner tissues gliding over his cock were magical. How could he envy or resent Ber when so much of her belonged to him?

But maybe it was he who'd fallen under her spell.

Rane had been matching his thrusts. Now her movements stuttered and then stopped, only to start up again. Studying her, he concluded she was trying to focus on Ber's needs as well as his, but this was *his* time. His dance.

Drawing in a deep breath that held traces of the storm, he captured her hard clit. Her muscles clenched. He picked up his pace. She tightened her grip on his wrist. Her head thrashed, yet she somehow kept her mouth around Ber.

Fire and flames coursed through Songan's body. He was lost. Gone. Past the point of pulling back. Beyond sanity.

"Now! Now!"

What Rane was doing no longer mattered. He cared nothing about Ber. Diving deep and then deeper still, he threw back his head and bellowed. The awful-wonderful pressure shattered, and he exploded inside his woman.

Chapter Eighteen

Arching as far off the bed as she could, Rane concentrated on Songan's shuddering release. God but she loved the feel of his hot gift speeding through her! Some had slipped past their locked bodies and was undoubtedly soaking the spread, but she didn't care.

Her lover—one of her lovers—had just blessed her in the most intimate way. His cock still pulsed inside her, and his fingers against her clit spasmed.

Any other time, she probably would have climaxed with him. She hadn't, because Ber's cock distracted her. She reveled in the feel of the newcomer to her world against her tongue, teeth and the insides of her cheeks.

When she turned her head to the side, Ber pulled back and leaned left and then right. Maybe he wanted her to focus on him, but Songan had been part of her world for years.

Still holding on to Ber, she managed to lock eyes with Songan. He looked, as she knew he would, like a man who'd lost touch with reality. His eyes were slightly glazed, and his mouth sagged. The fingers on her clit no longer moved. Releasing one of his wrists, she pushed against his belly to let him know she wanted him to back away. Take his cock with him.

To her surprise, he didn't resist, and as he withdrew, their shared juices dribbled down her crack. Wet heat reached her rear opening. Songan wiped his hand on her belly. Dizzy and lost, she tried to close her hand around Songan's cock, but it was so wet her fingers slid off. Her clit felt abandoned, discarded, unwanted.

Barely aware of what she was doing, she cupped Songan's balls and lifted. His cock glided over the space between her pussy and ass. What a fool she'd been to think he no longer had a use for her. Songan cared for her as much as he was capable of.

Ber. She still had him in her mouth and he was waiting for her to—to what?

She swallowed. Grunting, Ber pushed into her, his tip touching the back of her throat. She felt the sweet, rounded end of Songan's cock at her rear entrance.

Float. Yes, that's what she'd do. Just be. Exist. Let the men take care of all her needs. Embrace desire full on.

Thoughts of what she most needed spun through her. She couldn't drift after all. Her aching, demanding body wouldn't allow it.

Cool air touched her inner thighs. Songan had backed away so their bodies no longer touched. Telegraphing nothing of his intentions, he ran two fingers inside her. At the same time, he pressed down on her mons so she was trapped between the two sensations.

Wonderfully trapped.

Ber was at cross-purposes to her with his arms on one side of her head and his legs on the other. Keeping her in place. Offering her no freedom. He wasn't near her lower body, but Songan was.

Her jaw muscles started to ache, prompting her to push against Ber's belly much as she'd recently done to Songan.

Rounding his spine, the bear shifter lifted himself so she could turn her head to the side. She opened her mouth, and his cock slipped out.

Songan's fingers in her curled, causing the pressure on her mons to increase. If he kept that up, would his hands touch? Could he break her in two?

Not broken. More like coming together and becoming complete.

Reaching, she reclaimed Ber's cock and sucked it into her. She struggled to bring her legs together so she could acknowledge Songan.

Open and vulnerable, she tried to grab hold of Ber, but her arms had become heavy. Her ability to focus was shot. It was easier to cradle her breasts while Ber's shaft claimed her mouth and her lips slid over his length and Songan's fingers grazed her trigger.

One moment she knew who was doing what to whom. The next she was being sucked into a swirling vortex. Her jaw muscles tightened around Ber, her fingers captured her nipples, and Songan's knowing fingers fucked her. All three sensations collided, and she flew off in countless directions.

Crouched above Rane, Ber held his breath. He'd seen a few women climax, but it hadn't been like this. Rane trembled as if she'd stepped onto a downed electrical line. Despite his cock plugging her mouth, she whimpered repeatedly. Positioned as he was, he couldn't see her expression. Besides, her teeth raking his length nearly sent him on the same journey. The way her throat worked made him think she was trying to swallow him. Alert but not alarmed, he waited for her to relax a little before reluctantly drawing free.

This was her time.

Rocking back on his heels, he sat near her head and

studied what was happening to her. Her fingers continued to clutch her breasts, and her eyes had all but rolled back in her head. He didn't ask if she was all right because she probably couldn't hear, let alone answer.

Just as he wondered if she'd passed out, she sighed. She let go of her breasts, and her arms floated to her sides. After moistening his forefinger by putting it in his mouth, he lightly touched the base of her throat. She gave no indication she was aware of what he was doing. Moments ago her lips had been around his now lonely and air-cooling erection. Not giving himself time to question what he was doing, he kissed her. She sighed again.

"She's done," Songan said. "Give her time."

Reluctantly straightening, Ber looked at the kneeling elk shifter. Songan was stroking her thighs. If what glistened on the fingers of his right hand spoke the truth, they'd recently been inside her. No wonder she was done.

"I'm—all right. Just shaky."

Ber had spent his human time near Inuit women whose lives revolved around the basics of shelter, food and safety. They enjoyed sex, he knew that from personal experience, but he couldn't imagine any of them looking as used up as Rane did.

"Shit." She laboriously sat up. "I know you're both waiting for me to say something, but I'm said out."

She'd sagged so much he wondered if he'd have to grab her to keep her from falling forward. Glancing at Songan, he concluded the elk shifter was having the same thoughts.

Suddenly he understood why she'd said what she had. It wasn't finding words that was beyond her, it was saying the right things to the right man.

If she had to choose one over the other, which would it be?

Looking unsteady, she stood and walked over to the water jug. Picking it up with both hands, she drank. When she was done, she handed it to Songan, who did the same. After wiping the opening, Songan extended the jug to him. The water was stale but satisfied his thirst. By the time Ber had finished, Rane had picked up her panties and was stepping into them.

"I need a shower." She didn't sound as if she cared. "But it'll have to wait. Where's the flashlight?"

"Rane," Songan said. "We can't go outside."

Just like that, she was fully alert. "Why not?"

"It's snowing."

"So?" Not bothering with her bra, she yanked her top over her head.

"If there's anything left, any signs, the snow has covered them."

"No. Damn it, no."

Rushing her movements, she hauled her jeans into place.

"Listen to me," Ber said. His own nudity didn't bother him, but if Rane was determined to go outside, he needed to be ready, which was why he reached for his briefs. "We can't change the weather. I'm sorry, believe me I am. I know you wanted to try to find where—"

"It's not just that," she shot back. "Everyone thinks I'm crazy for trying to retrace my mother's last steps. Maybe I am. All I know is that might be the only chance I have to—there might be something, some clue the police missed."

"And if there isn't?"

His question hit her hard, but much as Ber wished he could take back his words, he'd said what he'd had to. Rane no longer resembled a woman who'd just been repeatedly fucked. Instead she looked as if she was being ripped apart.

Whimpering, she sank into a chair and covered her face with her hands. "You don't understand."

"Tell me."

Silence. Then: "I blame myself."

He'd been about to put on his jeans, but with her words, that no longer mattered. Like him, Songan's attention was locked on her.

"Why?" he asked. Should he try to comfort her or give her some space?

"We'd argued," she whispered, not looking up. "Maybe the worst disagreement we've ever had. She tried to get me to admit that these mountains are in my blood and I was being a fool for trying to stay away. I told her it was my life. She'd done her job. Now it was my turn to make my decisions."

"You were right," he ventured, though he wasn't sure about such things. "It is your life."

"Yeah. Maybe."

Barely able to hear her, he waited her out by turning his attention to getting dressed. Songan was doing the same.

"The thing is," she said at length, "Mom was right. I was a fool for not admitting she knew what she was talking about."

"Why not?"

She tried to blow a lock of hair off her face. "I was so damn sure I was doing the right thing when I left Chinook. That finding myself could only happen if I was living somewhere else. I didn't want to admit I'd wasted all that time."

"It wasn't wasted. You have a career."

"Yeah, the same one Mom did. Doesn't that say something? She and I are so much alike—were so much alike." She gnawed on her lower lip. "This forest never let her go. It kept her here. I think—maybe part of her envied me for getting away, but she absolutely believed I'd return. She wanted to spare me all that struggling."

Rane hadn't looked up during her speech. He wasn't sure how aware she was of his and Songan's presence.

"What are you saying?" he asked. Much as he wanted to spare her more pain, he didn't believe he had a choice but had to continue. "You think the argument made it impossible for her to concentrate on where she was or what she was doing? It made her careless?"

He didn't know how to comfort women, had never been shown how such things were done, and yet he had no doubt he was doing the right thing when he walked over to her and placed his hands on her shoulders. At least she wasn't crying. Tears undid him.

"Rane, your mother was murdered. Shot. We'll never know if anything she did or didn't do would have prevented that from happening."

When Rane looked up at him with agony-filled eyes, it took all he had not to apologize.

"She shouldn't have died."

"I agree. But you feeling guilty doesn't change anything. You can't bring her back to life. She wouldn't want you doing this to yourself."

"Easier said than done."

Much as he hated hearing that, at least her spark was back. "Were *you* able to function after that argument? You didn't take to bed and pull the covers over your head."

"Of course not."

"Then?"

When she shrugged, he reluctantly took his hands off her.

"I lost the most important person in my life under horrific

circumstances," she said after a moment. "Don't blame me because my thinking's messed up."

"We don't," Songan said. "We never will."

Rane looked at where she'd left her socks and boots. Much as he preferred her naked, Ber picked them up and handed them to her. She didn't seem as devastated as when she'd made her confession, but his guess was she still had a long way to go before she was at peace with herself. From the moment she'd learned of her mother's death, she'd harbored the hope that she could somehow redeem herself by coming here. A snowstorm would stop most people, but not only was she still determined, she wasn't alone. Songan and he were here.

"What do you think?" he asked Songan, who was tying his boots but hadn't yet put on his shirt. "There's more wind than snow. If we take off right now—"

Songan held up a hand and jerked his head at the window. "What was that?"

"The wind?" Rane asked softly.

"Maybe." Songan didn't look convinced.

Uneasy, Ber slipped over to the small window. The close-growing trees made studying their surroundings all but impossible. It was far from a whiteout out there but cold enough that the snow was sticking. He hated the idea of letting Rane go outside, but if the snow kept up, the ground might stay covered until spring.

I don't see anything, he wanted to say, but the words wouldn't form. Something had him on alert.

"What if it's *them*?" Rane whispered. "Whoever killed my mother."

Why anyone would come here in this weather made no sense—unless there was evidence to hide. As another possibility struck, he turned toward Songan.

"People knew she was coming up here," he said. "What if someone followed us?"

Songan shook his head. "We would have heard, sensed. But if they were already up here—"

"Doing what?" Rane interrupted.

Feeling his way, Ber voiced his theory that whoever had shot her mother and dragged her away from the kill spot must have been concerned he'd left clues behind. "You told some folks you were going to check out Wolverine," he told her. "If I'm right, and I don't know if I am, maybe they were already here when we arrived."

"Doing what? That's what I need to know."

Putting action behind her words, she shook out a sock and put it on. He longed to grab it, the other sock and her boots from her. That done, he'd hold her down and rip off her clothes. Then he'd caress her until they both forgot everything else.

Sensing eyes on him, he looked at Songan. *"You can't,"* the elk shifter silently warned. *"She needs to do this."*

But what if it was dangerous out there?

"Wait," he told Rane. "Let Songan and me check things first."

"No. No way. This is *my* agenda. My obsession." She tapped her chest.

Maybe it had once been, but sex and more had changed things.

"He's right," Songan said. "Even the way Ber and I are now, our hearing is keener than yours, our sight sharper."

Somehow he and Songan were standing side by side with the window behind them. No matter that they might be rivals for Rane's body, they'd just formed a united front.

"Wait here," he told her. "As soon as we know things are safe, we—"

Glass shattered, spraying shards everywhere. A muffled pop immediately followed.

"Someone's shooting!" Rane yelled, but he already knew that. So did Songan, who dropped to his knees at the same instant he did. Rane hit the floor on her belly, causing his heart to stutter. To his relief, he saw no sign of blood when she lifted her head.

A second shot followed the first. That bullet also tore a jagged hole in the door that was opposite the window. Cold air rushed into the cabin. In contrast to the sudden chill, heat raged through him. A roar exploded from his chest. His shoulders, chest and arms started to expand.

Fighting the drive to become a grizzly, he crawled over to Rane and hauled her against the wall under the window. Hopefully the shards hadn't cut her.

Also crawling, Songan joined them. The elk shifter's eyes were darkening, his nostrils flaring. He gripped Ber's forearm. "I don't dare shift. If I do, I could forget this."

"I won't."

"What are you thinking?" Rane insisted. "Damn it, no, you aren't going out there."

"If I don't," Ber said, "they might kill us."

Songan's grip tightened. "They might anyway."

"Stay with her," he said.

"You? No. I'm—"

"I'm the predator," he pointed out. "One of us has to stay with her."

"I'm not helpless," Rane said.

"Maybe not but you're not a shifter. You don't understand

survival the way we do."

That silenced her.

"I'm not going to tell you to be careful," Songan told her, "because that's a given. Roar if you need me."

Standing where he couldn't be seen from outside, Ber tore off the clothing he'd just put on. He still felt where Songan had grabbed him, and Rane's eyes were filled with fear and something else, but he didn't dare let those things distract him.

In the past, changing had always been a conscious effort, a move dictated by practical matters. Today was different. Unstoppable.

Barely aware of the two pairs of eyes on him, he moved as far as he dared into the middle of the room so he'd have more space in which to become a bear. As his neck thickened and thick brown hair began covering his human skin, he realized he wouldn't be able to get through the door once the transformation was complete. Songan must have had the same thought because, springing to his feet, the elk shifter yanked open the door.

The moment Ber stepped outside, snow and wind buffeted him. Glorying in what he accepted as nature's gift, he surrendered to the inner force he might never understand. Moment by moment he became less human and more animal. Bigger. Stronger. Solid. At home here.

As a bear, his eyesight wasn't as sharp as he'd like, but his sense of smell and hearing made up for it. With paws and claws instead of feet, he easily dismissed the cold, snow-dusted ground. Not even a blizzard could penetrate his thick fur. A heart capable of supplying a half-ton body sped blood through his veins.

Because the door was opposite the window, he doubted the shooter had seen him come out. But if more than one person was involved—

As if in answer to his question, another *pop* rocked the air. A bullet slammed into the just-closed door, sending wood splinters onto the snow. Grateful for the shooter's poor marksmanship, he whirled to the right and bounded into the trees. Whoever had shot out the window wouldn't have had time to run around the cabin, which meant at least two would-be marksmen were out there. As for whether whoever had just fired had seen him turn into a bear, hell, it didn't matter.

He'd heard people maintain bears were lumbering, clumsy creatures, but they were wrong. Given reason, he could move as silently as any deer. Lifting his heavy head and inhaling, he caught the stench of gunpowder and a hint of human. Much as he wanted to charge, he forced himself to be patient. To think. Plan.

Three shots, the first two twins of each other, the last sounding different.

Two would-be killers with separate weapons.

One knew he was out here and in grizzly form. The other didn't.

One had deliberately shot at Rane and come within inches of striking her. The second had fired at him.

Growling under his breath, Ber slipped through the trees heading for where the first shots had come from and whoever had tried to kill Rane.

Chapter Nineteen

"Why isn't he still shooting?" Rane demanded of Songan. "My God, if Ber has been hit—"

"He hasn't."

"How do you know?"

"We would have heard him."

Songan was right. There were rifles with enough firepower to bring down a grizzly, but that wasn't what had just torn into the door. Going by the sounds, she surmised the shooter was using a deer rifle, maybe a 30-30 since that was the caliber of choice for local hunters. Ber might be wounded but thank goodness not dead. No, not wounded. Ber would have let them know if he needed help.

"There's more than one man out there," Songan said.

"You're sure?"

"Yes."

Instead of asking for an explanation, she accepted what Songan had told her. So much had changed since she'd fed off Songan and Ber's bodies. Watching snowflakes enter through the shattered window, she ached to go back in time. "Two," she said unnecessarily. "Trying to kill us."

"Yes."

Instead of staying on the floor as he'd ordered her to do,

Songan had gotten to his feet and was pacing from one side of the cabin to the other and back again. Every time he reached the door, he cracked it open. She wanted to point out that the chance of seeing someone was slim; at least she wouldn't be able to.

Today was no longer about trying to solve her mother's murder and thus, somehow, win forgiveness. Neither did it have anything to do with exploring a level of sexuality she hadn't known she was capable of. Everything had become a matter of life and death. Even worse, her damnable obsession was risking the lives of the two most important men in her world.

"I'm sorry," she whispered. "I should have never let you come up here."

"I insisted."

Had he? She couldn't remember. No, that wasn't the truth. Despite everything she'd been through today, she couldn't deny a simple fact. She hadn't wanted to come to Wolverine alone. She'd told the men she'd appreciate their help in trying to determine where her mother had been shot, but that hadn't been the only reason she'd been grateful for their presence. She'd been afraid her emotions would swamp her if she was alone.

Now the laugh was on her. Her emotions had been swamped, all right, but not for the reasons she'd thought they'd be.

"Rane?"

Shaking off the useless thought, she realized Songan was handing her mother's rifle and to her. Why hadn't she already claimed it?

Instead of grabbing her pistol, Songan knelt beside her. "I didn't tell Ber the whole truth," he said.

"About what?"

"I can still think, at least a little, when I'm in elk form."

Songan wasn't darkly handsome like Ber, but there was a loyalty to him that had touched her from the moment they'd first met. Of course he was loyal. A bull elk was hardwired to put his harem's safety ahead of his own.

"I've told you some about how it is," he continued, touching her knee. "Even on four legs, there's more to me than instinct. I have a basic ability to reason and decide."

"What are you saying?"

He indicated the rifle. "Can you handle it if I go outside?"

Two evil men had tried to kill them. Right now Ber was outnumbered, but if a powerful bull elk joined him—

Shuddering, she covered Songan's hand with hers. "I couldn't stand it if something happened to you."

"*He's* out there. Is it different for him?"

Was Songan asking if he was more important to her than Ber? Didn't he know she couldn't answer that, might not ever be able to?

"No. It all happened so fast. Ber was gone before I could stop him."

"Even if you'd tried, you wouldn't have been able to. He's doing what he believes he must."

If she said the words Songan was waiting to hear, she'd be alone. Trapped in the cabin where her mother might have spent the last night of her life.

Her mother. For reasons she might never know, Jacki had come alone to Wolverine. Her daughter couldn't do less.

"He needs you," she whispered.

So do you, Songan's expression and the hand on her knee said, but she refused to go there. A short while ago, the two men had treated her as if she was something fragile and precious, but she was no longer that sexual creature. Damn it, she was a strong and competent woman. Just as her mother had been.

"I know how to use this." She indicated the rifle.

Songan didn't respond. After running his hand up her thigh and making a lie of her belief that she'd buried the sexual part of her nature, he again stood. As Ber had done, he took care to stay away from the shattered window while he undressed. Naked, he reached for the doorknob. She longed to say something but couldn't.

"I'll bugle when I return," he said. "That way you'll know who it is."

So you won't be tempted to shoot me, she heard.

More winter air rushed in when Songan opened the door. Then the big nude man disappeared, and she was left to imagine the transformation taking place in the storm.

"Be careful," she muttered. "I need you, both of you."

Despite the trees, Songan had seen Ber bound past the window opening. Obviously Ber had decided to go after the first shooter. That left the bastard responsible for the third shot. Filled with determination and little else, Songan left the stack of wood he'd jumped behind the moment he came outside.

Before he'd changed, he'd cringed under the wind's attack, but now he held his head and antlers high as he stepped into the trees. They closed around him. If circumstances were different, he'd be tempted to stay there, because despite the storm, it was still light enough for his intended target to see him. Speed, and what intellect he could hold on to, would keep him alive. Maybe.

Within seconds his nose alerted him to a human presence. Breaking into a run, he headed in the direction the last shot had come from. He made no attempt to be silent. In fact, he made a point of slamming his hooves against the ground.

Bam!

Snow exploded off a nearby branch. A moment later, the branch crashed to the ground. Furious and oblivious to danger, Songan plowed on. The closely spaced trees forced him to weave around them, and he tilted his head as he did. Pride in what he was capable of filled him. He inadvertently flattened a sapling under his weight, then slowed.

Facing him from maybe a hundred feet away with his back wedged against a thick, dark trunk and his rifle trembling stood a man dressed in camouflage.

Kill. End the threat.

Instead of surrendering to the animal command, however, Songan forced himself to stop. How would Rane react if he trampled the man? She needed answers, a confession, maybe words of regret. She might never forgive—

Something slammed into him, knocking him onto his haunches. His head rang, then throbbed. Struggling to his feet, he fought to keep his head up. Despite the pain and blurred vision, he realized the bullet had struck the base of his rack.

Reasoning shut down. He dug a front hoof into the ground. Challenge done with, he charged. He struck the enemy off center. As he spun the man around, the human's shoulder collided with the tree. Instead of withdrawing from the screaming creature, Songan continued to push.

Garbled and pain-filled sounds flowed around him. His heart rate kicked up. Fighting other bulls during rut felt right, something he'd been born to do. The rest of the time, unless a herd member was being attacked, he gave no thought to battle.

Today everything changed.

Elk and human were locked together. For as long as Songan wanted, the man would remain trapped between him and the tree. The man had dropped his rifle, not that it would have done him any good. He screamed repeatedly, and his flailing hands beat weakly at the air.

At length Songan grew weary of the one-sided fight and stepped back. Whimpering, the man slipped to the ground and curled himself into a ball with his back to his attacker.

Wishing the man had put up more of a struggle, Songan rose onto his hind legs and came down hard. The discarded rifle bent under his weight.

Done with what he comprehended was vital, he took another backward step. Only then did he turn his attention to the man who'd tried to kill him. The enemy's arms and legs were still tucked against his body, and he shivered as if cold.

Songan slowly shook his head. His vision was clearing, and his temple no longer throbbed. He tried but couldn't recall the emotion that had compelled him to attack.

Not caring what happened to his would-be killer, he turned his back on him. One thing he did know. His reason for shifting into elk form wasn't over.

Growling frightened the man who'd covered himself in a mix of brown and green clothing because he stupidly believed he could move undetected through the forest that way. Careful to keep trees between himself and the sometimes wildly swinging rifle, Ber silently laughed at the poor excuse for a hunter.

If he'd wanted to, he could have already attacked, but not

only did he respect the rifle, if the man was dead, Rane might never learn what role, if any, he'd had in Jacki's murder.

So keep him alive. Disarm him and force him back to the cabin when they'd wrench the truth out of him.

But first—

Keeping the sound low so hopefully the man couldn't tell where it was coming from, Ber again growled. He'd been chuffing and growling since locating the shooter and had discovered that beneath the camouflage lay the heart of a coward. The man had once believed that all it took to kill three people was to sneak up on them and fire repeatedly. Now he was learning how wrong he'd been.

"I know what you are!" the man shouted. "You ain't no bear. You're one of those damn shifters."

Ber waited for the man to threaten to kill him, but he didn't. Maybe the short speech had taken the last of his courage.

Ber let loose with a series of grunts the way he sometimes did when he found a beetle-filled log. Undoubtedly the man wouldn't know he was being labeled an insect, a bug.

"You stop that!" The rifle went still. "Think you can hide from me? You're wrong."

One thing about spending a great deal of his life as a beast but with human intellect was that Ber studied other animals. He'd learned from all of them, particularly the predators, and now handled himself like a cougar. A bear plowed through life. Ruled by its belly and made bold by its size, a grizzly took what it wanted. Fortunately almost anything the forest provided sufficed.

In contrast, cougars needed meat to survive. Toward that end, cougars stalked—just as Ber was doing now.

Carefully selecting the best ground to walk on, Ber silently made his way around and behind the shooter. Much as he anticipated watching the man's reaction the next time he growled, he didn't for a moment dismiss what the rifle was capable of. His enemy might be thinking the same thing, because his arms and consequently his weapon no longer shook. Something about him was vaguely familiar, and if the conditions were better, Ber might have recognized him. Now, however, survival and exacting justice ruled him.

When he was in position, he crouched behind a tree stump. The snow continued to fall. Anticipating smelling fear, Ber took a deep breath. He caught that, all right, but there was something else. A faint and distant stench that made the hair on his shoulders stand up.

Distracted and alarmed, he had to force himself not to stand on his rear legs to have a better chance of identifying the stench. Instead, belly nearly on the ground and shoulders low, he backed away from the stump.

"Where the hell are you? Stop whatever the hell game you're playing. Let's get this on."

The man who'd tried to kill Rane no longer mattered. And with the unsettling smell now coming hard on the wind, neither did Rane herself. Ber no longer cared about revenge and justice or even survival.

Turning his back to the man, Ber lifted his head and let the deadly but vital scent guide him. Wind gusts ruffled his fur, and snow landed on his face to connect him with his surroundings. This was his new home, the mountains destiny had brought him to. He shared it with the smaller black bears who in certain ways were his kin. Once he'd assured them that this was a safe place to live and eventually die, the rest of the Enyeto would join him.

He'd select a mate. The sow would give birth to what looked in every way like a human baby. Because his mate's body was incapable of nurturing such an infant, he would turn it over to a human surrogate mother.

Rane.

Her name and everything that went with it drew him back into the real world, and his cock responded. Then the unwanted smell again assaulted him.

Feeling the size, weight, and intellect that separated him from the area's indigenous bears, he reluctantly headed toward the smell. He still faintly heard the man he'd wanted to kill but that, like Rane, would have to wait.

Snow blanketed the rise ahead of him, and he concentrated on his route so he wouldn't slide. One step followed another followed by yet more until he lost track of how far he'd come. There were fewer trees in this area and many boulders. From what he could tell, there were more rocks than dirt underfoot. Only a handful of trees and few bushes meant he could take a direct route to wherever he was being drawn. Despite the ease of travel, he didn't want to be here. Dreaded what lay ahead.

Stopping, Ber looked back the way he'd come. Given the mountainous terrain, the man he'd been stalking couldn't have brought a motorized vehicle, which meant he couldn't quickly get away, but he might find a hiding place. If that happened—

More wind. More smell.

Walking again, Ber acknowledged a moment of envy for Songan, who didn't know the meaning of dread when he was in elk form. He even envied Rane, who was safe in the cabin with nothing to do except wait for her men to return.

Wind again. Smell getting stronger.

Lifting his head, Ber looked up and ahead. At first all he saw was the new snow carpet. Then he spotted a barely perceptible opening near the top of the rocky terrain. He wasn't yet close enough to determine whether what he suspected was a cave was large enough to shelter a hibernating bear. Even if it was, it was early in winter for a bear to be in hibernation. Besides, his nerves and nose had already told him that whatever was in there was dead.

Ber bared his teeth. Death was as much a part of these mountains as birth, nothing to shock or alarm him. Nothing new.

When the long climb was behind him, he stood in front of an opening large enough to allow a smallish black to pass through. After searching in vain for a reason not to do this, he began tearing at the earth. At first the rocks defied his attack. Then they gave way. Dirt and debris flew about to cover the snow. He was grateful for the cold.

The opening was now large enough to for him to enter. No choice but to go inside.

Dropping onto his belly, Ber wiggled forward until he found himself in a space with enough room for him to stand. Moving to the side, he let in as much daylight as possible. All too soon, his eyes adjusted. He saw what was responsible for the death smell.

An adult-size black bear lay against the back of the cave. Long-dried blood stained the fur over its chest. It had been gutted. Two smaller, still forms huddled near the adult's head. They too had been ripped open.

Wrenching pain closed around Ber's heart, and yet he couldn't fully wrap his mind around what he was looking at. The storm couldn't reach him in here; even the wind was little more than a whisper.

Peace should live in this place where a mother bear had given birth and nurtured her twins. Born in winter, the twins had undoubtedly nestled against their mother. At first they'd been tiny, nearly hairless and occasionally squalling mounds, but thanks to the rich milk that was their only food, they'd grown until they were large enough to venture outside and begin exploring the world beyond their home.

Tragically they'd never had the chance.

Maybe their killer had stumbled upon this place. More likely he'd watched and stalked the unsuspecting sow as she searched for food. The killer could have shot her outside and she'd crawled in here to die. It was possible he'd ventured into the cave and fired while she was sleeping, but Ber doubted that. The danger was too great.

So—Ber fought to wrap his resisting mind around the most likely scenario—despite her fatal wound, the mother had made her way to her cubs. Their safety had been foremost in her mind, but instead of protecting them, she'd led her killer to her children.

All three had died to feed some monster's greed.

Ber's intellect shut down. He no longer thought; he simply felt. His eyes hot with emotion, he inched forward and touched the large female's nose. Death touched him back. Despite the shock, he did the same to the two cubs. Then, heedless to the weather, he exited the cave.

Chapter Twenty

Sick with fear, Rane hammered the last nail she'd found in a catch-all drawer into the wall using the back of a metal stirring spoon. With four nails now holding up the corners of the blanket she'd placed in front of the window, the fire she'd recently stoked began warming the room. One edge of the blanket was so close to the window frame that she could easily pull it aside and peek outside.

Not that she could see anything.

Someone had shot at Songan. Twice.

The shooter had missed; he had to have! Otherwise she would have known, right? With Songan wounded or dead, the shooter would have come after her, right?

Picking up her rifle again, she went to the door and cautiously opened it. Just like the five or six times she'd already done this, she saw nothing. Much as she needed to call out to Songan, she didn't, because he'd told her he'd bugle once he'd accomplished his mission.

If he was alive.

Moaning, she closed the door and leaned on it for support. Try as she did to silence the sound, she kept hearing the horrid rifle shots.

"Be safe, Songan, please."

Not just Songan, but Ber too.

The bear shifter hadn't said anything about his intentions while he was stripping off his clothes in preparation for becoming an animal. She guessed he'd been determined to spare her the details. Either that or he'd wanted to downplay the danger. Had she begged him to be careful, told him how vital he'd become to her in the short time they'd known each other?

What had her final words been to Songan?

Her mind flashed to her mother. Not for the first time, she asked herself if her mother's murder was connected to what was happening today. Could it be otherwise?

Moaning, she returned to the blanketed opening and peered out. The two men who'd become her world were out in the wilderness trying to hunt down a pair of would-be killers. In contrast to their courage, here she sat inside a bullet-ridden cabin with nothing better to do than keep it warm.

Was the heat only for herself, or would it welcome Ber and Songan when they returned?

When, not if.

Songan wasn't sure why he was heading in the direction he was. All he knew was that this was what he was supposed to be doing. He vaguely recalled he'd come across tracks set down by both a man and a massive bear. When the two sets of prints separated, he'd followed the bear's. The bear needed him. The human could wait.

His head had stopped ringing, and his memory of being shot was fading. In contrast, the image of how the human who'd tried to kill him had looked curled up with snow blanketing him remained clear. As he tracked, he tried to imagine what, if anything, the human was doing now.

He'd hurt the would-be killer but didn't know how badly. If the human could get to his feet, he might be on the move. With his rifle useless and the temperature dropping, his primary concern had to be for his safety.

How does it feel? Does helplessness terrify you?

Surprise at his ability to relate to the man slowed Songan. He pondered returning so he could watch the struggle, but before he could make the decision, a wave of emotion distracted him.

Ber. Needing him.

So far he'd been holding to a measured pace to insure he wouldn't lose sight of the fading tracks, but with Ber's emotions now driving him, he trusted the unspoken communication to guide him to Rane's other lover. The poor visibility and terrain prevented him from running at full speed, and he had to keep an eye on his surroundings to insure he'd continue avoiding the trees.

He tried to comprehend why Ber had stopped stalking the human, but nothing made sense. He had no choice but to wait for the bear shifter to explain himself. The storm blunted the usual sounds, smells and sights, compelling him to trust that he was doing the right thing. He gave a half thought to what might happen if his trust was misguided. Maybe Rane wanted more of him than he'd been able to give her. Certainly she deserved larger chunks of him. But the forest and his place in it exacted their own demands. He could only be what he was and hope she understood.

Fewer trees grew here than where he'd been when he first *heard* Ber's thoughts. He vaguely recognized it as a place the elk avoided because there wasn't enough to graze on. The rocks and boulders forced him to slow even more, and the openness made him feel exposed and vulnerable. Just the same, his conviction that Ber was nearby kept him going.

A rock rolled under a hind hoof, causing him to stumble. He regained his balance, and when something large and dark separated itself from the white world he realized it was Ber standing motionless high on a rocky slope. Studying the grizzly shifter, Songan wondered at his ability to recognize Ber. His mind suddenly felt clear and sharp.

"What is it?" he asked. "What's wrong?"

Looking old, Ber swung his bulk toward him. *"They're dead!"*

"Who's dead?"

"A mother bear and her babies."

Death was part of the wilderness. An animal might mourn the loss of another of its kind, but grief didn't last long. He didn't tell Ber that, because the bear shifter hadn't told him about a sow and cubs. His emotions went far deeper.

"Where?" he asked.

Ber nodded at an opening in the slope Songan hadn't noticed. *"In there."*

"How did you find them?"

Still looking as if he was barely aware of his surroundings, Ber shook his head. *"The death smell."*

Songan inhaled deeply. Yes, there it was. Old. Sad. But the faded death stench wasn't the only thing that caught his attention.

"I smell humans," he told Ber. "Not recent."

Looking puzzled, Ber lifted his head. After a moment, his nostrils flared. *"Why didn't I notice that before?"*

"Because the other was more important," Songan ventured.

"It was. It still is. I hate—the three have been dead a long

time. The babies are so small—I think their bodies have been in there since spring."

"Scavengers haven't gotten to them?"

"No. The bodies are well preserved."

Even without looking into the cave, Songan knew what he'd find. *"They died together."*

"Not died; killed. Shot and gutted."

The mind conversation with Ber was straining his ability to think, and his headache was returning.

"Maybe that's the other thing we're smelling," he told the bear who'd become his companion. *"The lingering stench of whoever killed them."*

"No, it isn't old enough."

The scents were so faint Songan had to clear his mind before he could concentrate. Experience and instinct told him Ber was right.

"Three humans," Ber explained when they stood only a few feet apart with falling snow a gauzy curtain between them. "Two men. And a woman."

Now that Ber had pointed that out to him, Songan set himself to learning even more. One of the men's smell was similar if not identical to the stench of the one he'd attacked. Eyes closed so he could better concentrate, he struggled to make sense of what of herself the woman had left behind. The men-scent was a mix of sweat and other bodily aromas. In contrast, one thing dominated the woman's.

Blood.

Fully alert, he circled the area until he came to the spot where the blood scent was strongest. After waiting for Ber to join him, he touched his nose to the ground and inhaled.

"Jacki," he told Ber.

"*No doubt?*"

Not breathing, Songan stared into bear eyes. "*None.*"

Feeling too large for his bruin body, Ber retraced his steps. Most of the time, the massive elk walked beside him, but when the trail became too narrow, the elk slowed so he could go first.

Ber's mind pulsed as he struggled to process everything, but no matter how many times he came close to acknowledging what the various smells had told him, images of the three murdered and mutilated bears rushed to the forefront.

Revenge meant nothing to bears, but he was more than an animal, and the human in him wanted only one thing.

"*What happened to the second man,*" he asked Songan. "*Did you find him? Kill him?*"

Songan didn't reply, prompting Ber to stop and look over his shoulder. Something had changed about the elk, a dullness in his eyes that hadn't been there when they were near the cave and examining the telling scents.

"*What is it?*" he demanded. "*What are you thinking?*"

Head tilted to the side a little, Songan returned his gaze, but there was no comprehension.

"*Songan, it's me, Ber. Do you know what I'm saying?*"

Nothing. No hint the elk understood a word.

"*What about Rane,*" Ber pressed. "*Do you remember her? You fucked her today. So did I.*"

Something briefly flashed in Songan's eyes. Studying the elk with the largest rack he'd ever seen, he accepted the undeniable. When they were standing where Rane's mother had shed her blood, Songan's intelligence had equaled his. The effort must have taxed what little of Songan's human mind remained. He no longer thought. He'd again become pure animal.

In a way, Ber envied the other shifter.

Following the scents leading away from where he was certain Jacki had been killed should have settled him. Always before, he'd found a sense of peace in instinctive acts, but everything had changed. He didn't fully understand the rage that threatened to strip caution from him and could barely control it. Some of his fury came from the carnage inside the cave; the rest revolved around what he'd have to tell Rane.

Slowing, he struggled to form the necessary words to tell Rane what he and Songan had discovered. One thing he knew. He couldn't simply lay out the details. Rane deserved more.

So did the dead mother bear and her children.

Ber picked up his pace. Behind him, Songan did the same. Even with everything he was trying to process, he almost laughed at the thought of how they looked. A bear and an elk, no longer wary adversaries or enemies but united.

By the woman they shared.

Memories of how Rane's body felt against him lifted his cock. Instead of assuring himself that he was still following the faint blood trail, he drew one image after another from deep inside.

Rane, standing naked between Songan and him. Rane on her back on the too-small bed with her legs open and heat welcoming him. Rane taking his length and breadth into her core. Screaming her climax.

Something squeezed his heart. Forcefully casting aside what had given him his erection, he again dragged his nose over the snow dusting until the scents spoke to him. Once more single-minded and with his erection dying, he picked up his pace. The snow flattened under his paws. Behind him, the elk shifter's sharp hooves did even more damage.

He knew one thing. Several weeks ago, two men had taken turns dragging and sometimes carrying Jacki's body toward Wolverine. Only one reason for the effort made sense. The killers hadn't wanted her to be found near the cave.

Chapter Twenty-One

The camouflaged man trudged with his rifle slung over one stooped shoulder. His head was so low it looked as if his chin might strike his chest, and Ber concluded that his legs were in danger of giving out. When he'd followed him earlier, the man had moved at an impressive pace. No longer.

What did he care! This *creature* had savagely murdered three innocent bears.

That wasn't the only thing the bastard had done.

Despite his winter jacket, the storm that meant nothing to the shifters attacked the killer. Snow covered his shoulders and the top of his head, and Ber detected a shiver. Fighting the rage that showed no sign of abating, Ber pondered why the man was heading down-mountain. He and his companion had tried to kill Rane, Songan and him. Not only hadn't he fulfilled his mission, he apparently cared nothing for his companion's life.

A coward. Running away.

The babies, still and dead, cuddled against their equally dead mother's body. All three destroyed to feed a monster's or monsters' greed.

Rane's mother. Murdered maybe because she'd discovered the carnage. Deliberately silenced. Her body dragged away from the cave and then discarded.

Leaving Rane to mourn.

Blood pulsed in Ber's forehead. His world turned red. He heard only one word.

Revenge.

Rising onto his hind legs, he roared.

Silent and open-mouthed, the man whirled toward the animal sound. Yanking his rifle off his shoulder, he fired without first taking aim.

"Stop him!"

Propelled by Songan's command, Ber dropped onto four legs and charged. He struck the man in the chest, knocking him off his feet and landing on top of him. Looking down, Ber found himself face to face with terror-filled eyes.

"Oh God, oh God, oh God!" the man babbled.

The stench of loosened bowels filled the air. Instead of closing his jaws around the man's head as instinct commanded, however, Ber studied his captive. The collision had knocked the rifle out of his hands and sent it skidding across the snow. Out of the corner of his eye, Ber saw Songan step on the rifle.

"Oh God, please God!"

Maybe, in their own way, the mother bear and her babies had begged to be allowed to live. If they had, their pleas hadn't been heeded. The same might have happened to Jacki.

"Kill him. Make him pay."

Ber sensed the effort behind Songan's command, and when he again studied the elk, he saw the strain in the large expressive eyes. For the first time, he noticed that a prong on Songan's right antler was missing and the stub looked jagged.

"The other man did that to you?" he asked.

Songan nodded.

"I know who you are," the man blubbered. "A shifter." He struggled weakly, trying to crawl out from under Ber's weight. "First those damn elk. Now this."

Hearing the helpless fear behind his captive's words, Ber lost some of his rage. He still hated the man and everything he stood for, the horrible things he believed he had a right to do. However, Ber was no longer sure he wanted him to die at his hands.

Claws, he reminded himself. Today he was all claws and teeth.

A grizzly who would soon have to face Rane and tell her everything he'd done.

A muffled thud and crunching sound tore his attention to where Songan was. Lifting a front leg, Songan struck the already ruined rifle.

"Do it," Ber encouraged.

Gathering himself, the elk reared and came down. What was left of the rifle sank into snow and soil.

"Do it!" The man clawed at Ber's fur. "Get it the hell over with."

Propelled by the defeated plea for a quick death, Ber opened his mouth. It would be so easy to close his jaws around the man's shoulder, sink his massive teeth into helpless flesh and listen to bones breaking. He'd taste blood, feel—what?

Sensing something new from Songan, he once more looked at the elk.

"Don't."

You don't want me to kill him?

There it was again, Songan's struggle to reason. Paying little attention to the puny hands pulling on his hair, Ber waited for Songan to say more. The waiting stretched out. Then: *"Let the forest have him."*

Standing with her legs pressed against the bed for support, Rane watched Ber and Songan get dressed. They might think she was simply gawking, but her response went much deeper. Only by studying their potent bodies and serious expressions could she wrap her mind around reality and relief. They were safe! The horrid time she'd spent alone in this too-small space not knowing whether they were dead or alive was behind her.

Her lovers had returned.

Songan had a lump on his forehead, but as far as she'd been able to tell, that was their only injury. They'd said little when they entered, only took turns letting her grasp their naked bodies against her with all her strength. They'd come inside almost immediately after switching back into human form and yet that had been long enough for their skin to turn cold. However, instead of warming themselves by the woodstove, once they'd put on their jeans and shirts, they walked as one over to where she stood.

Taking her hand, Ber indicated he wanted her to sit on the bed.

"What is it?" she asked, her mouth dry. "Something's wrong."

The way Ber's jaw clenched and his eyes burned, she dreaded what might come next.

"You're safe," Songan said, while Ber only studied her as she scooted onto the mattress. "The shooters won't be back."

About to point out that the bullets had been intended for them as much as her, she decided to wait them out. Ber was still holding her hand, compelling her to squeeze his big, competent fingers. She wondered if she'd ever get used to his size and the magnificent beast he was capable of becoming.

The same held true for Songan.

"Are they dead?" she asked when the silence weighed on her.

"No," Songan said.

Too much. She couldn't absorb any more than that, and yet she sensed she'd soon have to.

Maybe understanding her turmoil, Songan lowered himself to his knees. Taking the hand Ber wasn't holding, he brought it to his mouth and breathed warm moisture onto her fingers. Her pussy tingled.

"We found both of them," Songan continued, looking over at Ber. "I went after the second shooter, the one who fired after Ber took off. He hit me." He touched the lump on his forehead. "I charged."

"Oh." What a stupid thing to say. "Of course you did. It was his life or yours. Thank God he wasn't a better shot."

"I didn't give him time."

Much as she needed to know the details, she first had to get the bigger picture. "Ber? Let me get this straight. As soon as you shifted, you headed after the man who shot out the window."

"Yes."

Was his short response as simple as Ber being the strong, silent type? Much as she needed to believe he'd acted on instinct, his expression said it went deeper than that. She thought about standing so she could wrap her arms around him and offer him comfort and her body, but not only might the gesture turn into more than comfort, Songan had hold of her other hand. She settled for leaning forward and running her lips over Ber's forearm.

She started to straighten when he too knelt. Barely believing what had just happened, she acknowledged that the two most macho men she would ever know were on their knees inches from her legs.

Thank God they were alive and safe.

"Songan, you charged the one man. Did you injure him?"

"I don't know. He no longer mattered."

"Just like that?"

Releasing her fingers, Songan bracketed her left knee with both of his hands. "I was an elk then. I did what instinct demanded."

"What—about his weapon?"

"Destroyed."

Was this really happening? Unlike the vivid erotic dreams she'd been having recently, this was reality. Songan and Ber had come face to face with evil and conquered it. Left the vanquished in no condition to cause any more trouble. More than that, the shifters had touched her in ways she'd never been touched. Had sex with her. Remembering those electric moments, her core swelled, loosened, let go.

As one, the men's gazes ran from her face to the join between her legs. She knew they'd smelled her response.

"I'm not going to apologize. It's beyond my control."

Ber's hold on her hand tightened. Much as she didn't want to call attention to the fact that he was hurting her, she tried to pull free. He briefly held on, then relaxed. Despite his growing bulge, his eyes still looked haunted.

"What is it?" She ran her tingling fingers over his cheek. "Please tell me."

He gave her a smile that didn't reach his eyes. "You get

turned on, it does the same to me."

"Me too."

Much as Songan's admission needed to be acknowledged, Rane kept her attention on Ber. She'd seen the same expression looking back at her in the mirror after learning her mother was dead. "What did you see?" she asked. "What happened?"

Ber started to pull back. Scared and determined, she clamped her hand over the back of his neck in an attempt to hold him in place.

"Don't keep it inside, please."

He told her then. Lost in his too-vivid words, she mentally pictured the three sad carcasses his grizzly sense of smell had led him to. Even with emotion forcefully stripped from him, she sensed his horror and understood his desire for revenge.

"You said they'd been cut open," she managed when he fell silent. Even though she already knew the answer, she had to ask. "What was taken?"

"Their galls."

Oh God, Mom, did you see—

Horrified by the unwanted thought, she closed and then opened her eyes. Looked around the cabin without seeing it. "Nothing else?"

"As far as I know, no."

Ber and she stared at each other while the ramifications of what had been done to the bears slammed into her. "Galls are worth hundreds of dollars to the right market." With every second, she felt more sick to her stomach. Was there no way she could hide from the possibility forming in her mind? "A reason to kill. At least that's what the poacher believed."

"Nothing justifies what I saw."

There was the emotion Ber had been trying to force down.

With the bear shifter's fury growing, she wondered if he'd killed the man after all but hadn't wanted to tell her.

Awareness of her physical response to Ber and Songan continued to make its impact, but even if they initiated sex, which she didn't believe they'd do now, she'd tell them to wait. Did they guess what she was thinking, that her mother's murder and the bears' deaths were connected? Maybe the same rifle or rifles had brought down the young elk.

"Where is the man you went after?" she asked Ber.

The men exchanged a glance. "After I knocked him down and Songan destroyed his weapon, I let him up," Ber said. "Let him run."

"Into the forest," Songan continued. "Unarmed with night coming and the storm continuing."

"He's going to die out there. They both are."

"Maybe."

Obviously Ber didn't care, not that she blamed him. Just the same, she was a compassionate and caring woman who'd never wished a slow and painful death on anyone, not even a ruthless bear poacher. Or did she?

Confused and conflicted, she got to her feet and walked to the opposite side of the room. Then she forced herself to face the men. She'd shared her body with them, taken everything they had to give and hopefully given them what they needed. They'd both fucked her and left themselves imprinted on her. It couldn't get any more intimate than that.

But, damn it, she couldn't condone what they'd done out in the storm.

Or could she?

Mom, am I thinking crazy, letting everything get away from me?

"How would you feel if it was you?" she asked, falling back on the woman she'd been before her mother's murder. "Think about it. Put yourself in the men's place. It's getting dark." She thought about pulling the blanket aside to make sure but didn't. "Your clothes aren't enough to keep you warm. You're disoriented. Maybe injured. You're afraid you're going to die, but it's going to take a long time. Is that what you want for those two, is it?"

"You don't understand," Ber said.

Chapter Twenty-Two

Ber's eyes were thick with more than had already been revealed. So were Songan's. She wanted to run, to go back in time, to throw herself at them and beg them to make love to her, anything but this. And yet it had to be done. "Tell me."

"They also killed your mother."

The strength left her legs, and she started to collapse. She was only vaguely aware that Ber had caught her and was carrying her back to the bed. Depositing her on the side, he settled himself beside her. Songan sat on her other side.

"How do you know?"

The explanation took longer than the one about the bears had. Hearing that they'd come to their conclusion thanks to their animal senses had her wanting to insist they couldn't be sure, but they were as much animal as they were men—maybe more.

If they believed her mother had shed blood near the cave, who was she to tell them they were wrong? After all, law enforcement and searchers had concluded that Jacki had been brought to where her body was found. Now, thanks to the two shifters, the pieces had fallen together.

"The tracking dog didn't find anything," she pointed out, not that it made any difference.

"It rained, remember," Songan said. "Rane, I wish I didn't have to tell you this but—"

"I wish you didn't either."

Songan sighed. "We found the kill spot."

Kill spot. Much as she hated hearing the words, she was used to Songan's direct ways. Besides, she'd guessed what the truth before the explanation came.

"The whole time we were returning to the cabin, we tried to find a way to make it easier for you," Ber said.

"You did. I wasn't doing much thinking."

Ber touched Songan's shoulder. "You did for a short while. Long enough for us to communicate what we needed to."

Songan's puzzled expression faded to be replaced by comprehension. She wished she knew more about what had happened, but that would have to wait. Right now the only thing that mattered was her mother's murder had been solved.

"At least you have some answers," Ber said. "A lot more than you did before you came here."

Grateful for his insight, she squeezed his knee. He covered her hand with his, and just like that, she remembered what it was to be a woman. As sensual warmth infused her, she leaned against Songan's shoulder and then Ber's.

"You're right," she admitted. "Knowing what happened to Mom is better than not."

Situated the way she was, she couldn't see the men's expressions but didn't need to. Songan's thoughts were on her one hundred percent. He cared only for her emotional health, wanted nothing except for her to be at peace.

Because of what he'd found in the cave, things were more complicated for Ber. In some regard, he would have to go through the same grieving process she had.

"We'll tell Gannon as soon as we get back," she said. "Let him know everything."

"We don't know who the men are."

She felt removed from the two who'd tried to kill her, Ber and Songan. For now, the men who'd shot her mother and three bears—more than three—were nothing more than faceless images.

Trapped in the storm.

Ber shrugged. "Someone won't come home, or if they do, they'll be in bad shape."

"Good!" she blurted. "He—they—deserve it."

Ber chuckled. The sound wasn't quite human. "Nature is the great equalizer."

Struck by his wisdom, she again bumped his shoulder. "The good guys won today."

She didn't expect him to offer her a high five. The conversation was too sober for that. Still, she loved having said what she had.

"Justice," Songan muttered. "Maybe that's what it all comes down to."

It was more complex than that, she acknowledged as the shifters' heat seeped through her. They were big, powerful, at home in the wilderness in ways she could never be. Despite that, the more time she spent with them, the more like them she was becoming.

For elks and bears, life sometimes boiled down to killing or being killed. Neither creature had much to fear in the wild, yet they saw the basics of life and death every day.

"What are you thinking?" Ber asked.

"I'm not sure." Yes, she was. "Maybe I'm putting my own spin on things because that's what I need to, but I think Mom would find gallows humor in what's happening to them." Her throat tightened, then relaxed. "She couldn't do anything for the sow and her cubs. She couldn't save her own life. But nature is exacting its own justice."

Leaving the bed, Ber walked over to the door and opened it. Winter rushed in. "The storm isn't letting up."

Trapped.

Shut up in a small, cozy space with the shifters who'd changed her.

"There's food in the backpacks," she said, even though she didn't care. "And someone left whiskey."

Songan's body touched hers. She felt him everywhere. Ber's hand was still on the doorknob, but he'd soon return to her.

"I'm still feeling overwhelmed," she admitted. "There'll probably be backlash, but right now I'm kind of numb."

"Are you?"

Determined to face Ber's question, she met his gaze. "I feel more alive than I have since Mom—that isn't numb, is it?"

"You accomplished what you wanted to. Got to the truth of what happened to her."

"I couldn't have without the two of you."

Ber nodded. "What happens now?"

"What do you mean?"

"Your job in Alaska."

"I don't know."

"Then you might not go?"

Confused, she told him she didn't want to leave until the criminal investigation had been completed. In addition, she had her mother's estate to deal with. "Her place is well built, but it needs some updating before I can put it on the market. I've tried to get started on that..."

Leaning forward, Songan stared at the floor. "If this was my cabin, I'd make it bigger."

"A lot bigger," Ber echoed. "With more windows."

"And space to move around."

Listening to the men, she silently thanked them for changing the subject. "A bigger bed," she offered. "King size." *Room for three.*

Standing, Songan touched her waist. She thought he intended to help her get to her feet. Instead, fisting her shirt hem, he drew it over her head. The heat from the woodstove brushed her newly exposed breasts. Her nipples hardened.

As he joined Songan and her, a sound that made her think of a bear slipped out of Ber. He tackled her jeans. Seconds later, she stood naked before them.

"Stand there." Songan pointed toward the wall where the window had been. "Let us look at you."

Elk weren't predators. They didn't stalk. Just the same, his eyes on her held her in place. It took all her strength to lift her arms enough to brush several strands off her face. Holding on to self-control with all her strength, she turned her attention to the bear shifter. He might be new to *her* forest, but he belonged here. This wilderness accepted him.

Barely aware of what she was doing, she cupped her breasts and lifted their weight. Offered them to her lovers.

"Will this be enough?" She looked at Songan and then Ber. "One woman for both of you?"

The storm pummeled the cabin's exterior, and the burning logs snapped. Except for those ordinary things, her world was silent. Ber and Songan studied each other, but she couldn't make sense of their expressions. She wasn't sure she wanted to. One or the other, not both? Could she live like that?

"We'll make it work," Songan said at length. "There will be times when I can't be around." He nodded at Ber. "When only he'll be with you."

"And times when the Enyeto need me."

"And times when you need me," she whispered, "To care for your kind's male babies."

"You're saying—"

"Maybe."

"You can do that? Give them up when they need to learn what it means to be shifters?"

The thought of handing a child she'd cared for and fallen in love with over to someone else made her heart ache and yet—"If that's best for the child, yes."

"Not a child; a bear shifter."

Too complicated! More than she could comprehend tonight. Looking down, she studied her uplifted breasts. "This is where I am. As far as my thinking will go."

"I'm not interested in thinking. Or speaking."

Watching Ber shed the clothes he'd recently put on, she wondered if he had any idea how magnificent he was. His pubic hair was as rich and dark as what was on his head. No weights-filled gym could produce muscles like his.

"Your turn," she told Songan. She was surprised she could speak.

"You're ready for this? After everything that happened today—"

"You got shot, not me." She indicated the lump on his forehead.

"I'm fine." He cupped his jeans-hidden cock. "Is this what

you want?"

"Are you saying I shouldn't, that the horror of it all—I just want to be. I need things simple. Intense."

"A break from reality."

Not long ago, Songan had been bothered by his reasoning limitations while in elk form. Now he was more than making up for it. Determined to let him know how important his words were to her, she stepped into his space. Despite her less than steady fingers, she unsnapped and unzipped his jeans.

Fortunately he then took over while she stepped back and watched. To her way of thinking, deer were more graceful than the heavier, bulkier elk, and yet Songan's every move was exquisite. Too slow but exquisite.

When Songan's nudity matched Ber's, she didn't compare them, barely gave it a thought. Instead, doing what maybe didn't matter to them, she retrieved a box of matches from the catch-all drawer and lit the candle she'd found and placed on the table. Deep red hues danced over powerfully muscled bodies.

"I'm not good at this." She licked her numb lips and wiped her sweaty palms on her hips.

"At what?" Ber asked.

"Right now, anything." She chuckled. Her cheeks felt hot. "I want both of you, at the same time, but I don't know how to make it happen. Or whether that's what you want."

Ber looked over at Songan. After a moment, Songan did the same. They nodded as one.

Two unique and special men, sharing her body. "I guess…" She couldn't think how to finish.

To her relief, Ber extended his hand. She did the same. Her fingers remained linked with his as he turned her so her back was to him. Before she'd caught on to what he had in mind, he'd wrapped his arm around her waist. Drawing her against his erection, he ran a hand over her hip and down her leg.

"I want to be gentle," he muttered. "After what you've been through, you deserve that."

Songan was in front of her, looming over her, looking down at her breasts and making her nipples harden so they hurt. His hands descended onto her shoulders. Suddenly he was so close she saw nothing except a blur.

"Gentle," Songan repeated. His breath washed over her face. "Healing."

Ber stroked the outside of her thigh, the touch not gentle but not rough either. She wanted to embrace both of them but couldn't remember how to make her muscles work.

"I, ah, don't know about the gentle part," she admitted in a whisper. "It's getting pretty hot."

"Just be," Ber said. "Let us take care of the rest." Taking a breast into his mouth, Songan bathed her nipple with his warm, damp tongue. A shiver assaulted her.

"Yes, yes," she bleated.

"Don't forget, you're in charge," Ber said from behind her.

Not tonight. "This. Oh shit, this." Arching her spine, she offered Songan more of herself. She tried to reach behind her so she could touch Ber, but her muscles still refused to respond.

Closing his teeth and lips around her breast, Songan straightened a little. The drawing sensation set off sparks all through her.

Ber's arm tightened around her.

"What—"

"Trust. We'll never hurt you."

I know she wanted to assure him but didn't. His hand left

her thigh then closed around her ass cheek, his nails lightly raking her there.

"God, you're killing me!"

"No," Ber said, "I'm not. Neither is he."

She'd regretted blurting what she had the moment the words escaped, but the mood might change if she said anything. Early evening in the middle of the snow-blanketed forest was all about emotion and sensation and the blending of three bodies. A minimum of thinking.

Legs on fire and feet going numb, she stood between the male shifters as Songan suckled and teased her breast and Ber repeatedly massaged her ass cheek. Every time Ber's nails teased her buttock or Songan lightly scraped her nipple, she gasped and twisted about. She didn't want to be free, never that! But the sensations—too much to stand still for!

At the same time, not enough.

"You're good for me," Ber muttered. "Exactly what I need today."

"I want to be." *Today and tomorrow.*

Songan opened his mouth, allowing her breast to slide out. She mourned, anticipated. Believed herself capable of flying. Capturing her other breast, Songan lightly sucked. Much more of this and the top of her head would explode.

Ber exhaled. His breath swirled over the back of her neck. "I never expected this," he said. "It's beyond everything—more than—you have no idea."

Think. Put your mind to what he just said. Help the three of us understand.

The effort wore her out. And yet twisting and shifting so Ber's heavy cock ground against the small of her back accomplished something vital. Essential. Light-headed, she pushed against him. "My offering to you. My body is yours to do what you want with it, what you need."

Fresh air suddenly assaulted the breast Songan had recently claimed. Looking up, she saw him looming over her. "You too." She meant it with all her heart. "Songan, I only have one pussy. Please understand why I want him to have it first."

"Tell me."

"You were wounded. If you'd been in human form, the bullet might have killed you." A tremor briefly silenced her. "But so was he."

"What do you mean?"

Filling her lungs didn't do enough to distract her from Ber's cock probing her tailbone and Songan's breath feathering through her hair, so she took another breath. "Not all wounds bleed. Some—maybe the most painful—touch the heart."

"And those wounds are?"

"What he found in that cave."

Songan didn't immediately respond. Going by Ber's labored breathing, she wondered if the bear shifter was so far into arousal that he didn't care what she'd just said. Maybe he was deliberately distancing himself.

"Do you understand what I'm saying?" she pressed. "What he's feeling?"

A low sound rumbled out of Songan. Cupping his hand under her chin, he lifted her head. His lips lightly touched hers. Pressure grew. Sensation spread. She cried out.

"Yes, I do." Songan's lips feathered over hers.

On the brink of thanking him, she lost her train of thought, because Ber was turning her toward him. As Songan had done, Ber cradled her chin so she'd look at him.

"I'm done talking or thinking tonight. I want to get drunk

on you. Only that."

Behind her now, Songan pushed her hair off her neck and nibbled. She swayed and might have lost her footing if not for Ber's steadying hold on her shoulders.

Her world and mind spun. Her awareness tunneled down until nothing existed beyond the formidable bodies bracketing her. Thinking to kiss Ber, she stood on tiptoe. Her mouth grazed his chin; then suddenly she was looking up at Songan again.

The men turned her in circles, keeping her dizzy, off-balance and turned on. One moment Ber's body grazed her breasts, belly and thighs. The next Songan's rangier form laid claim. They worked in unison, breathing as one, united in their task.

"This is crazy. Absolutely crazy."

"You don't like?" Ber asked. "You know the answer. But why—this?"

"Because we can."

Should she be concerned? They'd laid claim to her and were demonstrating their mastery?

If so, she loved it.

More being passed between them, more of her feet twisting on the floor, her breasts moving in waves. Tucking her arms around her middle, she gave up responsibility for holding herself erect. They were so damn strong, let them take charge. She'd swim in sensation.

Live for these moments.

"Enough," Ber said when she was facing him.

What do you mean? she wanted to ask. Before she could get the words out, his hands tightened around her waist, and he started to lift her. Guessing what he had in mind, she took hold of his neck and wrapped her legs around his hips. Head back, she arched away from him.

"Now," he commanded.

Delighted, she slowly collapsed against him. His hardness drove past her sex lips and into her, filled her with pulsing heat.

Ber began walking. She barely noticed where they were going, then struggled to remain locked with him when he started lowering her to the ground.

"My way," he said and pulled out.

She ran a trembling hand over her pussy. Wet heat met her. "Your way has to be quick."

Chapter Twenty-Three

Minutes, or was it seconds later, Rane found herself kneeling beside the bed. Her arms were in front of her and her elbows locked as she braced her upper body against Songan's thighs. She didn't remember the elk shifter getting onto the bed let alone positioning himself on all fours before her, and had no idea how she'd assumed the position she was in. His cock brushed one flushed cheek and then the other. Glided over her nose.

From behind, Ber's cock slipped between her legs. He too was on his knees on the floor, his larger body folding over her back, buttocks and the backs of her thighs. Reaching around her, Ber pressed her loose, hanging breasts against her body. He rocked forward and then back, his cock gliding over her wet folds.

Desperate for more but still trying to let him set the pace, she tried to distract herself by looking at Songan. This man's face was familiar, part of her past and integral to her future. Over the last few days, their relationship had become deeper, stronger, richer. Despite that, he still belonged to his herd. As she'd done in the past, she'd take what he had to give when he could and be content.

Content? Right now, far from that.

Ber's hot strength seared her spine and buttocks. She

started to look back at him, then went still as Songan's cock touched her mouth. She lightly kissed the gift. A heartbeat later, Ber's slipped into her from behind.

Opening her mouth, she welcomed Songan into her. Felt his length along her tongue and the roof of her mouth. The pressure against her sex grew. Flattening her fingers against Songan's thighs, she closed her eyes. Experienced.

Ber took her slow, slower than she believed him capable of. He nibbled at one shoulder blade and then the other before sliding his wet, heated tongue down the back of her neck. If not for Songan's cock gagging her, she would have cried out. Kneeling higher, she realigned Ber inside her.

Was she being touched everywhere? Even if she wasn't, she didn't care. Enough. Oh God yes, enough!

Ber fucked her pussy while Songan's cock probed and retreated. Simple as that. No contorting herself into a pretzel, no being asked to take someone in her ass. That might come later, another time and place. If she wanted.

The half thought splintered and blew away. Heat was everywhere. Male scent filled her nostrils. Ber continued to work her slow and steady, going a little deeper with every thrust. Much as she wanted to match him, having Songan's cock at her throat made her head swim.

Being double-fucked was making her drunk?

She slid her hands up from Songan's knees to his thighs. With every inch she claimed of his muscled body, she leaned a little farther forward. Maybe Ber was unaware of anything except his own pleasure. His measured pace started to increase, and she wondered if she could handle full force. His arm no longer held her breasts against her rib cage. Without her knowing when or how it had happened, his fingers now gripped the join between her belly and legs.

Inch by inch, Ber's fingers marched up her belly to further anchor her against him. That done, he rammed into her with so much force that if not for his hold on her, she would have been knocked face-first onto the bed.

No, no she wouldn't, because Songan's palms were now pressed against her collarbone. Anchored in front, attacked from the rear. One cock owning her hot sex, the other silencing her.

Burning wood snapped. A gust of wind made the window-blanket flutter. The sensations tunneled into her to join the storm already raging inside. She was helpless, caught between two wilderness shifters.

Wrenching strength from some inner core, she pushed back in time with Ber's thrusts. Somehow she suckled on Songan's cock. Sweat stained her body, and her muscles caught fire.

She came with her mouth and cunt filled. Screamed somehow. Jerked and shuddered and kept coming. *This is unreal. Any moment I'm going to wake up.*

Songan's fingertip trailing from her waist to her ass crack stilled Rane's thoughts. If asked, she'd admit she felt as if she'd been rode hard and put away wet. Following that, she'd willingly add she was ready for another round.

Not that she needed to say anything.

On her hands and knees on the well-used bed with Songan crouched behind her, she lifted her head off the spread so she could study what she could make out of Ber's form. He was standing in front of her and so close he could touch her without having to reach out.

He'd come inside her what, maybe five minutes ago? Going by his fierce, drawn-out explosion, she'd thought he might fall asleep. Instead, still breathing heavily, he'd pulled her up and back against him and held on until she'd regained a semblance of strength. Only then did she realize she'd stopped mouth-fucking the elk shifter.

One look into Songan's eyes back then and she'd vowed to finish what the two of them had begun. She wasn't clear on how the decision had been made for her to climb onto the bed near Songan and why she'd settled herself on her elbows and knees.

Yes, she did, she amended with Songan's fingers still on her ass cheeks. He was as much a creature of the forest as Ber. He too would take her doggy style.

"I love the way you smell." Songan swiped a hand over her wet, sensitive labia. He deposited what he'd collected on her left thigh.

"I smell like sex."

"But not of me, yet."

Shivering, she lowered her head and spread her legs. Offered herself up to him. She drew a vivid mental picture of what was happening. Ber, his cock satisfied, stood with his fingers tiptoeing over her shoulder and up and down her spine. The somber expression that had frozen her heart back when he entered the cabin was gone. In its place rested a look of contentment she hadn't known he was capable of. Sexual release was part of the change, of course, yet she'd seen something that went deeper. He was at peace with himself, fulfilled.

In contrast, there was a restless and agitated quality about Songan, nerves on edge. Having seen that look on him before, she knew what would quiet him. Sex. Their bodies uniting.

Songan's knees pressed into the mattress, while the fronts of his thighs touched the backs of hers. He'd leaned over a little, but as long as his fingers rested on her buttocks, he was in no danger of losing his balance. His swollen, throbbing cock lay against her inner thigh. Much as she needed it in her, she'd wait.

"Your skin's like silk," Ber muttered as his fingers trailed over her shoulder blades. "Softer than I knew any woman's could be."

This was Songan's time, his moments with her. He should be speaking, not Ber. But the elk shifter had never been one for sex talk. She'd accepted that he didn't know how or what words to use. In contrast, Ber seemed to have linked with her thoughts, found her needs.

They were different. Each precious in his own way.

"Feel me there." She wiggled her ass at Songan. "Inside. Tell me what you find."

"What?" His voice had a strangled quality.

Turning her head to the side, she tried to look back at Songan, but her hair and arm were in the way. "I'm ready. God, am I."

When Songan rocked back and away from her, she readied herself for penetration. Instead, his fingers slid into her already lubricated sex. Two fingers, she acknowledged as they stretched her. Two. Side by side, calluses rough. Giving up a mewling sound, she arched her spine and pushed back against him.

Unexpected pressure on her rear opening startled her. Then she realized Songan's thumb was against her there, and dove into the experience. Going deep and slow, Songan continued to finger-fuck her sex. At the same time, his erection pulsed against her inner thigh. The ass pressure backed off, returned, let up, demanded attention.

She couldn't breathe for the hair hanging around her, so she lifted her head and started to turn her head to the side. Maybe Ber was determined to claim some of her attention for himself. Maybe he simply wanted to see her expression.

Whatever the explanation, he took hold of her hair. His grip held her in place. Looking at him, she breathed with her mouth open. Splintered. Sliding a hand under her, Ber caught a breast between thumb and forefinger.

A sensation she knew all too well and was a slave to gripped her. Hoping to put off climaxing until Songan's cock was in her, she tried to shake free. Ber's hold on her breast tightened.

"I—don't!"

"Quiet." Songan lightly slapped her ass.

"Don't make a sound." Ber began drawing her nipple in small circles.

Quiet? Silent?

Desperate to obey the men, she clenched her teeth. Her arms were starting to ache from supporting her upper body, and there was a burning sensation along her spine. Any other time, the discomfort would have distracted her, but the shifters who'd taken ownership of her body knew her weaknesses.

Songan! Spreading his fingers in her and increasing the pressure against her pussy walls. His thumb no longer rested against her bung hole. Instead, it slid over the scant space between it and her sex, finding—oh God—her clit.

Triggering it.

"No, no, no, no!"

"Yes, Rane, yes."

She did as Songan commanded, surrendered. The hot, wonderful wash that was everything claimed her. Her inner muscles tightened spastically around Songan's fingers. Despite the awful/wonderful electrical charge consuming her, she didn't try to break free.

Still drawing her breast about, Ber nibbled the back of her

neck.

She climaxed. Climaxed again. She was still short-circuiting when Songan's fingers disappeared, and his cock took their place. He started pounding at her.

"Yes! Oh shit, yes!" she screamed.

Her body raged, her muscles caught on fire. She only dimly comprehended when the elk shifter spilled inside her.

Later, Ber opened the vacuum-packed stew packet, added water and put it on the woodstove to warm. When it was ready, they stood around the stove and took turns eating from the pan. Even later, all three dragged their clothes back on. Despite her insistence that they needed the bed more than she did, the men took turns sleeping on it while the other hung over the sides of the too-small recliner. She spent half the night curled against Ber, the rest with Songan's body around hers.

Even before first light, she knew the storm had lost its strength. Snow continued to fall all through the day but didn't hinder their hike back to civilization. No one said a word about what they'd left behind. They reached her truck before she'd decided what she had to do.

Chapter Twenty-Four

Planting his hands on her shoulders, Ber looked down at her. "No. You're staying here."

"Why?" she demanded, even though her muscles ached and she'd kill for a shower. "You two are going back." She jerked her head at Songan, who was talking to Deputy Gannon and the head of the county's search and rescue. "I know the area better than you do. Don't forget, I grew up here."

"Yes, you did." His hold gentled, but he gave no indication he might let her go. "Damn it, Rane, you've been through enough. You don't want to see..."

"We don't know what happened to those two men." Like Ber, she kept her voice low so the dozen or so people crowded inside the small city hall couldn't hear them.

She looked around but couldn't make herself settle on any of the faces. "They're probably still alive. Even if you can't find them, the search dog probably will."

As if aware that he was being talked about, the ninety-pound Doberman padded over to the door, clearly ready to get started.

"Then let him. We don't want you doing it."

By *we,* Ber was obviously referring to Songan. It felt strange to be talked about as if she belonged to the two men, strange and comforting and exciting.

"You don't want them to be alive, do you." It wasn't really a question. "At least the bear part of you doesn't."

"After what they did, they don't deserve to live."

Ber's voice echoed with conviction. Given what he'd seen in the cave, she couldn't blame him, but things were more complicated for her. She was more civilized, for lack of a better explanation.

Leaving the deputy, Songan joined Ber and her. He nodded at the door, then started that direction. Ber's hand remained on her as the three stepped outside.

"Gannon knows the whole story," Songan explained once they were alone. "For now he's going to keep it to himself."

"In other words," she said as she faced their imposing forms, "the volunteers think they're simply handling a search and hopefully a rescue."

The elk shifter started to nod, then stopped. "It's not that simple. They know who they're going after."

It hit her that those inside city hall, the whole town, probably, knew who hadn't come home last night. More than that, they saw the missing men either as friends or someone they preferred to avoid.

Running her hands into her back pockets, she concentrated on meeting the shifters' gazes.

"I need to know something," she said. "Do you blame me for telling Gannon what I did? If I'd said nothing about them being at Wolverine, no one would be looking for them. Nature could take its course."

"Let it," Songan said.

"Eye for an eye," Ber added. "They murdered."

"I know." Groaning, she rubbed her forehead. Then she

247

grabbed Ber's hand. "They murdered a sow and her cubs, creatures that mean a great deal to you."

"And your mother."

"And my mother."

"What is it you want?" Songan asked. "For the legal system to handle things?"

"I don't know." She couldn't remember when she'd felt this raw or when trying to get someone to understand her meant more than it did right now. "I couldn't live with myself if I did nothing and the men slowly died."

What she chose to believe was a softening in their expressions and their slight nods would have to be enough. And yet she had to ask one more thing.

"Maybe the dog will find them," she said, "but if you two are the first to reach them and they're alive—"

"Don't."

Shocked because they'd spoken as one, she wrapped her arms around her middle.

"You want to handle things the way civilized human beings do," Ber said after glancing at Songan. "We respect that."

"Even if that's not what you'd do?"

Ber brushed the side of her face with a rough hand. "It doesn't matter, Rane."

Rane waited until the searchers, the shifters included, had taken off in their four-wheel-drive vehicles before acknowledging Alice. The older woman stood with her arms tight around her middle much as Rane had done a little while ago. Instead of her usual grease-stained overalls, Alice had on faded jeans and an oversize men's jacket that somehow made her look even smaller and skinnier.

In contrast to Alice, who'd walked from her home above the gas station, Clifford Jones had driven his battered pickup and was leaning against it a few feet away. The last time Rane had seen Clifford, he'd been drinking at the Sawmill. Half drunk, he was full of bravado. Now he put Rane in mind of a trapped animal.

"You want to say it or should I?" Clifford asked Alice. He turned his attention to Rane. "The question is why. You know, don't you?"

Rane stuck her hands in her back pockets. "Only Dave and your brother can explain what they were doing at Wolverine. Maybe they'd learned Songan, Ber and I were going there."

"Songan's a shifter. Half human, if that." Spittle formed on the corner of Clifford's mouth. "The other one, Ber, he's the same."

She saw no reason to point out that Ber was a grizzly and not an elk like Forestville's residents were used to. "That's not the point."

"The hell it ain't." Clifford jutted his chin at her. "You think everyone don't know what's going on between you and those two mutants. Hell, makes me sick just thinking about it."

"Stop it! Just stop it, Cliff."

Shocked and yet heartened by Alice's outburst, she turned her attention to the mousy woman. "Are you all right?" she asked. "You look exhausted."

Alice scrubbed stained fingers over her face. "I didn't sleep. Hell, I don't know the last time I did. What's this about?"

"Do you really want to know?"

Shoulders sagging, Alice nodded. "It's going to come out sooner or later. I don't want to be the last to hear it."

"What about you?" she asked Clifford.

"I'll listen. That don't mean I'm going to believe you."

Several townspeople who weren't part of the search-and-rescue team were watching, but Rane didn't care. Right now all anyone knew was that Alice's husband Dave and Clifford's brother Chip were missing and presumably lost somewhere near Wolverine.

Her voice low, she spelled out everything that had happened at Wolverine yesterday. When neither Alice nor Clifford spoke, she continued. Her throat ached as she detailed what she believed had been the last minutes of her mother's life and why she'd been killed.

"You don't have no proof it was them what did Jacki," Clifford spluttered.

"Yes, we do. Stop it, please. Don't lie for your brother."

Like Ber and Songan, Clifford hadn't shaved for several days, but instead of looking sexy, his gray-flecked stubble just made him appear older. Worn out, beaten down.

Like Alice.

Propelled by a wash of emotion, Rane wrapped her arms around the gas station owner and held her against her chest. Thank goodness for the muscles that were a result of a lifetime of physical labor. If it wasn't for that, Rane might have hurt Alice.

"It isn't your fault," she told Alice. "I'd never blame you for what your husband did and tried to do."

Shuddering, Alice rested her head against Rane and took several deep breaths. Then she straightened.

"I hope you don't. I knew—" She threw a glance at Clifford. "I knew Dave had done something he shouldn't have. We didn't talk. We haven't talked for years."

"Then how—" Rane started.

"I know him. Maybe in ways he doesn't realize. For weeks now, about the time your mother disappeared, he's been acting different. Like he wishes he was anywhere except here when he always said this was where he was going to die."

Rane had stepped back from Alice so she could study her but still had hold of her hands. She wondered if Alice realized she was speaking about her husband mostly in the present tense when he might be dead. She also wondered if Alice was aware of the lack of emotion in her voice.

"I didn't want to put one and one together, so I didn't." Alice briefly closed her eyes. After looking over at Clifford, she focused on Rane. "I was wrong when I said things started bothering him when your mother went missing. He turned different months before that."

"When?" Rane asked. *When the bear poachings began?*

"What about it, Cliff?" Alice asked heatedly. "Last spring my husband and your brother started hanging around together. That when he stopped being close to you?"

Rane's temples pulsed. She would have given anything to walk away. Instead, she waited.

"He's my kin." Clifford shot an angry look at a man around his age who was walking toward him. "Later, damn it. Can't you see I'm busy?"

Shrugging, the man walked away. That seemed to be the trigger for the others, because one by one they headed for their vehicles. It would be hours before there was any word about the search, no reason to hang around.

"Chip and I've always done everything together." Clifford studied his chipped nails and scarred hands. "Ma kept saying she wanted us to stay in school, go to college. But we started logging soon as we got big enough, made damn good money. For a long time."

Much as Clifford's sad recital got to her, Rane didn't have the energy to hear the story again.

"So." She had to clear her throat before she could get going again. "When the logging jobs ended, you and Chip—and Dave—had to find other ways of paying the bills."

"Not no more. We got that logging contract."

"But before. And maybe in addition to."

Leaving Alice, she planted herself in front of Clifford. Although he didn't match the shifters in height or bulk, he was still bigger and stronger than her. Still, she *had* to get this out.

"I don't know about you," she said, "but I have no doubt your brother and Dave were making money selling bear galls." She swallowed again. "They poached, hunted out of season, trapped and slaughtered at least one sow and her cubs. The other day I came across a young bull elk that had had the same thing done to him. Killed for no reason."

"Damn him! Why the hell did I stay married to him?"

Alice's outburst had Rane pivoting toward her. Before, the older woman's face had been colorless. Now her cheeks were red and her eyes blazed.

"I suspected what was happening." Clifford's words were barely audible. "But I never asked."

"Why not?"

"Didn't want to know. Didn't want to hear that's what he and that old man were doing."

If Alice resented having her husband referred to as an old man, she gave no indication.

"Alice," Clifford muttered. "That's not all they did. They..." He stretched his hand toward Rane as if he wanted to touch her but didn't. "Your husband and my brother killed Jacki."

Rane tried to prepare herself for Alice's denial. Instead, Alice stumbled over to Clifford's dirty pickup and leaned against it. "Oh God. Rane—I wouldn't let myself think it. Looking at you, seeing what you were going through, I should have been stronger. Told the deputy of my suspicions."

Clifford placed his arm around Alice's shoulder. "So should I. Rane, you deserved better."

"I'm leaving him," Alice said. "If he's alive, I'll make sure he watches as I walk out. Leave here. Start over."

Still concentrating on the older woman's emotion, Rane wasn't sure Alice's words had anything to do with her. Then it hit her.

Unlike Alice, the last thing she wanted to do was leave Forestville and the surrounding Chinook mountains.

And the two men who'd stormed into her world.

Rio found what was left of Dave. Watching the search-and-rescue dog standing motionless next to the body with his hackles raised and tail tucked between his legs, Ber admired the well-trained animal's single-mindedness. Until he was given the command to relax, Rio would stay alerted on Dave.

Rio had frequently sniffed Ber and Songan during the hike up to the cabin, his tail wagging slowly. No one had said anything, but Rio's handler and the deputy's expressions had left little doubt of what they were thinking. Rio knew shifters were different from humans, more interesting, maybe more likeable.

Standing shoulder to shoulder with Songan, Ber studied Gannon as the deputy slowly approached the figure half hidden by snow. Regardless of what Gannon thought of what Dave and

Chip had done and tried to do, he was a cop. If the evidence proved that Songan's attack had caused Dave's death, Gannon would have to take the information to the D.A.'s office.

Putting Songan behind bars would kill him.

"Damn. Damn." Straightening, Gannon stared at Ber and Songan. The whites of his eyes looked enormous and his hands shook a little. "You have to see this."

Gannon added something to the effect that he didn't want anyone getting so close to the body that evidence was compromised, but Ber barely listened. Even before he joined the detective, his nostrils told him what he'd find.

Dave had been disemboweled.

The bear or bears responsible had defecated near their victim's head.

An hour later, Rio found Chip. Bears had gotten to him too.

Chapter Twenty-Five

Rane stepped outside so she could wave at Alice as the older woman approached in the small moving van she'd rented. Stopping, Alice rolled down the window, prompting Rane to walk over and squeeze her arm.

"Clifford will do a good job," Rane reassured Alice, even though it might not matter to Alice. "He's a decent mechanic."

"I just hope he can make the payments. Otherwise, I'll have to foreclose on him. It's going to be hard for him trying to wrap up the timber contract and keeping the station going for a while. Maybe he can get some work out of those cousins of his after all."

"You're all right, financially I mean?"

"I'll be living with my son for a month or so, but we need that time together. His boss is hiring me to do the books." Alice held up her hand. "No more grease under my nails. Once I get paid, I'm going to get myself a manicure, maybe those false nail things."

"You deserve it."

Alice sobered. "You mean it? After what—"

"We're not going there. The past is the past. We're both looking at the future."

A hammering sound had Alice looking toward the house

where Rane had grown up. "What are those two men doing?"

"Ask them. They just told me to trust them."

"I've known Songan for years. He's smarter than he looks, not that there's a damn thing wrong with his looks. If Ber's like him—"

"He is. And different."

"It'll work out, as long as you stay here. Never thought I'd be telling you that. I used to think your mother didn't know what she was talking about when she said you belonged in the Chinook Mountains. Now I know that's because I wanted out. Everyone's different." She nodded at the house. "The three of you are meant for each other. It'll work out. Look, I better get going."

"Stay in touch, please."

"If you want me to."

"I do. And I'll let you know how Clifford's doing."

"I'd appreciate that." Reaching out the window, Alice stroked Rane's cheek. "If I'd had a daughter, I'd want her to be like you."

Rane was still wiping at her tears as she turned back toward the house. Last week Ber and Songan had moved out the old woodstove and replaced it with a more efficient one. Between that and a strategically placed fan in a new wall cutout, the single wood heat source kept the whole house warm. Another stove would probably be needed to accommodate the addition of a master bedroom and bath, something the shifters planned to start on in spring.

She'd just stepped inside when the cell phone in her pocket rang. The construction sounds stopped, leaving her with yet more proof of Ber and Songan's acute hearing. Both men, shirtless, studied her as she said, "Hello."

"It's yours," the man on the other end said. "You start the first of the month."

Suddenly weak, she slumped against the nearest wall. Her gaze strayed from the men to the king-size wooden bed frame they'd been working on.

"I do?" She sounded stupid.

"As far as I'm concerned," Forest Supervisor Donald Cushing said, "this is exactly what should happen. Having you step into your mother's shoes is what the district needs. I'm sorry it took so long to deal with the red tape. And in case you don't think to ask, my recommendation carried weight. I pointed out that you changing your mind about Alaska had no bearing on your ability to do your job. Your mother was one of the most dedicated rangers I've known. I have no doubt you'll follow in her footsteps."

Following in her mother's footsteps, earning her own reputation for dedication to the Chinook Forest, safeguarding the trees and every creature that called these mountains home.

"You're quiet," Donald said. "Don't tell me you're having second thoughts."

Neither Ber nor Songan had so much as exchanged glances, yet she knew they'd heard Donald's side of the conversation. Past caring what they might think, she wiped at her fresh tears.

"No. None. Donald, thank you."

"No, thank you. The Chinook district is unique. The elk shifters make it so, and now—any idea when those grizzly shifters are going to get here?"

Ber was taking off tomorrow. He intended to travel to Alaska as a human and then shift and lead the rest of the Enyeto to their new home. He'd told her that the month he expected the return trip to take would give the others the time they needed to adjust to the change in their lives.

Instead of telling Donald everything, she said she expected to see the Enyeto shifters before Christmas. "They'll be going right into hibernation. Spring's a wonderful time here. They'll fall in love with their new home."

"They will as long as you're the bridge between them and the locals. Look, I'll let you go for now. We'll hook up in a couple of days to discuss that in detail and finalize the paperwork. Welcome aboard. Your mother would be proud of you."

Rane had put her phone back in her pocket but hadn't figured out how to push off the wall when two blurry hands reached toward her. She took them.

"You okay?" Songan asked.

"I think—yes."

"I hope so. Haven't seen you cry since your mother went missing."

The men were still holding her hands, which meant no wiping away the tears she wasn't quite done with.

"These are different." She sniffed. "Kind of happy, a bit overwhelmed."

"Think you can put your mind to something else?"

For a moment she thought her mood was making Ber uncomfortable and he was trying to change the subject. Then she realized her lovers were guiding her to the bed frame.

"We want to finish this tonight," Ber explained. "With me being gone for a while, we want to break it in first."

"We? You feel the same way?" She directed her question at Songan.

The elk shifter nodded. "There's details to be worked out, the whole sharing you thing, but this"—he indicated the frame—"is a start."

She could point out that some of the time only one of them would be sleeping under this roof, in this bed with her, but that could wait.

Pulling free, she folded her arms over her breasts. "Then finish," she said in her most take-charge tone, "because I'm more than ready to see what kind of craftsmen you two are."

"That's not the only thing we're good at." Ber made his point by cupping himself. Smiling, Songan did the same.

She agreed. And several hours later with three sweating, naked bodies tangled together, she agreed even more.

About the Author

A fast-fingered writer of erotica, Vonna Harper loves penning stories set in remote locations where her characters can give into primitive impulse. Throw in a little capture and/or bondage and she's a happy camper. Her website is www.vonnaharper.com. She's also on Twitter and Facebook and loves connecting with readers.

*Desire is their only connection.
Love may be his only salvation…*

Night Hunter
© 2011 Vonna Harper

Locals call the highway Alligator Alley. Emerging jeweler Mala Bey sees it as a storm-tossed road to a bright future. When a black-clad motorcyclist pulls alongside, thrilling her with dark eyes that promise raw, wild sex, her system goes into overload. Moments later, the stranger loses control and crashes into the Everglades.

Horrified, Mala desperately searches for the compelling man, but it's as if the thick vegetation swallowed him whole. Yet she hears his voice calling for her—only his voice.

Caught in a portal filled with disembodied voices calling him backward in time, Laird Jaeger clings to his only lifeline to the present—the woman with gray-green eyes. A mystical thread connects their thoughts as ancient forces drag him deeper into a nightmare, farther back into a past only his Seminole blood remembers.

A mysterious, panther-like creature guides Jaeger toward a past life as Thunder, the ancient tribe's one hope of survival. Even as the past wraps tendrils around his soul, his and Mala's connection endures. Its power is enough burn a fiery path of desire through time, but their growing love may not be strong enough to break destiny's spell.

Warning: Sex in the Everglades. Lots of hot sex with no bugs. Or snakes. But some rather judgmental Seminoles.

Available now in ebook from Samhain Publishing.

To break this curse, they'll have to turn the heat up. Way up...

The Yearning
© 2011 Tina Donahue

Jasmine Dante prowls Key West's nightlife, fighting a losing battle against a jealous rival's curse that forces her to seek carnal pleasure, no matter the danger. Weakened from lack of sleep, driven by insatiable lust, she spots a man who stirs her desperate craving, and begins yet another dance of seduction.

Except the dark stranger who returns her direct stare is no ordinary lover. Inside his powerful body lies a raw sexuality that just might be enough to break her curse. There's only one way to find out: imprison him in her bed and feed on his passion.

Former U.S. Marshal Mike Stearn is many things, but he's no woman's sex slave. The deadly telekinetic power he ruthlessly suppresses comes alive again at Jasmine's touch. Beneath her bold, potent sensuality he senses vulnerability and desperation. He may be in handcuffs, but she's the one who's enslaved.

As Mike resurrects his power to free himself so he can find the curse's source and defeat it, Jasmine revels in his masterful rule. Her ravenous yearning evolves into rapture as she surrenders to his hunger, her darkest needs—and the emotional connection that lies beyond. Unless the curse takes her life first...

Warning: Tons of steamy sex, smoldering passion and a to-die-for love story with a hot Alpha hero who finds himself imprisoned by one sultry and desperate babe.

Available now in ebook and print from Samhain Publishing.

www.samhainpublishing.com

*Green for the planet.
Great for your wallet.*

It's all about the story...

Romance

HORROR

www.samhainpublishing.com

CPSIA information can be obtained at www.ICGtesting.com
Printed in the USA
BVOW041025070213

312666BV00001B/5

3119202043 0334